What Lurks in the Shadows

A Novel

by S.C. Shannon

Dorrance Publishing Co
585 Alpha Drive
Pittsburgh, PA 15238
Visit our website at *www.dorrancebookstore.com*

ISBN: 978-1-6386-7004-9
ESIBN: 978-1-6386-7953-0

Acknowledgements

First and foremost, I have to thank all my family and friends who have been involved in this labor of love. This was something I began approximately three to four years ago. I kept on revisiting the project, but life always seemed to get in the way. Then 2020 came, and suddenly I regained my sense of inspiration, and was determined to finish what I had started so many years ago.

First, I have to thank my brother, Michael. When the pandemic hit, he had suggested I use the free time to write, and only about a month later I was finished with my first draft. To all of my test subjects who were willing to read the very first drafts: Mom, Tiffany, Maggie, Rachel, and Danny, your feedback was invaluable. I am grateful for the time and effort you put into this project to make it a reality, and the story evolved into a much more complex narrative that I am very proud of.

Tiffany, thank you for being my very first fan, and enduring multiple revised drafts of the story. It was fun being able to brainstorm with you, and get feedback from a person who really enjoys this genre of storytelling. I am so fortunate to have friends like you! Maggie, I could not have done this project without you! Being able to work with you on this was really enjoyable, and it was nice having the time to bond as cousins. To one of my dearest friends, Sarah, thank you for always reminding me to follow my dreams (and buying me really amazing vintage typewriters to keep me excited about the writing process). Finally, to my parents, thank you for always pushing me to reach outside of my comfort zone, and motivating me to do more. I am fortunate to have a family so supportive of my creative endeavors. It has been a wild ride this last year, and I look forward to engaging in this process with all of you again.

"WHOEVER FIGHTS MONSTERS SHOULD SEE TO IT THAT IN THE PROCESS HE DOES NOT BECOME A MONSTER. AND IF YOU GAZE LONG ENOUGH INTO AN ABYSS, THE ABYSS WILL GAZE BACK INTO YOU."

FRIEDRICH NIETZSCHE

Prologue

Day 635

I read once that, "Extinction is the rule; survival is the exception." I don't remember where I read it, or who said it, but today as I pen these thoughts onto paper I can't help but laugh. It is strange how the brain fires off random tidbits of information when one is confronted with conflict. Extinction really is the rule, isn't it? Our entire childhood is spent learning about the history of extinct creatures and fallen civilizations, and the eventual species that take their place. Life is one continuous cycle of people thinking that they are untouchable; that they are so much more advanced than the others that came before them. Yet, it is that very way of thinking that has ultimately led to our demise. For some reason, humans always destroy each other. There is always someone or something bigger and stronger waiting to take our place. Complacency is our downfall.

I don't know what will happen tomorrow. Here within these pages, I've documented every experience since my life changed forever. What I realized is that when something ends, something better has to take its place, and I want to be the exception to the rule. I want us to survive. Every being on this planet has a weakness; it is just a matter of recognizing what that weakness is.

My name is Grace. I am the youngest daughter of John and Susan Baker, and I have a brother named Stephen. Everything I am I owe to my parents and to my brother. They taught me to be strong; they taught me to be smart;

they taught me to never give up trying. It is in their memory that I attempt this venture tomorrow. I refuse to live like this any longer. There has to be a better way. There has to be more to this life. There just has to be a reason that all of this is happening. I refuse to be scared. I refuse to hide any longer. I know in my heart that I would rather die with courage, going out fighting, than live a life in hiding as a coward. God Bless.

Chapter One

Before

I was twenty years old when I had a front row seat to the end of the world.

Like any twenty-year-old, I was trying to figure out who I was and what I wanted to do with my life. I was taking some junior college classes to get some general education credits while I determined where my path in life was going to take me. I was working a part-time job at a local police station while I figured things out. I had a great family, with parents who taught me that success is only earned through hard work and perseverance. My older brother spent most of his time picking on me, though he always looked after me. I felt like I was just getting the hang of things. I was managing working while going to school, all while living on my own for the very first time. Then, like a sudden bolt of lightning, everything changed.

I was a SoCal girl, and while I really did not care for the big city life, I grew up there and it was where I was comfortable. Contrary to popular belief, however, living in Southern California did have its drawbacks. The summers were hot, and with the heat came rolling blackouts and wildfires. That is how it all really started, but we did not know any better. It was a particularly hot summer, and being the fifth straight year of drought conditions, it was dry and it was unbearable. First, we blamed the fires. It was not a summer in Los Angeles if the hills were not set ablaze, torching everything in its fiery path, especially all our power lines. We had grown accustomed to the way the smoke filled the air with its ominous orange fog, causing the sun to shine down on us with its sinister vermilion hue. Every time we left our homes, the aroma of burning brush from the nearby hillsides was carried in the haze, alerting us to nature's fury. It happened every year for as long as I could remember, and we had adapted to such conditions.

Eventually, we began to think it was the overuse of the air conditioning units. The news insisted that we needed to spare the electricity, but no one trusted the media anymore. Plus, we had grown so accustomed to the electric companies just shutting off the power with their random brownouts whenever they felt the need to. It was nothing we hadn't encountered before, so we didn't heed their warnings.

Despite having experienced these occurrences for most of my life, I had this foreboding sensation that something bigger was happening. No matter how hard I tried to quell my nerves, I could not make sense of the anomalous events taking place. Blackouts were common in this part of the country. We would get warnings and alerts to prepare us for sporadic energy interruptions. They would last for a couple hours, here and there, never for much longer than that. The first were what we expected, and what we were used to. Eventually they grew longer, until we went days without power. Shortly after that, we found out it wasn't just Los Angeles, but appeared to be nationwide. Both major cities and small rural areas were experiencing these blackouts with no real explanation. Whenever you called and asked the power companies for answers, they had a prepared generic response.

Naturally prepared for earthquakes, my family and I were always prepping for the next big one. My parents always ensured we had basic supplies to last us if the freeways collapsed like they did during the Northridge quake back in 1994. They had insisted that we had an emergency preparedness plan so that we would not be victim to whatever emergency presented itself. Unsure of whether it was truly overuse or a real weakening of the power grid, my parents wanted us to be prepared just in case there was some other unimaginable threat approaching. Who knew how people would react if our way of life was threatened? We knew we had to prepare in case people started hoarding basic necessities, like they did during the Coronavirus pandemic. Humans and their fearmongering always led to unpredictable responses. You never truly know what people will do in times of a crisis. Would something like that happen again? Would there be chaos? Riots? Overwhelming civil unrest? No one really knew. This was unchartered territory, and no one could prepare themselves for something of this magnitude.

I remember the last time I listened to the news before it all ended. Conspiracy theorists discussing how terrorists had gained access to the power grid. They insisted unknown entities were doing systematic tests to see if they could control us. We would destroy each other given those circumstances. Technology had taken over our lives at this point. Everyone had become reliant upon "smart" phones, "smart" TVs, "smart" cars, and "smart" appliances. We became a culture so vain and obsessed with social media that we were truly losing a sense of what mattered in life. All people seemed to care about was how many "likes" they could get on their Instagram or Facebook posts, and they had seemed to lose all sense of dignity in the process. The modern-day Sodom and Gomorrah; no wonder the world was in desperate need for a reset. We needed to find the values we had lost, and somehow realize what was truly important again.

No one can foresee when the world is coming to an end, and I was no exception. The last day of my regular life was like any other. It wasn't until I watched the President of the United States give a nationwide address, telling us not to worry, that I knew something major was coming. Every essence of my being knew something very grim was about to materialize. He stood there polished and articulate. He was the leader we needed in such uncertain times. His words were full of hope as he remained calm and tried to dispel any rumors that could have led to the inevitable chaos. Everything was under control, he assured, and America would persevere. He emphasized that as a nation we would overcome this and be stronger for it. He reminded us of all that we had endured thus far as a nation, and that this was an inconvenience, but not the end. Did they know already? Looking back, I wish I would have studied his body language. I wish I had been able to read between the lines to understand what he was really telling us. I wish I had seen the warnings hidden within his words.

My brother and I met at my parents' house, just as they requested. Honestly, I didn't mind being there with my family. While I did feel like they were overreacting a bit, I at least felt a sense of safety; false security of being with my family, I guess. We could all feel the shift in the air. It was undeniable. Within hours of the Presidential Address, the power was out. We knew something was coming, but didn't realize it would happen so suddenly. We thought we would have more time. Just as we suspected would happen, though, disorder ensued. It did not take long before the looting and rioting began in the streets. Once people realized the severity of what had transpired, they did not know how to act. With tremendous sorrow, I knew we could never come back from this; not at least within this generation. The world was no longer a safe place.

We knew we had to get away from Los Angeles. We had to get away from any big city. So, we packed everything of necessity and drove north. We left late at night because we knew there would be fewer people on the streets, and fewer people trying to steal whatever we had. We also knew there would be less carnage for us to encounter, and I don't think my parents wanted us to witness the worst of humanity. We were about an hour north of Los Angeles when our dire circumstances escalated beyond comprehension. There in the sea of black sky, a beam of amber incandescent flame trailed behind a giant metal projectile. The orange, fiery light painted itself across the dark canvas as if it were a giant meteor heading toward downtown, eagerly delivering our annihilation. The explosions were visible in the distance. Within seconds, the ground beneath us began to violently shake. Despite being in a land of constant tremors, this was unlike any earthquake I had experienced before. And that was it; everything I had ever known was gone.

Unsure of whether the event was isolated to Los Angeles or spread nationwide, we knew we had escaped just in time. But what had been destroyed? Was there anywhere to go? My dad drove us a few hours north to a small town just outside of Lake Tahoe. There was an old family cabin, hidden deep in the woods, that was hard to find even when you were looking for it. It was like we were hiding in plain sight, which in these troubled times seemed like the safest place for us to be at the moment. It appeared to be undisturbed. No evidence of what we had witnessed hours before occurred here. It seemed safe for now.

That next morning, we attempted to find a radio station with news on the battery-operated radio we had. We sat anxiously waiting to hear if it had only been Los Angeles that was destroyed. Finally, we found a radio station and listened as a male with a southern accent began to speak. His words were spoken with despair, and it was evident he was distraught.

"I don't know if anyone is still out there and can hear me. I survived, somehow, but the majority of my loved ones did not. I have just learned it is all gone. All of it. Much of the country has been destroyed in multiple air strikes and bombings. The damage to the other countries is anyone's guess, but prior to the attack on American soil, nuclear missiles were fired at the terrorist countries that destroyed our power grid. We have literally destroyed ourselves. For those of you hearing this broadcast, you cannot lose hope. We need to rebuild. We need to do better. Please do your best to survive. God bless you. God bless what is left of America. May God have mercy on your souls."

Then silence. In a matter of days, we went from the most prosperous nation to nothing but ashes. It was all gone.

We did what we could to pick up, start over, and build a new life. We felt like it was happening, too. We had encountered savage humans from time to time, but we had some feeling of peace. Our new life was one in which we were closer as a family. We went out and scavenged for supplies. My mother and I learned how to fight off possible attackers. We learned how to hunt for our food and find non-poisonous berries to eat. We gathered up what we could of the lives we had left in the ruins, and we pushed forward. We laughed; we cried for what we had lost; we became new people. Our family unit was unbreakable. All we had was each other, and we were happy with that because we had somehow survived all the bad that happened. For 226 days we managed. We had a routine; we had a purpose. Then on day 227 the monsters came.

Chapter Two

Present

Keep running. Don't look back.

My lungs are on fire, and every muscle is cramping. I am almost home, and I cannot stop now. I try to look back, but the trees make it impossible to see if I have been followed. Just keep running. When I look forward again, I am startled by a branch that hits my face. It disorients me but I have to keep moving. I feel warmth drip down my cheek, and I know it is blood. Unfortunately, it is a feeling I have strangely become accustomed to.

I am almost there. I jump over a fallen tree and make the final sprint to the cabin. I open the gate, push through the bushes, and I run around the back to the hidden entrance. I stop and try to control my breathing before I enter. My heart is racing, but I close my eyes and I listen. Thunder rumbles in the distance, as I hear raindrops striking the trees up above. No other sounds. I am safe. Thank God.

I drop to my knees, reach below the wall, and unlock the door. I push it slightly open, crawl in, and lock it behind me. Leaning against the wall, I let out a deep sigh of relief. That was too close for comfort. I cannot make these mistakes. I know better.

I put my backpack down in the living room of the cabin. I grab a towel lying on the table to wipe the sweat off my forehead. When I pull the towel from my face, it is bright fire truck red. I roll my eyes. "Just what I need," I murmur to myself. To assess the damage, I walk into the bathroom and turn on the lantern. It is worse than I thought. There is a gash just below my hair-line above my right eye that has to be the length of my pinky finger. The blood has caused my normally light brown hair to turn into a gothic burgundy color. My face looks notably pale, almost a ghostly white, and I don't know if it is from the contrast of the dark red on my face against my skin, or due to an actual loss of blood. I lean in closer to the mirror, and it doesn't look like it is quite deep enough to need to suture it closed. Finally, some luck.

I wipe the blood off the wound as best as I can. Pouring rubbing alcohol on a cotton pad, I wipe the wound to disinfect it, and I apply some tape to allow it to heal. It's days like these I really miss Band-Aids. I don't think I will ever get used to the feeling of sticky tape on an open wound.

To be honest, I hardly ever think to look in the mirror anymore, and when I do, it is always shocking to see how frail I have become. My brown eyes look black against my skin. The bags under my eyes have only grown larger, and my cheek bones seem to be so pronounced against the hollows of my face. The longer I stand there looking at the changes, the more it reminds me of when I applied Día de Los Muertos makeup for Halloween one year. There is no need to dress up anymore, now that I just always look like this. Every day seems like Halloween now. I don't recognize myself anymore. This new life has prematurely aged me.

After I fix myself up, I go back into the living room. In the first few months we were here, it was more like we were just camping. We opened the windows and looked at the world out there. This little piece of Heaven seemed untouched. There was no sign that the world had been destroyed. It was like all of that had been a bad dream. Now, however, there is no looking out anymore. On the outside, it is still a cabin hidden among the trees. But the windows have been replaced with metal siding that we were able to find in old, abandoned businesses in town. The doors have been sealed shut, except for the hidden entrance in the back. Once inside, I am completely isolated from the world, and from the monsters that stalk me from the shadows.

I grab my canteen of water, my notebook and pencil, and head to the basement. Normally I have more time before I have to hide myself away for the night. Due to the onset of nimbus clouds, the color of newly wet cement, serving as a barrier to the sunlight, nightfall has presented itself sooner than usual. I lock the basement door behind me as I descend the steps, walk toward the back corner, pull up the door in the floor, and take the steps down into my sanctuary.

This is my bedroom now: concrete walls, shelves filled with some necessities, and a cot replacing my soft queen-size bed I used to have. On days like these, my sanctuary has more than enough space to feel comfortable rather than claustrophobic. Back when this just was a cabin, this area was used for a wine cellar. Barrels and expensive bottles lined the shelves, aging to perfection, until they were ready to be drunk. Now it serves as a way to protect me from what is out there. Down here I am hidden. Down here I am safe—or at least that is what I have led myself to believe.

I sit on my bed, grab my notebook, and begin to write:

Day 620

I almost got caught in a storm today. I cannot be so reckless. I felt the overwhelming need to go to town today and see if there was anyone new traveling through. One cannot be too careful these days. I made my way toward the town and found myself spying on a group of people that were walking the desolated streets. I could hear them talking. I could hear them laughing with one another. I had not seen this group of people before, and I just sat there, hidden in the trees, trying to figure them out. It had been so long since I heard laughter that I got transfixed in it. They had no idea I was there, which made me wonder how they had survived this long. Suddenly, the sun disappeared behind the clouds, and I ran for my life. This time I made it, but I have to be more careful next time.

From what I could tell there were five people in the group: four males and a female. Based on their rugged attire it seemed like they had been traveling for a very long time, with no real home base. Their demeanor suggested that they haven't encountered too many savage humans. The fact that they are still alive made me think they probably haven't encountered too many monsters either. I wonder if wherever they came from they have encountered what lurks in the shadows here. Maybe it really is time to relocate? Only time will tell. I will have to go back tomorrow. If they survived, maybe they can tell me what is going on out there. I need to investigate further.

I put my pencil down and close the notebook, placing it on the ground beside me. As I lean against the wall, I look at the shelf, tilting my head to the side as I decide what to read tonight. I choose one I had already read many times before: *Odd Thomas*. I open the front page, and I can't help but smile when I see the piece of paper with handwriting on it. I have used that scrap of paper as a bookmark ever since I found it. The note was written back when life was much simpler; when life was on the verge of changing, but hadn't changed yet. I turn to the first page of the book and begin to read.

A few hours pass and I can feel myself getting tired. So, I mark the page with the piece of paper, close the book, and put it back on the shelf. I pull my knees onto the cot, wrap my arms around them, and rest my head. The silence is what plagues me now. Being all alone, just trying to survive. It is as if I am in a state of constant mania; unable to truly calm my nerves to relax. I cannot allow myself to sprawl out and get comfortable. Once it is dark, I have to be ready to fight. Even though they had not found me down here, I have to be alert. I have to be still so I can listen for them.

Each night as I attempt to recover from the events of the day, it is in this stillness that I feel myself going mad. I close my eyes, and no matter how hard I try to fight it, I am reminded of all that I have done. As if it were my own personal movie trailer of every macabre occurrence I have contributed to. Gruesome images flashing in my subconscious, evoking contrition night after night as I try to cope with all that I have lost. Over and again I attempt to justify my actions, but my guilt consumes me.

I am the last Baker standing because my family sacrificed themselves to save me.

Chapter Three

Before

It is the perfect night. The air is warm with a cool intermittent breeze. I sit in my favorite spot, which just happens to be next to a white stone fire pit with glowing Edison lights hanging from the trees. It is peaceful here. Here, I do not feel like I'm in a big city. A hidden café in the industrial part of town. This place is just quiet enough for me to get lost in whatever book I am reading, and the aroma of coffee and fresh baked pastries comforts me. It always reminds me of being a kid; of how my house would smell when my mom baked homemade chocolate chip cookies as I did homework in the living room adjacent to the kitchen.

It is dusk, and I can see the sky has already transitioned from orange to crimson. I curl up in the most comfortable oversized chair on the outdoor patio, which I had unofficially declared my very own spot. I drink hot chocolate with just a sprinkle of cinnamon, and just take in the atmosphere. This place serves as my escape from the big city, and the responsibilities of being an adult. I always become so easily engrossed in what I am doing or reading that I never notice the time. Today is no exception. The sky is already black and absent of stars when I look up and see Nick walking toward me.

"Here, Miss Baker," he says as he places a mug in front of me on the fire pit. "Thought I'd top you off with another hot chocolate before we close up. It is pretty chilly out here tonight."

I look down at my phone, and it is 10:55 P.M. "Where does the time go? I was just getting to the good part of my book, too."

He smiles, "What are we reading today, Miss Baker?"

I would be lying if I did not acknowledge how striking Nick is. I don't even think I could create a man as handsome as him in my own head even if I tried. He is tall with dark brown hair and brown eyes, with a perfectly bronzed complexion. When he smiles there is a natural sweetness to it that seems so pure and genuine. He has an athletic physique, and always presents himself very professionally. Not only does he possess such handsome physical qualities, but he is undeniably kind, and I think that makes him even more attractive.

I close the book and show him the cover. He sits down in the chair next to mine.

"Stephen King," he smiles. "We all float down here!"

I laugh. "Well, Mr. Gates, I didn't peg you for a fan of horror novels."

"Well don't let my boyish good looks fool you. There is a lot more going on in my head than in this pretty face of mine," he says winking and then letting out a small laugh. "I remember seeing *It* as a kid. Then when I got older, I decided to read the book. It was one of the first books I ever really got into. Then it made me wish I would have read the actual book before I saw the movie, because it was so much better!"

"Nicholas!" I gently slap his knee. "Books are always way better than the movies! They never do them any justice. Despite their best attempts, Hollywood often ruins great books. They spend too much time trying to add action or sex appeal, that they take away the best elements of the stories!"

He lets out a small chuckle, "You're right, they are always trying to add completely unnecessary elements. I didn't know it back then, though. Plus, to be honest, I don't think my mom would have let me read Stephen King as a kid anyway. There is no doubt that his stories are not kid friendly."

I giggle, "My mom used to let me read that stuff as a kid, but I guess she was just happy I was reading to begin with. I knew it was all make believe so I never got too scared, anyway."

He looks around like he is about to tell a secret and leans in to whisper, "Sometimes I still have nightmares about Pennywise," and he begins to laugh.

I place my hand over my eyes and shake my head in a disapproving fashion. "Wow, I would have never guessed that you were such a… what is the word I am thinking of? Oh yes, a wimp!"

He opens his eyes wide, "Really? Name calling, Miss Baker? I am no wimp. I am just a small-town boy, not a big tough city girl like yourself. We really didn't have storm drains like you guys have here."

I look at him and smile, "Ok, I guess you have a point there. I am sure seeing a creepy clown in a drain would freak you out if you didn't realize that they aren't big enough to actually pull you down there."

He points his hand at me. "See! I never even thought of that before. Even if I can't be dragged down there, I'll still always try to avoid walking past them. I just can't shake this deep fear that I am going to feel something grab my leg as I walk by," he says as he reaches out and grabs my shin.

I start laughing, "Well your secret is safe with me. I guess I'll just have to safely escort you past the drains from now on because you are going to have a rough time trying to avoid them—they are literally everywhere. You won't be able to get anywhere without me!"

I feel my cheeks begin to flush as I realize I had just inadvertently suggested that I would accompany him anywhere outside of this establishment.

He looks at me with a sudden smile and extends his hand, waiting for me to reciprocate a handshake. I reach out to his, and we shake in agreement. "I like that. Sounds like a deal. You protect me from monsters, and I will keep bringing you free hot chocolate. Seems like a fair trade."

I feel my cheeks warm even more. Our banter is broken when someone walks out to the patio from inside. Nick looks back at them and then toward me. "Well I guess that's my cue to get back to reality, considering I am supposed to be working right now," he says as he places his hands on his thighs. "Once again, thanks for the conversation."

He stands up and walks to the door, looks at me, and smiles, "And you better not think that you can back out of our agreement. You shook on it, and a deal is a deal, Miss Baker."

Before I can answer, he walks back into the café. I will admit that one benefit of coming here is the friendship I had begun to develop with Nick. Never in a million years would I ever imagine I would playfully flirt with the cute boy at the café, but he made it so easy. Our friendship always felt organic. It didn't feel forced at all. I wasn't trying to impress him, and I don't think he was trying to impress me. He just seems to get me and my reasons for being here all the time.

It didn't take me long before I noticed the way the girls stared at him. It was impossible to ignore the ways they would fake laugh to get his attention, or go out of their way to talk to him. What was a tad perplexing was that despite all the attention he got he never seemed interested. He would politely smile, and do his best not to be rude, but no matter how beautiful the women were, he always maintained his professionalism.

My friendship with Nick is just an added benefit to being here so frequently. I value our conversations, and even though there are moments when I ponder what it would be like to see him outside of this environment, I never feel the desire to pursue it. I want to maintain what we have, and asking for anything more is a risk I'm not ready to take.

I grab the hot chocolate and take a sip. I smile when I realize there is just a hint of cinnamon. He always gets my order right, even when I don't actually place one. I put the hot chocolate down and grab my book. I curl my feet onto the chair, flip open the novel, and begin reading where I had left off.

Chapter Four

Present

Grace, honey, it's time to wake up.

I open my eyes and I am blinded by the light. Once my eyes begin to focus, I can see I am in my childhood room, and my mom is sitting on the side of my bed. When I was younger I always hated having my mom wake me up, but now I treasure it.

"Good morning, Mom," I say, still half asleep.

She softly brushes my messy hair off my forehead. "Dad said I should let you sleep in, but I was hoping we could do a little mother/daughter bonding today."

I let out a long yawn and stretch my arms overhead. "Sounds good. I'll be down in a minute."

She kisses my forehead and gets up to leave my room, closing the door behind her. I can hear my dad and Stephen talking in the kitchen below my room, and I turn to the dresser beside my bed to check my phone. No messages, like usual. I put the phone back on the nightstand and slowly try to stand up. I walk to the bathroom, throw some warm water on my face, grab the towel, and pat my face dry. After I quickly brush my teeth, I throw my hair up in a messy bun.

When I walk downstairs, I can immediately smell coffee and bacon. As I round the corner into the kitchen I can see that my mom, dad, and Stephen are all sitting at the table, and there are several plates of food. I sit down and am surprised to see the big brunch style spread on the table. Bacon, eggs, Belgian waffles, pancakes, and my favorite homemade mini-cinnamon rolls.

"Did I miss something?"

My dad looks up from reading the paper, "What do you mean, Grace?"

"This just seems more like a celebratory breakfast, or something we would eat on a holiday. What is the special occasion?"

Everyone starts laughing, except for me because apparently I am not in on the joke.

"Grace, we always eat like this, silly girl," my mom says as she sips her coffee.

Still very confused, I just smile and then start loading up my plate with a little bit of everything. I look up at Stephen, and it is the first time I have seen him at the breakfast table without his phone.

"Did something happen to your phone?" I say with a mouth full of bacon.

He looks at me with a smile, "Why would I have my phone at the table? That would be rude."

I almost choke on my bacon. "What? You always have it at the table—"

Before I can finish, my mom interrupts, "So I was thinking we could go to lunch and see a movie today at that new, fancy theater with reclining chairs. What do you think, Grace?"

"That sounds great, Mom!" I hear the phone ringing in the other room. No one seems to notice it, so I get up from the table. "I'll get it."

I walk into the living room, and I pick up the cordless phone. "Hello?"

Click-click-click-click.

"Hello? I'm sorry, but I can't seem to hear you."

Click-click-click-click.

"Whoever this is, I think something is wrong with your phone. Why don't you call back when you have better service?"

Click-click-click-click.

Right as I am about to hang up the phone, I hear a loud crash from the kitchen. I drop the phone and turn around to run back to my family. When I cross the threshold, the scenery changes. No longer am I standing in my brightly lit kitchen. The walls have been replaced with towering redwood trees, and the ceiling has been replaced with a midnight sky embellished by the stars. I realize I am standing in a forest. I look down, and I am still in my pajamas, completely underdressed. The air is so cold that I can see my breath. I cross my arms to try to keep warm, and I turn around looking for my family as I feel my limbs begin to shiver. They are sitting just as they were at the table. I stand there looking at them as they continue to eat their breakfast like nothing is going on.

I run to the table, "Oh my God! What happened? Where are we? What is going on?!"

"What do you mean, Grace?" my dad says, completely oblivious to the fact that we are in the middle of a forest.

"Umm... HELLO!" I scream at them as I lift my arms and point to the trees. "Look around! How did we end up in the middle of the forest?"

"Grace, stop being silly. Sit down and eat your cinnamon rolls, honey," my mom says calmly.

Before I can answer, I hear the same noise I heard on the phone, now coming from behind where Stephen is sitting.

Click-click-click-click.

"What is that noise?" I ask.

"Stop being weird," says my brother.

Click-click-click-click.

"How can you guys not hear that?"

Click-click-click-click.

"Hear what—" before he can finish his sentence, Stephen is lifted from his chair. Blood is pooling all over his green shirt, transforming it into a dark brownish gray color. Before I can make sense of what is happening, he is pulled backwards from the table into the darkness as he lets out a horrifying scream. I scream too and run toward my parents, but before I can reach them, they are simultaneously pulled in different directions into the blackness of the abyss. I stand there in shock, lose balance, and fall to my knees. I am aghast at what I have just witnessed and am completely silent. The fear has paralyzed me, and all I can hear is the clicking sound resonating around me.

Click-click-click-click.

Chapter Five

Before

We had another blackout last night, and this time it lasted until morning. My fridge has been pretty much empty since the summer started because these blackouts were causing all my food to go bad. No electricity means no coffee maker, and there is no way I can start my day without my coffee. I always forget how dependent we are on technology now. Pretty much everything requires charging or plugging it into the wall, and hardly anything is battery operated anymore. Seems like we are going to be in for a rude awakening if these blackouts continue.

I start my car and make my way toward the café to get a drink for work. I have a really good job doing clerical duties at the local police station. The job basically entails filing and inputting crime information into the database, and it's actually very interesting to see first-hand what is going on in the city. It is also fascinating to hear all the stories the police officers share with me while they are waiting for report incident numbers. They always tell me stories of car chases, foot pursuits, and saving people's lives. Yet every time they do something extraordinary, they always insist it is just part of their job. Their lives are so exciting, and I cannot imagine what it is like having that constant state of adrenaline surging every day that you are at work. I admire that even though they act heroically, they remain humble. No wonder there are always so many shows and books written about their profession. Honestly, the stories they share with me I feel could not even be fabricated into fiction. You seriously cannot make up the things they encounter every day.

When I arrive at the café, it is packed. I have to park three blocks away, which is unusual for this part of town. As I make my way toward the café, I can see a homeless man. He has shoulder length white hair, with a matching white beard. He is wearing a long sleeve shirt that once was white, but now is covered in dirt making it a dusty brown color. His jeans are worn, with holes in both the knees, and he has no shoes on. The man is standing with a sign made of cardboard, and black marker written on it. The sign does not ask for money or food, all that is written is: The end is here. He looks toward me as I offer an awkward half-smile, look away, and quickly make my way inside.

This is the busiest I have ever seen it in here. People chit-chatting about the blackouts and how much it inconveniences their busy lives. People are complaining about how they aren't able to charge their tablets, laptops, and phones. I overhear a couple behind me talking about how all their social media has not been working since the blackouts started.

"I don't know what is going on, Jeff. Like I can't refresh my feed. And anytime I try to post something it just says it can't upload," says the woman.

"Well maybe it has something to do with the blackouts?" says the man I assume is Jeff.

"I'm telling you, like, it has to be some government censorship. There is, like, no freedom of speech anymore."

"Why do they care about what you are trying to post, Chelsea?"

"Uhh… obviously, they are trying to coverup whatever is causing these blackouts, Jeff!"

"You think that the government controls your social media?" I hear the sarcasm in his tone.

"Obviously. Like, why else can't anyone upload anything. All the posts are from, like, five days ago. They don't want us to be connected."

"I think you are reading into this a little," he says as his patience is wearing thin.

"I am just saying that the same major company owns pretty much all of the social media platforms and not a single one has been working for days. They are trying to keep us quiet."

"Chelsea, I highly doubt that the government is in cahoots with social media companies to keep you from being able to do your social media influencing."

"Oh my God, Jeff. You never take anything I say seriously," she says as she begins to throw a tantrum.

"Well, you do sound a little ridiculous."

"No! You are ridiculous!"

I stand patiently in line waiting my turn, trying not to laugh at the conversation I am eavesdropping on.

"Grace!" I hear someone call from behind the counter.

I shift my view around the tall person in front of me and see Nick waving me over. I look at Jeff and Chelsea, and politely ask, "Do you mind saving my spot?" They just look at me, and continue their debate without acknowledging my request.

I walk to the end of the counter and greet Nick. "I can't believe how busy it is here today. It's crazy."

"I know! These blackouts sure are good for business. What are you having? I'll sneak you in front of line," he says as he's wiping off spilled coffee on the counter.

"Are you sure? I mean, I don't want to be rude," I say quietly looking to see if anyone heard me.

"No way! You, my dear, are our best customer and so you obviously get priority. Like the café V.I.P."

I look down and smile, "If that's the case when do I finally get a parking spot?" He laughs as I continue, "I'll just take a coffee with extra room for cream please."

"My pleasure." He turns around, grabs a cup, pours some coffee, and then walks back over. "Here, it's on the house."

"Really? Thank you so much!" I grasp the cup and begin to turn around, when he grabs my arm from across the counter.

"Wait! I almost forgot." He reaches below the counter, pulls out a book, and then continues, "Look what I found!"

I smile, take the book, and look at the title: *Odd Thomas.*

"Finders keepers!" he says, grinning. "I told you I'd save it for you if I ever came across it."

"I can't believe you remembered! Thank you so much, Nick. Means a lot to me."

He smiles once more, and I pull out some single dollar bills to toss them into the tip jar. I turn and walk out of the café with a smile on my face too. Sometimes I forget how kind people can be in an urban environment like Los Angeles. I walk back to my car and drive away. With everything going on I decide to turn on the news rather than listen to music. There is some guest on air that I don't recognize, and he is talking about the blackouts.

"Listen, no one thinks it's odd that all of a sudden we are just having these blackouts? Yeah, I get it, it is Southern California. Blackouts happen all the time, but it isn't just California. It is everywhere," the man says.

"Everywhere? How do you know?" says the host.

"Trust me, I have been doing my research and I am not some crazy anti-government conspiracy theorist. These blackouts have been systematically happening all over the country in major cities for the past six months. What reason would some of these cities have for blackouts? When was the last time New York City just went dark? It is real. It is so much bigger than us. Not to mention, there has been social media silence across the board. Have you noticed how it won't refresh, and how you can't upload anything? All those social media sites are owned by the same company, and conveniently they all aren't working? It is a way to keep us from not knowing what is going on nationwide. They are in on it, too." I guess Chelsea is not the only one being paranoid about the social media silence. Maybe she did have a point, I think to myself.

"Ok, I hear you. If that is the case, then who is behind it?"

"Well you know the government will say that it's terrorists. It is always terrorists. They gain our approval by labeling the threat that way, and then use that as a method to do whatever they want for whatever secret reasons they want. They know there won't be pushback or lengthy investigations if they just call it terrorism. All of a sudden, they are sanctioning all these countries for reasons that no one seems to understand. They act like we are in control—by we I mean the U.S.—but we aren't in control. We haven't been in control for a long time. They want us to believe that we are the only nation capable of sending nuclear missiles, but it's all lies. These blackouts are other countries demonstrating their power over us. We are just fleas in their circus, and the show is about to end—"

Suddenly, I hear a loud honk, which snaps my attention away from the radio. I see a large red pick-up truck fly through the intersection right in front of me without stopping. I slam on the brakes, which causes my car to begin skidding until I am almost sideways. The car comes to a complete stop, and I look up to see my light is still green. I catch my breath, slowly drive out of the intersection, and pull over. What is going on? People are losing their minds.

Chapter Six

Present

I wake up screaming. Still sitting up with my hands clutching my legs, my arms are completely drenched with sweat from my forehead. I lean my head against the wall, and wipe my eyes, as I feel them swell with tears. I am deluged with sorrow. Days like these I miss my family so much it physically hurts. It always happens the same. The dreams start out happy. My family is always there, and I am always in my childhood home. It is an absolutely ordinary day. I am content, and it feels like what I believe Heaven would be like for me now. Then, without fail, the dream turns into a nightmare and I am constantly reliving the loss of my family. I don't know what would hurt more: waking up from these dreams realizing I can never experience that happiness again, or losing them over and over again. I don't know what I did to deserve this torment.

I grab my notebook and begin flipping through the pages. On my worst nights, I like to revisit what I have learned. It's important to review what I have done, and what I have had to overcome since this all began. Plus, it helps take my mind off the horrors. I also like to review my research though. So far, I have been collecting data from my travels and encounters. Eventually, I will take my data and apply it to actual experiments. It is just difficult right now because there is still so much uncertainty. My dad always taught me that for every problem there is a solution. First you must figure out what the problem is, then you conduct your research, then you develop a plan, and finally you execute. From there you should have a solution to said problem. Research, Plan, Execute. He made it sound so easy, didn't he? If only he were here to help me figure all this out.

My notebook somehow became my survival bible. Every night, I wrote about what had happened that day. It was also a way to keep track of how much time had passed since the world as I knew it came to an end. Some days I write entries. Some days it serves as notes. Some days it's my only companion; my escape to pretend like I have someone to talk to. My way to leave behind something to show I existed before it all went bad.

DAY 1

So much can change in one week. A week ago at this time, I was probably at my favorite café drinking an overpriced latte, reading a book, while listening to hipsters complain about how the café didn't offer enough vegan non-dairy bakery items. Today, everything I know is gone. I am completely cut off from whatever was left in the aftermath of the bombings. I fear that everyone I know is dead.

There is nothing left. Everything I worried about a week ago is no longer a concern. The stress of paying bills, the missing out on social interactions due to school or work, the trying to constantly lose weight to have that summer beach body I was never going to have anyway, the trying to get the cute boy to like you… it is all completely irrelevant to my current situation. I wasted so much time trying to get to a point in my life where I could be successful, and here I am now. It was for nothing. I have nothing but memories, and even those I should have tried harder to make. I wasted a lifetime preparing for a future that will never happen.

I could sit here and be completely down about what has happened. I mean, after all, life as we know it is over. But I refuse to be that way. I am with my family and that is all that matters. There are other survivors. We cannot be the only ones who made it this far. We will rebuild. I'd like to think we have learned our lesson, and can rebuild the right way, with the right intentions. We have to do better next time.

I always forget how much optimism I had that first week. I don't even recognize the girl who wrote that. So much has changed since that first entry. I am brought back to reality when I hear my stomach growl, and it is about time that I get the day started. I take my notebook and put it on the shelf. I stand up and raise my arms above my head to stretch as high as I can. I walk to the door, open it, and listen. It is quiet, like always, and I illuminate the basement with my flashlight. I begin to walk up the stairs, unlock the door, and slowly open it. Once again, I listen.

Silence.

Who knew silence could sound so pleasant? I look around, and it is undisturbed. Another night I survived without being found.

Once I am upstairs, I take the old camping stove and light the burner. I do not usually take the time to make a real breakfast and use what little resources I have left, but I know today will require actual fuel. I have a long day ahead of me. So, I pour some water into a pan, and wait for it to boil. Pouring some old oatmeal into a bowl, I wait until the water is ready. To kill the time, I look at the package and it is long past the expiration date. I have been eating expired food for years and it has yet to make me sick. Seems moronic these days that I used to make such a big deal about eating expired food a day after it went bad.

You have to go back. You know what you have to do. The time is now. It isn't safe here anymore.

I pour water into the bowl and wait for the oatmeal to soften. Part of me knows I shouldn't risk making the trek back to town, especially with strangers around. Yet, part of me knows I have to determine if they are dangerous. Do they live nearby? After all, what if they had figured out a way to overcome them? I have to know! Then again, a part of me is so incredibly scared. What if their presence draws more of them to this area? I am the only person here now. I have no allies. No friends to help me fight them. It is just me. All alone. I can't risk them bringing more of them here.

As I eat my oatmeal, I can't help but remember the first time my family and I encountered the savages. While it may not be politically correct to call other human beings savages, there is no other way to describe them. It was on a supply run to town when we had our first real encounter. It had been about a month since the attacks, and we had been spending most days scavenging for what remained in the town and cabins nearby. We knew we had to get as much as possible back to the cabin before others found our quaint little town.

The plan had been to systematically check for supplies in each business. The first couple days we had just grabbed the absolute necessities. Then as days progressed, it was gathering what we thought we may have use for in the future. The town had been looted, but not the way you would see in movies. No windows broken or the skeletons of burned cars lining the streets. The doors to the businesses were ajar, and most of the goods were gone. But it almost felt like there was a sense of civility among the madness, if there were such a thing.

I can still remember it as clear as the day it happened. I close my eyes, and I am taken back to that scene. We are in the pharmacy rummaging through what is left. I hear the sound of a gun being cocked behind me. In the silence it is deafening. I look up and see the fear in my parents' eyes, so I just slowly put my hands up. The universal sign of surrender.

"Looks like we have a family expedition goin' on here. Hey, Rick! We got us a whole family in here," the man with the gun says. He is a large, fat man, with balding red hair. His plaid shirt is ripped and has different colored stains on it, some resembling blood. Several open wounds freckle his face, like even though the world has ended, he still indulges in smoking methamphetamine.

My dad, attempting to maintain his composure and negotiate accordingly, responds, "We have no weapons. We are just here for supplies." My dad does have a weapon though, so why is he lying? Maybe it is some attempt at de-escalation?

The man who must have been Rick chimes in from a distance behind me, "Did you hear that, Bob? No weapons!" Rick is scrawny compared to his overweight companion. It is hard to tell in the mirror, but it looks like he has long straggly hair, an overgrown beard, and appears to be missing some teeth. He is wearing a brown shirt, and some torn overalls. He is exactly how I would picture some post-apocalyptic savage to look. Good job living up to the stereotypes, guys.

"Now who the hell would come to a town, looking for supplies, with no damn weapon?" Bob says.

I can see the men in the mirror behind the counter where my dad is standing. My mom is behind the counter as well, and my brother in the corner. It appears that there are only two men, Rick and Bob, and Bob seems to be the only one with a weapon. Research, Plan, Execute, I tell myself in my mind.

"Now aren't you a pretty little thing," Bob says as he leans in and smells my hair. "And, I'll be damned, you smell good too. Rick, come smell." He reeks of old cigarettes, beer, and body odor. I feel myself gag as they get closer to me.

Rick comes closer, leans in, grabs me by the hair with his hand, and takes a whiff. "Oh, she smells real nice. How long has it been since we seen a pretty girl around these parts—"

"Don't. Please. We'll leave," my dad pleads with them.

"Well, hell, Pops, I don't think that's gonna work for us. We could use some female… companionship." Bob then places the barrel of gun against the side of my face as he presses his body against me and licks the other cheek. The gun is cold against my skin, and his tongue is rough, like sandpaper. His body is soft and doughy, and I just stand there trying to decide what I should do.

Research, Plan, Execute. There are only two of them, but four of us. One has a gun. If I can distract them, maybe I can get the gun before the other one even realizes what is happening. I need a weapon.

"What do you say, little lady? You come with us, and we let the others go…" Rick says.

"Or you choose not to come with us, we kill your family, and then we make you come with us," Bob says. "It's your choice really."

Oh really, that was a choice? I think.

I can see the fear in everyone's eyes. This is my only chance to do something. I look over to my left and see a barrel full of umbrellas. That will have to do for now.

"Wait… Is there…" I say as I begin to whisper.

Bob leans in to hear better, and I head-butt him so hard it makes me dizzy. It is successful, as I feel his grasp loosen around me. I am able to free myself, and I quickly run toward the barrel. I grab an umbrella, spin around, and hit him as hard as I can in the head with the handle. Just as I suspected, Rick is caught off guard, and Bob drops the gun. I dive for the gun as Rick jumps on top of me, grabbing me by the hair to lift my head up. He then slams my face to the ground as hard as he can. I can feel blood dripping from my nose, and my head is throbbing with intensity. I have to get the gun.

At this point, my family has all joined in fighting with Bob, as my brother runs toward me and kicks Rick in the face. He kicks him so hard that Rick falls off and lands beside me. I hear Bob scream out as my dad takes the knife and stabs him in the stomach. I get up, grab the umbrella, and swing as hard as I can, striking Bob in the face once more. I run toward the gun and pick it up. I point it at them, but they are both lying on the floor unconscious. So, we all just run. We run as fast as we can until we feel safe.

"Grace. Oh my gosh, Grace Tiffany!" my mom says as she grabs my face and starts giving me kisses on my forehead like I am a little kid.

"Mom—I am fine."

She begins wiping the blood from my nose on her sleeve.

"Grace, I am so proud of you. I could see you working something in your head, but that was so dangerous," Dad says.

Stephen chimes in. "Not bad, little sis. I guess me kicking your ass all of these years did you some good," he says as he begins to laugh.

"Stephen Patrick! This isn't a joke! She could've gotten really hurt." My mom always had a way of using both our first and middle names to really get the point across to knock it off.

Finally, after a brief pause, my dad looks at us and says, "Susan, kids, this is what people are going to be like from now on. We have been very fortunate that we have not encountered this sooner. We got complacent. You have to understand that morals, compassion, basic human dignity… none of these things are going to exist anymore. We are in a dog-eat-dog world out here; every man for himself; survival of the fittest. It has been a blessing that this didn't happen sooner, but this is a reality check. We must prepare ourselves for people like this. This is our new life."

We all stand there in silence as Dad's warning kicks in. He is right.

I remember that day like it was yesterday. It was the first of many encounters with the savage humans. As time progressed, it only got worse. As what was left in the town dwindled to nothing, people became more heartless. You could not trust anyone. Any form of kindness shown to a stranger was seen as a weakness. Dad was right; in the end it was every man for himself.

We did what we could to prepare after that incident. Dad and Stephen taught my mother and I how to fight. We would have about an hour of training a day. Different scenarios were presented, and we had to think on the fly—

like I had done in the pharmacy—and do what we could to survive. I knew it was valuable training, and I took it seriously. I guess because I felt like I had my parents with me, and my strong older brother, that everything would be ok. I just assumed that they would always be there to help me get through it. I never thought I'd be doing this alone. God, how I miss them.

Chapter Seven

Before

I am still half asleep when my phone rings. I grab it and look at the caller ID. It is my mom.

"Hello?" I say, a little groggy.

"Grace, your dad and I were talking, and we think that maybe you and your brother should come over and stay with us until all of this craziness dies down a little bit."

"Mom, they are just blackouts," I say with a yawn.

"I know, dear, but still. Like your father always says—"

I interrupt her, "I know, failing to prepare is preparing to fail. But I don't know how this applies to all of this."

"Well, Stephen already agreed to come, and I think it would make us all feel better if you could come, too. Just for a couple days. I don't want you getting stuck in any riots or anything."

I roll my eyes, "Mom, I don't think they are going to riot just because of some blackouts."

"Please think about it."

"Ok, I have to work today, but I'll try to come after work. Ok?"

"Thanks, hun, we love you."

"Love you too, Mom."

We hang up. While I think they are overreacting, I can't blame them for being worried. People are behaving in a peculiar manner these days. Not to mention, you never know what will happen in a big city like Los Angeles when and if things do not go according to plan.

I drag myself out of bed, attempt to turn on the lights in the bathroom, and yet again, another power outage. I roll my eyes once more. Of course. I grab my toothbrush, put toothpaste on it, and turn on the faucet.

I am immediately disgusted when I see that the water coming out of the faucet is brown and thick like mud. I turn it off. When I walk to the shower to turn it on, it is also brown. Seriously, this is getting ridiculous. What can possibly be wrong with the plumbing? I am going to have to have a serious talk with my landlord when I get back. I grab the bottle of water by my bed and use it to brush my teeth. I throw my hair up in a ponytail, put on some sweats and a t-shirt. I guess I have to take a shower at work today.

I pack a quick go-bag to take to my parents' house in case I decide to go there after my shift. I know they will be upset if I don't come. I feel compelled to take some of my meaningful items with me, too. I grab a couple books, my laptop, a cross necklace my parents gave to me for my first Communion, and throw them into my backpack. As I walk into the living room, I see the book Nick had given me, so I grab that too. Clumsily, I drop it on the ground. When I go to pick it up, I see a small white piece of paper on the ground beneath it. It's a hand-written note addressed to me.

Grace,

So, I have to be honest. I have never done anything like this before. I just have to tell you that even though I don't know much about you, somehow you have made this crazy place feel like home. Honestly, my best days are the ones that we get to spend time together, even if it is just for a few hours a week. There is so much I want to say, but for now, just know that even though you try to hide yourself from the world, I see you. I would love the opportunity to learn more about you and take you on a real date (not just coffee at the café) if you are willing to give me the chance. Hope to see you soon.

—Nick

I just stand there reading the note over and again. I don't know what to say, or what to feel. Who does that? Who writes notes and leaves them in books for girls to find? That's like something you would only read in a story. There is so much going on, and my head is spinning. "Seriously? The world must really be coming to an end if I am getting notes like this!" I murmur to myself.

I feel my phone vibrate in my pocket. I pull it out and read that it is a news alert: Breaking News: Authorities Have Confirmed Blackouts Appear to be Nationwide. I put my phone back in my pocket, and am thrust back into the reality I am living in. I put the note back into the book and put the book into my backpack. I'll revisit what Nick said later, when I don't feel like my entire world is falling apart. I grab my go-bag, my backpack, and am about to walk out the door when I stop to turn around and look at my home. For some reason, I feel this pain in my stomach, a nauseous sensation, that somehow I know this may be the last time I ever see this apartment. I sigh to myself, and then walk out and lock the door.

Chapter Eight

Present

I tie my hair in a ponytail and put on my boots. On the table I see my knife, which is secured in a brown sheath, so I grab it and attach it to my belt. Also lying on the table is a second smaller pocketknife, so I pick that one up, and slip it into the side of my boot. Scanning the room, I look for my backpack, which is hanging on a chair, so I walk over and swing it over my shoulders. I walk to the door, crawl out, reach under and lock it, then I stand up. As I listen, I realize that the woods are eerily quiet this morning; no animals prowling on the yard. I walk slowly as I look around. All clear for now.

I make my way down the hill toward town. These walks are always dangerous. I have to be careful to watch for those savage humans. I have to be cautious about people who can hear me before I can hear them, just waiting to attack me. Most importantly, I have to be careful about the monsters. I have not encountered one since my brother was killed about six months ago. That was when it was all so new. Mom and Dad were already gone. Stephen and I had learned that these monsters could not be seen and they attacked in hours of darkness, but we always knew when they were around because we could hear them clicking in the trees. On the night Stephen was killed it was like he was attacked by a ghost. Whatever it was came out of nowhere. It lifted him high above the ground as it began to tear through his flesh. I still don't remember how I got away, but I remember hearing them. The way their feet touched the ground, making some sort of scratching noise: Click-click-click-click. Like their nails were rubbing against each other. I could feel their presence. It was that feeling of someone watching you; the eyes beating down on you, but I couldn't tell where from. I would just get this sick feeling in my stomach; I knew I was being hunted.

We had been fishing in the lake that day, trying to get some food for dinner, and time just escaped us. In this new world, losing track of time became a cardinal sin that often resulted in penance. We had grown so close those last few months since Mom and Dad had passed away. After all, we only had each other. We had spent hours reminiscing about being kids. We talked about Mom and Dad and how much we missed them. We had been discussing what this new life was going to be like with just the two of us. We even started to discuss whether we should stay here, or try to move on to somewhere new. I think we wanted to move on and find a new place to start over that didn't have such bad memories. However, the idea of leaving the last place we had been with our parents just didn't seem right.

Hours had passed, and then suddenly it was dusk and we knew we had to get home fast. We were quiet like always, walking along the path but not on it, just in case someone was waiting for us. We were only about a quarter mile from the house. Then we heard it. First, we heard deer darting into the trees and birds screeching and flapping their wings, warning their fellow creatures that something was here. We could hear them fleeing the area scattering along the forest ground, and the random animals screaming as they were attacked.

The memory immediately transports me back to that night in haunting detail. As we are quietly walking through the forest, I can feel it. I feel its eyes on me, and I look at Stephen with fear in my own, just as he looks at me with desperation in his. We are in danger. We are too late. I begin to scan the massive redwood trees, but there is nothing to be seen. Dusk has transitioned into nightfall, with just a residual glow of sunshine hidden beyond the horizon. Cautiously, we take each step trying to minimize the sound of our feet striking the forest floor. My breathing has slowed as I take short shallow breaths to remain as quiet as possible.

But in the stillness, I can hear it. Click-click-click-click. At first, it sounds like it is coming from the right side of me. Click-click-click-click. Now it sounds like it is coming from my left. I look around and can see nothing in the darkness. Where are they?

Click-click-click-click.

Wait, is that coming from behind me now? I can feel my hands start to tremble. My heart begins to palpitate, and I can no longer control my breathing. I am overcome with trepidation.

The sounds are echoing around me like some form of forest surround sound heightening my senses. I want to scream at the top of my lungs. I feel my heart tightening in my chest, and it is making it even harder to breathe. I grab Stephen's hand; a scared little sister. We walk faster, and the faster we walk, the louder the clicking gets.

Click-click-click-click. Now it sounds like it is right in front of us. We both stop in our tracks. Click-click-click-click. Stephen looks at me, and for the first time I can see the panic on his face. He doesn't look like the jovial brother I had grown up with. His face is pale, and I can feel his hands begin to quiver.

He whispers, "Grace, I need you to run."

"No, we have to stay together!" I whisper loudly in return.

"Grace, stop being a pain in the ass and do what I tell you for once."

"No, Stephen. Please."

Click-click-click-click.

He looks around, "Grace, please don't make me ask you again."

Click-click-click-click.

"Please, don't leave me. Please! I can't do this on my own," I protest.

Click-click-click-click.

"Grace. I love you." Click-click-click-click. He lets go of my hands, and screams at the top of his lungs, "Run, Grace! Run now!"

Obeying his request without hesitation, I take off in a full sprint. I hear Stephen release a scream that I will never forget. Terrified, I look behind me and see his elevated body in the air. He has fresh gouges to his torso, and blood is staining the front of his gray hoodie. Suddenly, he is quickly yanked into the darkness of the woods, absorbed by the shadows of the trees.

I keep running. Without even realizing it, I still have the fish in my hand from the lake. I throw the fish we had caught on the ground, run through the gate, and toward the hidden entrance. I slide under the door, lock it behind me, and run directly to the basement. I sit in the wine cellar and wait. Please Stephen, please come back. You cannot leave me here all alone. Please.

I continue praying for Stephen to give the secret knock, notifying me of his presence; that somehow he escaped the monster's clutches to be with his petrified little sister. The knock never comes, and I know he is gone. Just like that I am all alone, trying to make sense of how I could just run and leave my brother to die.

I feel a tear roll down my cheek as I remember that day. It is a scene that haunts my dreams. I should have fought back. I should have tried to save him. But how can you fight something you cannot see?

Chapter Nine

Before

As I drive to work, I see dozens of people packing up their cars like they are leaving town. They are hurrying around throwing bags into the trunks of their cars and loading up supplies. I try to ignore it, but it is like every street I turn down there are more people packing to leave. Where exactly are all these people planning to go? Do they all know something that I don't?

After I get to work and rush to the locker room to shower and get ready, I return to my desk, turn on the computer, and begin my workday. I look over and see a stack of reports already on my desk that have to be inputted into the police database. I grab them and start looking at what the titles are so I know which ones to prioritize. There are at least twenty reports, and all are mental illness holds. We have a lot of crazy people in this area, but I have never had that many holds in one day.

"It's like there's a constant full moon out there," says a voice from behind me.

I turn around and see that it is Officer Rodriguez. I met him my very first day, and he has been nothing but polite ever since. Whenever I needed help, he would never hesitate to lend a hand. While some officers came off as arrogant or unapproachable, Officer Rodriguez was always friendly and smiling. I look at him and ask, "What is with all of the holds?"

"You know how it goes, the weather gets weird, the power goes out, and it brings out all the crazies. We had so many holds that all four area hospitals are at max capacity."

"No way!"

"I've been here for ten years and I have never seen that happen either. We have nowhere to send them."

I glance at the pile that has at least ten or fifteen files and sigh before asking, "So what are you doing with all of them? Obviously, they pose a danger to themselves."

"The powers that be authorized them to be booked at county jail until the space is available at the hospitals."

"That is horrible. They need medical attention. They don't need to be in jail with real criminals."

He nods, "Yeah, it is really sad, but we can't risk them being out there and hurting someone else."

"True. I don't know. There is just something in the air these days," I say as I take a sip of my drink.

"Yeah, pretty much," he pauses. "I don't mean to bother you, but do you mind getting me a report number on this?"

"Oh, of course." I put my coffee down.

He hands me the report, and it is for a missing person. I input the information to the database, while I overhear him talking to other officers about some of the day's more exciting events. It is unbelievable to hear what has already gone on so far. A few police pursuits, and a few uses of force with people who appeared to be under some drug that they described as being worse than PCP. There were even two separate officer-involved shootings with people who were under the influence of the drug.

I hand the report back to Officer Rodriguez with his report number, "Here you go, Sir."

He takes the report, "Thank you, Grace. Be careful out there. I feel like something is coming. Take care of yourself."

"Of course. You be safe, too."

He smiles and walks away. I grab my coffee and walk to the Watch Commander's office to see if they need anything prioritized for input. As I round the corner, I can see through the glass window leading into the office. Everyone is standing in there watching the large TV screens hanging on the wall. I walk through the door and look to see what they are watching.

A large banner on the bottom screen reads: A Presidential Address to the Nation. We stand there quietly and watch as the President approaches the podium:

Good morning, my fellow Americans. I am here to address you regarding the recent blackouts plaguing this great nation. First and foremost, I urge that you not be frightened. There is no need to be. I have seen many reports that this has been a deliberate attack on our soil as a way to test the strengths and weaknesses in our power grid. These terrorists are using our power grid in a calculated manner of creating destruction and disorder among our citizens.

After meeting with my most trusted advisors this morning, I can confirm that this, indeed, is true. We have linked these systematic attacks on our power grid to multiple anti-American terrorist organizations. We will not stand for this blatant disregard for the well-being of our citizens and country as a whole. As I stand here before you, I beg all of you to recognize that it is essential that you do not give into what they are trying to accomplish. Civility must remain among us all.

In a joint session of Congress, we have decided to do what is necessary to protect our American citizens. Do not be alarmed. In no means is this a declaration of war; we are merely emphasizing that we will not tolerate any disruption to the safety of our citizens, and we will utilize whatever methods are needed for a resolution. Those responsible, these terrorists, will be handled through a demonstration of strength and resolve. For those terrorists watching, understand that our patience has worn thin, and the red line has been crossed. I beg Americans to remain calm. Those of you wanting to flee the major cities, please reconsider. We come to you with this transparency to give you the confidence that we are protecting you. There is no immediate danger, and I urge you all to continue your lives as you normally would. We are all in this together. I am once again asking for your patience. While this all may seem somewhat concerning, there is no real threat here.

As a nation we have survived so much more than a mere electrical disruption. We have overcome global pandemics, Pearl Harbor, two World Wars, The Great Depression, and 9/11 just to name a few momentous struggles in our history. We are strong, and we can overcome anything with our ingenuity and resoluteness. There is nothing we cannot do as long as we remain steadfast and true to our American principles. We will get through this together as a nation. God bless you all, and God bless America.

He turns around, walks away, and the broadcast goes back to what was on before.

The Watch Commander looks at everyone, "This is bad." The phone rings, and he answers.

"Watch Commander, Lieutenant Sanchez speaking."

He responds with multiple "Mmm-hmmms" and "I understand" before hanging up.

He looks at all of us and then states, "That was Captain Parsons. Per Chief of Police, the entire city is on tactical alert. Notify everyone to be ready with their crowd control gear. They think this is going to be just like 1992 again."

I look at him, shock on my face, "Sir, umm, is there anything—"

"Grace, there is no need for you here today. With the tac alert there's no need for data input." He smiles and then continues, "Go home. Be with your family. I don't have a good feeling about this."

"Ok sir, please, be safe. Yeah?"

"Of course. Thank you so much for your hard work, Grace. You've been a true asset here." The phones start ringing off the hook as I walk out.

At my desk, I grab my purse and my phone. I have three missed calls from my mom, and about ten text messages from various people. I walk out of the building and call my mom right away.

"Hey, Mom. Sorry, I was away from my phone."

"Grace, please tell me you are on your way. We just saw the Presidential Address."

"Yeah, I saw it. I am leaving work right now. I should be there within the hour. I love you."

"I love you, too, hun. Please drive safely."

Chapter Ten

Present

I am almost to town when I decide I should approach from a different side. I try to change up my routine from time to time just in case there have been people watching my movements. I always prefer making my way from the north side of town, because I feel like I have a better advantage. Today, however, I make my way from the south side.

There is an old gas station that is at the very south end of town, so I slowly walk around it and listen. It is a decrepit stone building, with the windows broken out, and only four gas pumps rusting in the lot. In the silence, I can hear crows cawing in the distance; always an ominous feeling. I don't know why I always feel that way, but I guess the years of reading Stephen King and his obsession with crows has instilled that as a warning mechanism in these circumstances. To be honest, this town looks exactly how I imagined the cities were like when I read *The Stand.* The streets are desolate. What once was full of cars and people, is now just a graveyard of abandoned vehicles, trash, and broken glass. I listen longer, and it doesn't sound like anyone is around. The only thing that would make it more appropriate would be dust blowing in the gusts of wind, with a few tumbleweeds making their way down the Main Street corridor.

I slowly walk up the street. As silent as I can be, I pause at every building, peer into the windows, and take temporary refuge in the alleys. As I get closer toward the middle of town, I can see a tent that had not been there yesterday. I try to get closer, being as quiet as possible, and I can clearly see the tent has been ripped to shreds. Pieces of brightly colored vinyl line the street nearby, with clothes scattered along the sidewalk. I have seen this play out before. I let out a sigh because I know there will be nothing left. I tip-toe toward the tent, constantly assessing to make sure no one is lying in wait anywhere. As I get closer to the tent, there is blood spray everywhere, and the smell of iron is overwhelming. There is blood on the ground, on the tent, and trailing behind the old, abandoned liquor store.

I get close enough to the tent to peer through one of the slits, and it is empty. Did the monsters get the entire group? What a shame. I look down and I am surprised to see that the trail of blood does not appear to be from someone being dragged, which causes me to feel a little excitement. Maybe someone was actually able to escape the monster's clutches. Rather than lengthy longitudinal striations of blood, the trail consists of varying sizes of globules.

I follow the trail of blood to the back of the store, large droplets leading the way. Whatever caused these droplets, they came from someone trying to escape. Multiple red spots of blood lined the sidewalk. I look up and see a bloody handprint on the wall. At this point, I am unsure of what I will find, or if I will find anything at all. I pray that nothing is here, because that would mean someone was able to fight back and actually escaped these creatures. As I gaze around the corner, all hope perishes. Pieces of bloody clothing line the walkway. Just like I saw on the tent, there are streaks of blood covering the walls of the businesses. It is a massacre. Even though I have seen this many times, I cannot get used to it. Did they not know what was out there? Are there no monsters where they came from? Is there anyone anxiously awaiting their arrival in vain? It truly is heartbreaking.

As I get to the rear of the building, I stop and listen. This is my life now. Always stopping, always listening, and always on guard. As I listen, I can hear the pounding in my chest, unsure of what I will see. I can hear movement, and the sound of crows. I cautiously peer around the corner, and there on the ground lies what remains of the travelers. I cannot even make out how many were there, or what is left. There are chunks of fatty flesh, and broken bone scattered on the pavement, as if they were a grotesque jigsaw puzzle waiting to be assembled.

A faint gust of wind blows the smell of the rotting flesh in my direction, and I cannot help but gag when it hits me. The crows are devouring whatever is left of the bodies. There is nothing left for me to do now. Maybe that feeling that I could learn from these travelers was just a big mistake. I don't know what to make of my senses anymore. There is no point in trying to investigate now. Whatever answers I was seeking will not receive solutions today. Maybe being alone for so long is messing with my head. It is making me see things that are not really there and hear things that are not really being said. It is making me mistake coincidences for signs. Maybe I have finally lost it. There is nothing left to do here.

I turn around to head back home, and I am stunned when I see a large knife pointed directly at my face.

Chapter Eleven

Before

I am a creature of habit. I wake up at the same time every day. I start my day with a glass of water, while my coffee brews. I drink my coffee and eat a banana while I catch up on the news. Once I feel like I am all caught up, I get ready for the workout of the day, and then I get to it. Once that is done, I either go to work or school, and finish with either reading or homework at the café. I am kind of shy and keep to myself. I do not do well with change. Yet here I am, driving to my parents' house, possibly about to throw all of those routines out the window. I live in a fantasy world; dreaming of adventure. Living vicariously through the protagonists of the stories I read. I never thought I might end up in my own real-life adventure. I guess you could say my life had been mundane up to this point. I know I could have tried harder to create excitement, but you always think you have more time. Change is coming; I just have no idea how it will play out. Will it be for the better?

I have never been one to admit when I am scared. I like to pretend I am stronger than I really am. In my family, we do not show weakness. Fear gives strength to your predators. We do not really talk about our feelings, unless it is with my mom. Dad always told us it was necessary to our survival to hide any emotions that may undermine your strength. If we are scared, we find solutions to overcome that fear. If we are sad, we put that emotion into finding happiness. If we are unsure, we educate ourselves until we have validation. Dad always stressed that nothing in life can be controlled except our feelings. It was always up to us to choose how we were to handle any given situation. I guess for some people that may come off as a bizarre way to live. To most people, it may not even seem real. Like we are constantly trying to conceal our emotions. Some people may even wonder what kind of life is it to always have to be so tempestuous. In my family, though, that was a way of life. We showed each other we cared, and we were real with one another, but we just did it in different ways than most families. Dad was always prepping us for survival, and I knew that whatever he had been through that his lessons were from his own experiences.

I guess the reason I always liked to read was because it allowed me to escape into a life that was not mine. Most of the books I enjoyed dealt with mystery or the paranormal, but usually they had a character who needed to be strong to avoid being a victim, and to overcome all obstacles. Who doesn't love a great underdog story, though? Someone who has to work against all odds to survive. We all have our own struggles, and it is paramount that we learn to overcome them. There is just something great about a story when the good people win. I guess the reason I was always drawn to these types of stories was because they were predictable. The good guys always win. Despite whatever shortcomings they may have, or the impossible situations that present themselves, the hero somehow finds a way to save the day. Let's face it: That is not real life. The good guy doesn't always win. The girl doesn't always get the guy. The world doesn't always escape destruction. Real life sucks in comparison to what the human mind can fictionalize for a reader's entertainment.

I kick myself because I always felt like my life was so monotonous. It is like you spend your entire life waiting for the next chapter to begin. When you are a kid, you cannot wait until you are older so you can make your own rules. Once you feel like you are an adult, you cannot wait until you have a good job so you have money to do everything you always wanted. You look forward to the adventures you probably will never go on. You look forward to meeting someone who you feel will complete you. You are always grasping for something, and never really just taking it in. You are always wanting something more. I regret the moments I never stopped to enjoy, but rather I took for granted. Too often life is about rushing toward a destination, rather than appreciating the journey and recognizing the lessons along the way.

I guess in the end when you feel like life will never be the same, it is time for reflection. As I drive to my parents' house, I can see the mayhem starting to fill the streets. People running from store to store to grab whatever last-minute items they may need. I see smoke in the distance from various fires being set in the horizon. People honking more than usual, and people driving more recklessly than I am accustomed to. Is this really what the end is like?

I pull up to my parents' house, and my brother's black truck is in the driveway. Several neighbors are filling their vehicles with supplies. Running back and forth from their garages with boxes and gallons of water, much like I saw earlier in the day. I grab my bag and walk up to the door. I go to open it and it is locked, which I would expect given the circumstances.

I ring the doorbell, and Stephen answers the door. His attention is fixed on the television, and as I walk in I can see my parents grabbing various supplies and putting them into boxes too. I walk over to my mom, and she stops and gives me a big hug.

"It is going to be alright, dear," she says trying to comfort me.

"I know, Mama. It is just crazy around here."

"Grace, did you pack enough supplies?" Dad says as he comes over and gives me a hug.

"Just a few things. I think they're just being overly dramatic," I say as I watch Mom stuff another sweater into a box.

"No way! It's about to be World War 3, you dummy," Stephen chimes in.

Mom gives Stephen the death stare, a look only a mother can give, and he turns back around and continues watching TV.

"Your dad and I think we should go ahead and try to get out of here for a few days. Just while it all settles down. You know? We haven't been to the cabin in years," she says as she hustles around.

"Whatever you guys think is best. Do you need help with anything?" I ask Mom.

"No, we're almost done here. Just relax with your brother."

I just give a half-smile and go over to the couch to sit down. Stephen looks behind us to see where Mom and Dad are, and then whispers to me: "They really think this is it. They are freaking out, but they don't want you to be scared."

"Who says I am scared?" I ask defensively.

"Relax, little sis, despite whatever we may all say or how we act, we are all scared."

I look at him, surprised to see how much he is trying to comfort me.

I go back to looking at the television, and they are showing the looting all over the news. People covering their faces with bandanas and rags, and wearing oversized hoodies to help conceal their identity. People throwing garbage cans and breaking the windows to the shops, as they flood the interior for non-essential items to take as they please. Cars are on fire, as people are spray-painting the walls with ominous messages about the end of the world. People running down the street in mobs, as groups of people swarm to attack the helpless victims attempting to protect their businesses. I cannot believe what I am seeing.

"This is really bad," I say as I look at my big brother.

"They have done this before, you know. Don't you remember the pandemic?"

"I know, but this is really scary. What if it really is World War 3?"

He pauses, then looks at me, "Well we survived the other two wars, so what makes you think we can't get through this one, too?"

Surprised at his optimism, "I guess you are right. Sometimes I forget you aren't always an idiot," I laugh.

He punches me in the arm, and I laugh once more. I shift my attention back to the news, but I can't help myself from drifting off into memories of the first time we were at the cabin.

Chapter Twelve

Present

The man holding the knife is covered in blood. He has ragged shoulder-length brown hair, knotted with blood and dirt. He reeks of sweaty body odor, and he is sweating profusely. His hand is shaking as he holds the blade close to my face. His eyes are black, and he looks hopeless.

"Sir, please…" I say as I start trying to develop a plan.

"Don't move," he says, his voice trembling.

"Please, I don't want to cause any trouble."

"How are you out here by yourself? What do you know?" he says as he begins frantically looking over each shoulder to see if I brought a companion.

"What do you want from me?" I say as I attempt to get my knife out without him noticing.

"Get your hands up! I will use this!" he says, thrusting the knife closer to my face. "Where the hell did you come from?!"

My hands are up in the air now in my go-to surrender position, "I was just passing through. I—I am not from this area."

He looks at me, like he knows I am lying. "You expect me to believe that? Where do you sleep at night?!" He takes the knife and slices my cheek, "Don't lie to me!" His voice cracks.

The laceration burns, but it is nothing I haven't had to deal with before. Pain is temporary. You know what you have to do. Research. Plan. Execute. He is by himself, distraught, and terror-struck. He is more scared of me than I am of him. I can tell by the way his voice cracks when he speaks. He thinks he has the upper hand, but I can see his trepidation. I have to make a run for it.

I shift my eyes from his to look past him, to make it look like someone is behind him. He turns to see what I am looking at, and I front kick him to the stomach. He is caught off guard and bends forward as he lets out a loud grunt. With all my might I push him, which causes him to fall to the ground. I run away as fast as I can. I only have a small head start, and I cannot risk looking back.

I hear him scream, "You bitch!"

I keep propelling myself forward, but he closes the distance quickly, faster than I expected considering his condition. I suddenly feel my ponytail yank from behind, bringing my forward motion to a halt, as he pulls me backwards causing me to land on my back. The wind is immediately knocked out of me and I let out a groan. As I am trying to catch my breath, he jumps on top of me, and strikes me with the handle of the knife one time to my forehead where I was already cut from yesterday. I plant my feet and use the strength of my legs to try to buck him off me, but he has to outweigh me by at least 150 pounds. I elbow him once to the face, as he continues to repeatedly strike me with the handle of the knife. Every time I make contact with his face, it does not appear to faze him, even though I can see blood dripping from his face. I can't reach my knife, and at this point I am shielding my face with one arm and doing my best to elbow and strike him with the other.

The attack feels like it will never end, and I am starting to get physically exhausted. A few minutes of fighting feels like an eternity, and I feel my muscles begin to spasm from the adrenaline. I know I need to try something else, because I will not be able to overpower him, especially after getting the wind knocked out of me. Is this the way I am going to die? I can feel my face begin to tingle as it swells, and the blood tickles my cheeks as it cascades down my face. I have to try to get to my knife. I take a deep breath, and then with all the remaining strength I have, I buck with my hips as hard as I can, using all my body weight, and it is just enough to make him fly forward. As he regains his balance, I have just enough space to grab the knife in my sheath. I pull the knife out, and just as I am about to stab him, I am momentarily distracted as I see something moving in the distance.

A blur of movement runs right toward us, and the newcomer causes my assailant to fly off me as he tackles him to the ground. I look over and I see that they begin to wrestle one another. They are throwing multiple punches, and I hear an assortment of grunts as they make contact with various body parts. Slightly dazed, I see the stranger reaching for the knife, pleading with my attacker to stop. Maybe it was one of his companions?

I get up and run, until I realize I have to help the stranger that helped me. As I look back at the pair on the ground, I can see that the stranger is now on top of my attacker and punching him in the face. I jog back toward them right as I see the knife go into the stranger's side as he lets out a loud scream. I grab my knife and push the stranger off my attacker. I stomp as hard as I can on the attacker's hand that is holding the knife. He lets out a loud agonizing howl, and with one quick motion I stab him in the eye. All his motion ceases as the blood begins to pool around his head.

Without allowing myself to think about it, I pull my knife from his eye socket. I wipe the excess blood on my pants and return my knife to its sheath. I grab the knife he had in his hand and throw it into the front pocket of my backpack. Wiping the blood from my face with my shirt, I cautiously walk over to the stranger.

"Thank you for saving me. Sorry—I am sorry if that was your friend."

He is hunched over, kneeling, looking at the ground. His hand is on his side, but it is bleeding badly. I can tell by the way the coagulated blood is seeping through his fingers. He is cut deep and won't make it much longer without some form of first aid. I kneel beside him and gently lift his hand to gauge the damage. It is just as bad as I suspected. I feel awful. I can't let him die, after all he did to save my life.

"Here, let me help you. I—I—have a place nearby with supplies."

He looks up at me.

You have got to be kidding me.

Chapter Thirteen

Before

We have been driving for hours. Stephen is being super annoying because he keeps playing some game in which he punches me in the arm whenever he sees an out of state license plate. I try to drown him out as I listen to music on my iPod. Mom and Dad want us to go camping at the family cabin this weekend, because they said we need to "reconnect" as a family or something. I think maybe it is just because Stephen is a teenager, and I am practically one too, since I am already twelve now.

It is very pretty here. This time of year is fetching because all the leaves are changing colors for fall. Sometimes as I stare out the window at the trees along the highway, with the music playing in my ears, I feel like I am in my own music video. I am zoning out when suddenly I feel a hard punch to my arm.

"Oregon!" yells Stephen.

"Ouch, Stephen! Mom! Stephen hit me again."

"Kids, can you please stop hitting each other. Your father is trying to focus. We are almost there."

Stephen just looks at me, mad that I tattled on him. I don't want to play his stupid games all the time. I look back out the window, when I see that Dad is turning onto a dirt pathway. The trees are very dense and the path seems very narrow. Luckily, we have a small car, or I don't think we would even fit. I can feel the air change, because the windows already feel drastically cooler than when we were on the highway. I shift from looking out the window so I can see through the front windshield. There is nothing in front of us but trees, and I begin to wonder if Dad made a wrong turn. He starts to turn left, and I am confused because I do not see where we are going. He continues to drive for another minute or so, and then stops the car.

"Ok, kids, we're here," he says.

Stephen and I look at one another confused. "Dad, I don't see anything. I thought there was a cabin here?" Stephen says.

Mom and Dad laugh, and then Mom says, "It is here, sweetie. You just need to know where to look. Come on, we'll show you."

We exit the car and all I see are trees and giant bushes. I have never seen such large shrubbery. They are at least six feet tall, or at least they feel like they are. There are no pathways to walk on, or a driveway, just a small open area barely big enough for the car. I stand right next to Stephen, because it is a little scary out here. Mom and Dad lead the way. They walk up to a big tree that appears distorted. Instead of standing tall, it is curving and bent. We get to the broken tree, and my parents turn right and start walking directly into the bushes.

"What are you doing?" I yell at them.

"Oh, Grace, you'll be fine," Dad says.

"But, Dad! What if there are spiders in there?"

"Stop being such a wuss. Come on." Stephen grabs my hand and pulls me toward the bushes.

My dad takes a key and inserts it directly into the bushes, then pushes open a door hidden inside. I realize that the bushes are actually intertwined with the fence, which is why they seem so large. With my eyes squeezed shut, I run through the bushes until I feel that I have cleared them completely.

The sun is peeking through the massive trees and warms my skin when I emerge from their shadows. It smells so different here, like wet dirt and pine needles. The air also feels clean and fresh compared to the smoggy L.A. air that I am used to. I finally get close enough to see the cabin, and it is large and beautiful. It has a flawless wood exterior, with a cute wrap around porch with rocking chairs and large windows to expose the beauty of the woods to whoever is inside. As I get closer, I can see a small cleared out area, with a round fire pit, and stacks of stone probably used as chairs. I didn't know places like this exist in real life.

My parents walk past us to the front door and open it. We follow them, and when we walk in I am surprised by how nice it is. I already feel comfortable here. Everything is made of wood, and there are oversized leather couches. I walk toward the living room and am amazed by the giant stone fireplace, and the deer head hanging above it. I guess it would not be a cabin if there weren't dead animals displayed on the walls.

"Alright, kids, we'll go get your bags. To prevent you from fighting, your mother and I have decided that Stephen will have the room on the right side of the hall, and, Grace, you will be on the left side. They are the same size, so no need to argue," my dad says sternly.

I walk over to the giant couch and plop down. It is so comfortable. Way better than the couch we have at home. Stephen walks out of the living room, and I imagine he is checking out the rooms. I continue to sit on the couch and stare out the giant window. It is strange that a cabin would be this hidden from the world. Disguised by rows of giant trees and bushes I had never seen before. It is peaceful though. Maybe someday this cabin will get passed on to me too. But knowing my luck, Stephen will end up with it.

My parents walk in with the few bags we have. Since we are only here for the weekend, our trip did not require a tremendous amount of luggage. Stephen walks back in from the hall and sits on the couch as well.

"I noticed there aren't TVs in any of the rooms," he states with annoyance in his voice.

"That was the point. We need to spend time as a family. Too many distractions these days," my mom says.

We continue to have small talk about everything that has been going on with everyone. I tell them about all the drama that has been going on between my friends, and how some of the girls were secretly dating the other girls' boyfriends. It has all been very scandalous, and way too much to keep up with. We are still just kids, I don't know why they are in such a rush to date boys anyway. After all, it's not like they can go anywhere without their parents taking them in the first place, and what kind of date is that?

After my junior high gossip, Stephen slowly begins filling my parents in on everything going on with his sports. He is a really good baseball player, even though I would never actually tell him that. He's on the varsity team, and it's a really big deal, I guess. Everything he does revolves around baseball. It is cool to see him so dedicated. Dad thinks he really has a chance at getting some college scholarships out of it.

It is already dark outside when my dad pulls out a box from the shelf and brings it to the table. "Alright, everyone, gather around. I thought we would play a game we haven't played in years," he says.

I look at the box and am filled with delight when I realize it is one of my favorite childhood games: Yahtzee.

We must have been playing for hours, because it seems even darker outside now than before. There are no curtains, and all I can see is the blackness of the forest out there. While it is stunning and secluded during the day, I feel exposed now. I feel like anyone out there could be hiding and watching us. It makes me feel uneasy. But being with my family, I know Dad would never let anything happen to me. So I turn my attention back to the game, happily playing Yahtzee with my family.

Chapter Fourteen

Present

The face is one I had grown to like very much in a different lifetime. The hair is longer, and much more disheveled than I had ever seen before. His face has only grown more ruggedly handsome with his scruffy beard, and his eyes are still the kind brown eyes I could never forget. He is thinner than before, but has still managed to keep his muscular frame.

"Grace?" he says with a startled look on his face.

"Oh my God, Nick. What are you doing here?" I say, grabbing onto his arms with my hands.

"What are you doing here?" he says as I feel his hands tighten on my arms in return.

"I've been here since this all started."

"I thought you had died for sure when they bombed L.A. I am so glad you are safe." He gives me the biggest hug, squeezing me tightly, like he didn't want to let me go. I am surprised how comforting a hug can be now. I am even more surprised he can hug so tightly after sustaining such a deep wound in his side.

"I am glad to see you made it out as well." I say to him as I pull back from the embrace.

"We lucked out and got out right before the bombs hit."

"I can't believe you are here!" Overcome by this serendipitous reunion that has brought me a friend, I give him another hug, tighter than before, and feel him flinch. "Oh my God, I am so sorry. I didn't mean to hurt you."

"You could never hurt me! I am just glad I found you when I did." He looks around, and his smile slowly drops, "Are you here alone?"

I look down and stay silent for a moment. "Yeah, it's just me now..." I pause briefly before changing the topic, "Look, I feel so horrible because I got you stabbed. I have to get you back to my house so I can bandage that up. It needs stitches." I look over to my attacker, "And—and I am sorry about your friend."

He looks at my attacker, "Sorry Ken tried to kill you. I wouldn't have let him hurt you. He was just scared, you know? He wasn't going to last much longer anyway, you probably did him a favor. Better than being ripped to shreds by those things out there."

He attempts to walk and then falls hard on the ground. I kneel beside him, "You are going to be fine. Do you mind if I check it out? I should probably bandage it before you lose too much blood."

Hesitantly he says, "If you insist."

I put my backpack down, pull out some old Purell wipes and some gauze and tape. I rip open the package of Purell wipes and lift his shirt to expose the cut.

"Ok, this is going to sting reeeeaaaaalllyyy bad, but you don't want an infection." We stare at each other for a moment, before he gives me a thumbs-up to let me know he is ready.

I press the wipe against the laceration, and I can feel his body wince with pain. I look up and can see him tightening his jaw.

"Almost done..." I lie, but a false sense of relief never hurt anyone.

I continue to wipe the semi-dried blood away from the laceration, before wiping the cut itself. I hold the wipe against the cut as I grab the gauze. I quickly trade the gauze with the wipe and continue to apply pressure. I grab the tape and apply a few strips to hold it in place until we can make it back to the cabin. I pull his shirt down.

"Ok, that should work for now. We have to try to hurry, though. With all of that screaming, I don't know who else could have heard."

I help him get onto his feet, and he trips a little bit. This is going to take forever with a wounded person. I am deep in contemplation because I recognize that this may be a really bad idea. I don't even know whether any of his friends are still alive and possibly watching us. I have so many thoughts racing through my mind—so much can go wrong.

I feel a heaviness in my chest as well, because killing that man was so effortless. He was scared. He was acting how anyone would act if they were in the same circumstances. He was trying to save himself. He didn't deserve to die. I should have just helped Nick fight, but I saw the opportunity and I reacted.

"Miss Baker," Nick says as we continue toward the cabin. "Did I say something to offend you?"

I look over at him, "No, why would you think that?"

"You're just very quiet."

I stop, which causes him to stop too, and face him, "I killed your friend, and you are worried if you said something to offend me?"

I can see he's taken aback by my stern tone, "You killed him to save me."

"I still killed him."

He pauses, "Do you want to talk about it?"

"Honestly, we don't have time for this. I need to get you back home, and it is going to take forever."

He opens his mouth to speak, but closes it before any words come out. After a brief pause, he goes to speak again, "Sorry I asked. Thank you for your help."

We continue walking toward the cabin, and I am angry at myself for my reaction. I can't take my anger out on him. He is trying to be nice and trying to make it not seem like such a big deal. I look at him, and he is just looking at the ground. "I'm sorry. I shouldn't have reacted that way."

His eyes meet mine, "There is no need to be sorry. I mean, what is there to say after something like that happens, right?"

"I know, but you saved my life, and I saved yours. So maybe we just leave it at that?"

"I think that is fair." He looks away, and back at the ground. I guess if I am going to have company, I need to re-learn how to properly socialize.

Chapter Fifteen

Before

It is shortly after 9:00 P.M., when my parents come rushing into the living room bringing me back to my reality and causing the memory to fade. The power is out now, and my parents have flashlights to illuminate the living room. In the distance I can hear screaming, explosions, and gunshots. I am so terrified. I look at my phone, and there is no signal. I realize we are completely cut off from the outside world. For the first time in my entire life we have no way to contact anyone to determine what is really going on. We have no idea what is happening, or how bad it really is out there, and the sounds are reminiscent of something you would see in a movie about the apocalypse. Is that what this is? Am I experiencing the end of mankind as we know it? I feel a sudden sense of dread in my stomach.

"Kids, grab whatever you can carry on your back. The car is full, and it is time we leave," says my dad impatiently.

Stephen and I both look at my dad without a single protest and nod our heads in agreement.

I go to my room, grab the few things I had gathered from my apartment, and quickly return to the living room. My parents are both anxiously waiting there, and Stephen comes in shortly after me.

"Ok, kids, time to go," my mom says in her usual comforting tone.

We make our way to the Suburban parked in the garage, and suddenly I feel so scared. My hands are trembling with fear, and I feel queasy. What are we going to see when we get out there? Is it going to be worse than what I had seen on my way over here? Will it be worse than what they were showing on the news? Are people going to try to attack us? The fear must have been written in large letters on my forehead because I feel Stephen grab my hand as he gives it a squeeze. I look at him and he whispers, "It's ok, little sis, we'll be alright."

I just give him a half smile and try to prepare myself for whatever I am going to see out there. The garage doors open, and Dad slowly backs out of the garage. I am staring out the passenger window, and it is unbelievable how dark it is. No streetlights to illuminate the pavement. No ambient lighting from the houses lining the yards and sidewalks. If it weren't for the headlights of the car, we would be in complete darkness.

The radio is off, and no one says a word. We cautiously drive down the streets, making our way to the closest freeway. As we get closer to the city, disorder has taken over. There are loud crashes of broken glass as people are looting the businesses like we had seen on the news hours earlier. Cars and trash cans overcome with giant flames. The smell of burning metal and chemicals inundate the interior of the car as we drive down the street. The closer we get to the city, the more screams we can hear, and the louder the gunshots become. I cover my ears, like a frightened child, and close my eyes. I let out a scream when I hear something strike our car.

"It's alright, Grace," says my dad, "someone just threw a rock."

I continue to cover my ears and close my eyes. I don't want to see anymore. We have to be close to the freeway by now. With every sudden swerve of the Suburban, I know there is something Dad is trying to avoid in the street. Is it bodies? Is it fire?

This is the end. This is how I always pictured the end. People losing all sense of civility among the chaos. I had read about it, and I had seen the movies, but no description could accurately represent what I was seeing at this very moment. What I never expected was the amount of fear I truly would feel.

We continue driving north, and once we get on the freeway it isn't so bad. I finally open my eyes again and can feel myself starting to relax. I guess I had anticipated traffic as people tried to flee the city like we were, based on how many people were loading their cars today. Yet, seeing the freeways so empty made this whole thing feel so much scarier and very dystopian. But really, where is anyone going to go? The threat is everywhere. We know our only chance is at the cabin, and that is where we are going. Hopefully it is undisturbed. Hopefully we have somewhere to call home.

We have been driving for about an hour. I finally find the courage to look out the window again. It is so strange to see the city lights out. Nothing to separate the hills from downtown. There are random orange spots where fires had begun in the distance, with just a hint of black smoke trailing into the sky prior to being soaked up by the darkness. There are so many stars in the sky that I had never been able to see before due to the bright city lights.

Suddenly, I see a huge fiery radiance in the sky. I close my eyes, and open them again. It is getting brighter.

"Oh my god, what is that?!" I say as I place my hand on the window.

"Oh no! John, dear, is that what I think it is?" My mom says.

"Susan, kids, look away. You don't want to look directly when it hits."

I knew what he meant by that. I was looking at a missile headed directly for downtown. Haven't we been through enough already? I can't bring myself to look away. I know it is moving fast, but it suddenly seems as though it is moving in slow motion. It gets closer and closer, inching its way toward its target. The hills that stand between us and downtown are now illuminated with an eerie fiery glow. As if a sudden burst of sunlight broke through the darkness, shining down on everything in its path. The light is hidden momentarily beyond the hills, and instantaneously, a huge explosion erupts. Despite the movement of the car, we can feel the earth shaking below us. I close my eyes, because I know there is nothing to look at any longer. It is all destroyed.

Where do we go from here?

Chapter Sixteen

Present

Making this trip is much harder with someone who is wounded. I can see how much he is in pain, and I can see he is already bleeding through the bandage. I have so many questions. Like number one, how did he survive last night when nearly his whole group was murdered? Had he figured out a way not to be detected by the monsters?

Also, I have not talked to someone in almost six months now, and I am dying to know what was out there. I am so anxious to know what kind of knowledge I had been shut off to by being cloistered up here. I want to know how he found this place to begin with.

It is different though. The years past have aged us so much already. There is pain in his eyes, just like there is pain in mine. I knew him before all of this happened, and the people we were are not the people we are now. I have killed people since the world unexpectedly ended, but every time it happens it takes more from me. Is this what we had become in this world? A life is a life, and there is still value in that. We were destined to destroy each other, but how many lives can I take before it consumes me and turns me into a monster?

"Grace… you haven't said a single word. You ok?"

"Yeah… I… I haven't talked to anyone in a long time, so I am still processing all this. It just feels like a dream." I continue looking forward even though I can feel his gaze on my face.

He puts his hand on my shoulder as we continue to walk, "That is terrible, I'm sorry."

"It's ok, I just want to get you home so we can get you all stitched up. Then we will have time to catch up." I am trying not to be rude, but he keeps trying to get me to talk about things I do not want to discuss.

He smiles, but I think he knows I am not ready to get into the entire conversation about how I ended up here alone. I am overwhelmed, I guess. Plagued by the improbable chance that this is even happening now. That somehow in a world long forgotten—a world destroyed from within—a familiar face would appear, under the circumstances he did. I have to remember that the Nick I knew before the end is not the Nick standing here now. I have to keep my guard up. It is so dangerous even considering bringing him back to my house. But I owe him. A life for a life; he saved mine and now I have to return the favor. I have to figure out what he knows, or doesn't know.

My thoughts are broken when I hear something just off the path. I stop and grab Nick's shirt collar to stop his momentum. I put my finger over my mouth to tell him not to make a sound. I point to the right and then to my ear as I mouth "listen" to him. He nods his head up and down, indicating that he understands. I hear the noise again, but this time from behind us. I spin around scanning the area, but I see nothing. I slowly walk toward where I heard the noise, just waiting to hear the familiar clicking sound. I have never encountered one during the day. How is this even possible? What if Nick and his companions really did draw more of them to this area?

Nick grabs my shoulder and points to where I originally heard the sound. Could there be two of them? If that is the case, we will never survive. I walk closer, listening for the clicking. I quietly remove the knife from my sheath, and I can hardly hear anything over my heart drumming in my chest. I can feel the sensation of sweat slowly dripping down my back as I make it closer to the sound. I hold my breath, afraid to make any more noise, and cautiously look around the tree.

Suddenly, a rabbit darts out of the bushes toward me and across the path. I jump and let out a small scream. I wipe my forehead with my sleeve, turn around, and can see that Nick is still focused on whatever we had originally heard. He is standing completely still, just staring in that direction. I walk closer but hear nothing. He looks at me and his face is completely pale. I am confused, I don't know what he sees. Then he takes his hand, puts it underneath my chin, and gently tilts my head up until I see what he is looking at.

Where the branches meet the tree trunks are what remain of dozens of bodies. Mangled pieces of flesh and tattered clothing strung along the trees. Where are we? I had walked this path hundreds of times. How could I have not seen it before? How could I have not smelled it? This has to be new. There has to be more than just one monster here. I was right, this place is no longer safe. We have to get out of here.

I grab Nick's arm and pull him forward so we can begin a light jog. I know he is hurt but we have to get inside. We have to figure out what the hell we just saw. We have to come up with a plan. I am certain those bodies had not been there earlier. I would have seen them. We have to get home as quickly as possible. Our lives depend on it.

Chapter Seventeen

Before

When I wake up, I am hoping everything I just witnessed was a dream. To my disappointment, it is not. We are still driving, and I look over at Stephen and he is sleeping. We must have been driving for hours, because I can see the sun starting to rise. Which means we are almost at the cabin by now, since we have had none of our usual road trip stops. My parents are talking quietly, but I eavesdrop since they think I am still asleep.

"What are we going to do, John?" My mother asks.

I see my dad grab my mom's hand, "We got out in time; we are going to be fine. We'll get through this."

"I know, but what if there is another series of bombings?"

"We are far enough away, no one will even think to bomb up here. Not enough casualties. This is the safest place we could possibly go. The cabin is poised for living in a rugged environment. We have everything we need there."

After a momentary pause, my mom says, "This is just really bad. I knew there was a possibility of this happening, but I really didn't believe it would happen this way. Did you?" I can sense the emotion in my mom's voice.

He lifts my mom's hand and kisses it, "No, I really didn't think so. I thought we had learned our lessons, but we just seem to keep repeating history. At least we are all here as a family."

"I am just so grateful the kids came, and we were able to get out together. Imagine if Grace was still at work? Or stuck out there all by herself? I couldn't have my baby girl out there to endure all of that."

"Honey, I have been training her for years. She is a smart, and very capable girl. We have great children. We are lucky."

"I know, but maybe we should have prepared them better? Maybe told them more of what we know?"

"Susan, there was no way that we could have ever imagined any of this was actually going to happen. We did the best we could to prepare them based on what little we did know. They are going to be just fine, dear. We all are going to be just fine."

"I know. I just worry. What if anything happens to us?" I see her move her head to look out of the window.

"That is exactly why we trained them the way we did. They need each other. They will learn to work together."

"I just worry about them. Grace is so smart and capable, but she is always doubting herself. Stephen, on the other hand, can be so smug and sometimes condescending with her. They need to be able to get along."

Dad lets out a sigh, and then says: "We have been hard on our children for good reason, and look how they have turned out. I have seen them work together, and comfort one another when the opportunity presented itself. We have good kids, Susan. Not to mention we are all together. Pretty soon they will understand the importance of family, if they don't already. Trust me."

I see my mom smile, "Oh look, we are almost there."

I stay quiet and try to process everything that has happened over the last twenty-four hours. I also try to process what my parents were just talking about. I know he had top-secret clearance in the military, but I never stopped to ask him exactly what his role was. Did he know this was going to happen someday? I know he always saw it as Stephen being the brawn, and me having the brains. He always made sure that Stephen was strong, and ready for any physical task; whereas, I was the one to solve the problems. Is that why he trained us the way he did? Was it his way of making us dependent on one another if some catastrophic event like this happened? Has he been prepping us our entire lives to be able to take care of each other? What do my parents actually know?

Looking back, how old was I when he started introducing me to his puzzles and riddles? I could not have been much older than six or seven. I can't even remember those first lessons. I can only remember, vaguely, his explanation for why we had to do the lessons.

Dad looks at me sternly, "Grace, I know this will not make sense because you are so young—"

"Dad, I am not a little girl anymore!" I protest with my hands on my hips.

"Don't interrupt me, Grace, this is important. While you may think that you are not a little girl, you still have much to learn if you want to be a big girl already."

"Then why do you treat me like I am a little girl?"

He pulls me closer to him, and puts his hands on my shoulders, "Because, you are my little girl. You will always be my little girl. I want you to be safe. Do you understand that?"

"Yes, Daddy," I say with a pout.

"I need you to take all of this serious, because by the time you are a big girl the world might be a different place, and I need you to be able to take care of yourself."

I roll my eyes, "I still don't understand why we are doing this."

He pats me on the head, "I know, sweetie, and that is why it is time we start doing some of these lessons. It will all make sense someday, I promise." He extends his hand out to me with his pinky in the air. I smile and wrap my pinky around his.

"Pinky promise," he says with a smile.

"Pinky promise!" I respond with a giggle. "But, Daddy, I don't understand. What lessons?"

He sits next to me. "Grace, the world is a confusing place. Sometimes things happen that we can't explain, or that we don't understand. Sometimes we are put in dangerous situations and have to think quickly on our feet. Sometimes we have to figure out how to survive."

I just sit there looking at him, trying to understand the riddles he is speaking.

He stands up and walks to the closet where Mom keeps some of our craft supplies. As he pulls out our portable standing whiteboard, Dad continues, "I think it is important that we develop a set of skills so that, no matter what type of situation you are placed in, you can figure a way out. Does that make sense?"

I shrug my shoulders, "I guess."

"So we have to remember, everything in life can be summed up in this formula, so pay close attention. Whenever there is a problem we feel we need to solve, we begin with identifying what the problem is. You cannot solve a problem if you do not even understand the problem you are trying to solve. So rule number one: Identify what the problem is. You tracking with me?"

"Yes, Dad."

"Good." He turns to the dry-erase board and hurriedly scribbles in red ink, Rule 1: Identify Problem. He faces me again and continues, "Ok, rule number two: Research what you need to know about the problem. For example, what resources do you have available to you, what are the strengths and weaknesses of either you or the person or problem, and what advantages and disadvantages are there?" Dad pauses for a moment to add Rule 2: Research Problem to the board. "Still following?" he asks over his shoulder.

"Oh my gosh, Dad, yes!" I start getting impatient.

"Don't bite my head off, this is important. Ok, rule number three: Once you have developed your plan, you need to conduct trials, if practical. Applying theories or different aspects to your plan to see what works and doesn't work. This one is really important because sometimes you won't have the luxury to experiment available to you, and you will have to think of all the things that can go wrong and can go right with your plan even without trials. So when it comes to conducting your research, you cannot leave any components out."

"Okkkk, Dad." I impatiently read his list back to him, "Identify the problem, research the problem, and experiment. Got it. Can I go now?"

"No. Alright, once you have figured out your problem, conducted your research, did trials if plausible, then all that is left—" he turns to write Rule 4: Execute under the others, "is to actually execute your plan."

"That sounds easy enough. I already told you, Dad, I am a big girl now, I can handle it. I know how to follow instructions."

"Grace, I cannot stress this enough." He returns the cap to its pen and looks straight at me, commanding my attention. He spins the white board so that I can't see the writing on the other side. "Whenever you come across a time in your life when you feel like something bad is going to happen, I need you to remember this: research, plan, execute. Can you remember that?"

"Yeah, Dad."

"Repeat it."

I take my hand and put my pointer finger in the air, "Number one is research." I put my middle finger up to join the pointer finger, "Number two is plan." Finally I put my ring finger up, "And number three.... Umm... number three..."

"Grace! Focus."

"I'm sorry, Dad. One more time."

"Research, plan, execute."

"Oh, yeah, that's right. Research, plan, execute." I say with confidence.

"One more time."

"Fine, research, plan, execute. I got it."

He walks over and gives me a huge hug before kneeling on one knee to look me directly face to face, "One more time, Grace."

"Research, plan, execute."

"Such a smart girl," he kisses my forehead.

"Can I go out and play now?"

He laughs, "Yes, you earned it. We'll talk more about this later."

I can remember that very first lesson like it is happening right now. I was so young, and I can still see the seriousness in his face. Hearing him talk to my mother right now, and remembering everything he has been teaching me, chills me to my core. Dad, did you know this was coming all along? If you did know, why would you keep it from us? We had a right to know what was coming.

Chapter Eighteen

Present

We enter the cabin through the secret entrance. After locking the door behind us, I escort Nick to the couch. I grab my first aid supplies in the bathroom to get him stitched up, put the supplies on the table in front of him and walk to the cabinet to grab a bottle of whiskey, placing it on the table beside the supplies.

"I hope you are planning to drink the liquor after you stitch me up, Miss Baker," he says with a smile.

"This isn't for me, it's for you. I don't have an actual suture kit, so I'll be using just a needle and thread."

His face turns white when he processes what I just said. He reaches for the bottle and takes a big swig, shaking his head when the whiskey hits his throat.

"I forgot the sting of whiskey."

"It isn't the best quality whiskey, so I apologize. Unfortunately, I can't just order the good stuff for delivery anymore," I say as I shrug my shoulders.

He laughs, "Oh man, do you remember that? Being able to order anything you wanted and have it delivered by the next day usually. I miss that." He takes another sip.

"There is a lot more I miss than just Amazon Prime. Like actually going to a doctor for stitches," I say as I show him the needle and thread.

"Do you have any experience in this?"

"I had to do it to myself about six months ago."

I stand up, lift my shirt, and show him my stomach. Nick leans in closer to see the scar, and then takes his hand to feel it. I flinch at his touch, partially because his hands are cold, and partially because it has been such a long time since I felt human contact.

"Hmm… I'd give you a B+. Not bad for doing it on yourself, but definitely could use some practice."

I smile, "Luckily I haven't had to practice too much. This was an unfortunate accident where I impaled myself; it was a much harder wound to close. It will be a lot easier to close a knife wound than what I was working with on myself."

He looks at me with his mouth open, grabs the whiskey bottle, and takes another gulp.

"Ok, I just need you to lie more on your side. Do you want me to give you something to bite down on, to help with the pain?"

He shakes his head no, and then tries to reposition himself on his side. I move the table away from the couch so I can kneel and have the laceration eye level. I grab the alcohol and some cotton pads.

"This is going to hurt even more than the Purell wipes, ok? But I'll try to be gentle."

He takes a deep breath, "Ok, I trust you."

I don't know why he would trust me. I hardly trust myself doing this. I guess desperate times call for desperate measures. I pour the alcohol on the wound, and I can see his body tighten up. I start blowing on the wound, like a mother tending to a child, as I wipe the blood with the cotton pads. I continue wiping until the dried blood is gone. I grab the needle that was already pre-threaded in case of an emergency.

"Umm… you ready, Nick?"

"Ready as I'll ever be."

I squeeze the skin surrounding the laceration together and take the needle to his skin. He immediately lets out a loud shriek, but I cannot stop. I pull the needle slowly through his skin, trying not to tug too hard, but it is impossible not to induce more pain. With each pull of the thread I can feel his body tense as he tries to maintain whatever is left of his tough exterior.

"I am almost done, I swear, just keep being strong. You are doing great." I say to him while tugging on the needle.

I pierce the needle through the final edge of the laceration, pull on the thread to make sure it is tight, and knot the thread. I take a pair of scissors and cut the remaining thread, go over the treated area one more time with alcohol, and then cover it with some gauze and tape.

"It is going to hurt for a few days, but this will prevent it from getting infected."

He just looks at me and I can see how much pain he is in. I feel terrible because it is my fault he got hurt in the first place, but there was nothing I could do to make him feel better.

"Oh, I forgot." I lift his shirt, and kiss the freshly threaded wound, "That is the most important part. All better now." I smile.

He smiles, and then grabs his side in pain, "You wouldn't have anything to help with the pain, would you?"

"So demanding, Mr. Gates. Just have some more whiskey." I hand him the bottle and he takes another sip.

"You should be careful getting me all liquored up, you know. I am probably a cheap drunk now."

"Even better," I say with a smile. "You really should get some rest, though. The couch will work for now. There is no need to go out until you get better. I think we have enough supplies to last a little bit."

I stand up and turn around to walk away, when he calls out to me.

"Grace, I really am sorry about what happened."

I really wish he would just drop the issue already. I turn and look down at him lying on the couch. He looks so innocent. "Don't apologize. You didn't do anything wrong. I am just glad I could help."

He pauses before responding. "I'm glad I found you. I just wish it had been under better circumstances," he says.

I don't know how to respond, but after a moment I say: "Things work out the way they are meant to work out. Just get some sleep, ok?"

"Will you be here when I wake up?"

I laugh, "I don't have anywhere else to go. This is my home now."

He smiles, and then closes his eyes. I walk down into the basement so I don't disturb him while he sleeps. My sanctuary welcomes me, and I lie down on the cot. I want to give Nick some time to rest before it is time to come down here and lock up for the night. I am completely beat as well. I had so many surges of adrenaline that I feel utterly gassed. I try to keep my eyes open so I don't fall asleep. As I lie here, I cannot believe the bizarre change in events that have occurred over the past twenty-four hours. Last night, I was completely alone, and now Nick is here. How many times have I revisited the moments we spent together? How many times have I wished life wouldn't have ended before I could tell him how I feel? How many times did I read that note when I was alone and could not bear the silence? Does he know that he has helped me get through the last couple years? He can't possibly know any of this. It is just all a crazy, ridiculous coincidence.

I must have fallen asleep, because I awaken to the sound of a page turning. I look and I see him reading my notebook. Startled, I jump up and grab the notebook from his hands.

"Nick! What are you doing?" I yell at him.

He looks surprised, and then says, "Oh geez, Grace. I'm sorry. I didn't want to wake you up because you looked so peaceful. I saw this on the shelf. I didn't know—"

I interrupt him, "You didn't know not to read a female's journal? Was that allowed before the world ended? Because I am pretty sure it was not acceptable back then either."

He looks at me, speechless. "I—"

I interrupt him once more, "You what?"

He looks away, and down at the floor. "You're right. I'm sorry. I don't know what I was thinking."

I can tell he's being sincere. I take a breath before speaking to try to sound more level-headed, despite my outrage. "It's just—it seems so personal to have someone else read it. I did not give you permission to read this. I didn't mean to yell at you, I just feel like it is such an invasion of privacy."

"Grace, trust me, I know it is a total invasion of privacy, I screwed up big time. But hear me out—"

"Hear you out? I brought you back into my home, and you repay my generosity by reading my journal?" I say with a sarcastic laugh.

I go to stand up and walk away from him, but he grabs my arm. "Grace, please—" His eyes are pleading with me.

"Please, don't look at me like that," I say to him.

"Grace, please. Just listen to me. I know I don't really know you, but I know you are private. You are always trying to hide whatever you're feeling. When I saw what this was, I knew that if I didn't read it, you would never tell me what really happened."

I pull my arm away from his grasp, "So you think since I won't talk about it, that you can just read my thoughts, and I would thank you for it?"

"No, not exactly." He looks away from me.

After a moment, I sit down next to him, "You're right, I am not that person who is going to talk about my feelings. You need to respect my boundaries."

He looks down, averting eye contact. "Ok, I was wrong."

I take a deep breath, "Listen, I have this giant wall up, and I get that. I just need you to trust me, that if it is something worth talking about I will—"

He tries to interrupt me, "But—"

"No. No interruptions. Just listen, please? We were raised completely different. I have reasons for being this way, and I respect that you are more open to talking about things. All I ask is that you please give me time. I will discuss what transpired when I am ready. Do not rush me, because I am still dealing with a lot of traumatic stuff that I am trying to figure out. Is that too much to ask?"

He looks me in the eye now and quietly responds, "No, it isn't at all. I am so sorry for all you have been through."

"I am sure you have had your fair share of loss and hardships as well. And if it is something you want to talk about, then I am here to listen. I just don't want to talk about what happened with me. It is over with, and there is no sense in reliving it over and over again."

"I know, but to read it in your own words… I just don't know what to say."

"Please, don't say anything. It is over with. It is all just growing pains. We will get used to this new situation and learn each other's boundaries. That being said, we have a few hours before we have to call it a night. So I think we should go back upstairs and get some food."

I walk into the basement as he follows me, and I grab a bottle of wine from the corner of the room. "This used to be a wine cellar. Might as well open a bottle if we are sharing secrets." I look at him and force a smile, and we walk back up to the main living area.

CHAPTER NINETEEN

BEFORE

We get to the cabin, and luckily, it's still standing. We haven't been up here in years, but nothing about it has changed. Before we enter, Dad wants to make sure there is no one taking refuge inside. So he makes his way through the cabin, clearing it for potential unwanted visitors, and alerts us when it is safe to enter.

I grab the few items I brought, and I take them to my room. I am devastated by everything that has transpired in the last twenty-four hours. All that is left from my life before are a few items of clothing, and a backpack with some meaningful possessions. All that I know is gone. All that I wanted to be doesn't exist anymore. What have we done to ourselves?

I am sitting on my bed, holding onto the book Nick found for me, when my mom walks in and sits down next to me. She takes her hand and wipes the tear rolling down my cheek. She then uses that same hand to tuck a loose strand of hair behind my ear.

"How are you doing, hun?"

"To be honest, Mama, I am not doing so well," I say as I try to choke back my tears.

She puts her arm around me, and I lay my head on her shoulder, "We are a strong family," she assures. "We have each other, and we will make it through this together. You know that."

"I know… I just never thought this stuff happened in real life, you know?"

She kisses the top of my head, "I love you, Grace. It will get easier."

I lift my head from her shoulder and look at her, "I love you, too, Mom."

She takes both hands and places them on my cheeks. "You are a strong girl. We will get through this."

I feel another tear spill from my eye, "But, Mom, what kind of life is this? I mean, what does all this mean? We are just going to spend the rest of our lives pretending like we are on a camping trip indefinitely?"

"It means we are lucky, dear. This is just a bump in the road. There will be a future for all of us." She removes her hands from my face and gently grabs my hand that is on my lap.

"How do you know, though?" I say looking at her.

"I just know. Think of it as mother wisdom." She smiles at me and looks down at the book I am holding with my other hand. "I see your friend finally returned your book."

I sniffle, "No, actually this was given to me by my friend at the café. I told him about it one day, and when I saw him a few days ago he had it for me. Said he found it while he was cleaning up."

She looks at me and smiles, "Oh, is that what he said?" She wipes another tear from my cheek. "Well it sounds like he was a very nice boy."

"He was, and now I will never see him again." I bury my head into her shoulder once again.

She begins to run her fingers through my hair, "Well you never know, Grace. Life has a funny way of working out. Maybe when all this is settled you will see him again."

I lift my head and look into her eyes, "Mom, you know that isn't true."

"Honey, I know things are hard. They will continue to be hard for a while. But we will get through this. We will pick up where we left off, and we will have a new life. Just stay positive. That is all we can do now."

"I am trying to be strong."

"You aren't trying, Grace. You are doing it. You are being strong. Emotions like these are expected. Everything will work out in the end. Trust me." She gets up and walks out of my room. She is right. We are all together. If anyone can survive the apocalypse it is the Baker family.

I put what is left of my former life in the drawers and the shelves. I take a look around and recognize that this will be my life now. I cannot be a scared little girl anymore. I have to be strong. Now more than ever I have to control my emotions. Fear is weakness. I have to play my part so that we can survive as a family. Research, plan, execute. I must research how to survive, then plan how I am going to survive, and then survive. This isn't a book, and this isn't a movie. I need to expect the unexpected. I have to train myself to no longer dream, but live in each moment. This new life is going to be difficult. Whoever remains out there will not care about consequences. They will not be deterred by laws. There is no one left to enforce laws. Everything is going to be different.

I walk out into the living room, and everyone is sitting at the table. I join them, and my dad begins to talk as I sit down.

"Just in time, Grace. I just wanted to talk to you guys about some important matters. I think we can all agree that things are going to be very bad for a very long time. We need to remember that people are no longer people anymore. They will do whatever they can to take from us, and to hurt us if necessary. From now on we stay together. No going into the woods alone. Do I make myself clear?"

In unison, Stephen and I reply with, "Yes, Dad."

"No one was prepared for something like this. Everything people have grown accustomed to is gone. They will not hesitate to take from us to ensure their survival. There is nothing to stop them from hurting us. We are our only protection now. We have to be smart if we want to survive. Do I make myself clear?"

Once again, in unison, we respond with, "Yes, Dad."

"It is going to take some time to get acclimated to this new way of living. I am telling you kids now that it is not going to be easy. It will be hard work, but we will get there. We will have a normal life again, as long as we make some sacrifices to begin with. I know that is asking so much from you, considering all the sacrifices you have already made, but I need you to pull your weight."

Stephen and I nod in agreement.

"I know we are all tired, but we have to get to town and try to gather whatever supplies we can get before it is all gone. I don't even know what will be left at this point, but we have to try. How are you kids feeling? Do you think you will be able to handle yourselves if anything happens?"

We nod our heads yes once more.

"Normally I would not recommend taking a car for this sort of thing, but we don't have much time. Plus, we need to load up whatever we can. So, grab something that you can put supplies in, and be ready to go in a few minutes."

We all stand up and Stephen and I look at one another. What is going to happen when we get to town? Is it going to be as bad as Los Angeles? What kind of horrors await us there?

Chapter Twenty

Present

I laugh so hard that I snort, which only makes me laugh even harder. Which in turn makes Nick laugh even harder. He grabs the bottle of wine and pours more into each one of our glasses.

"Ok, your turn," he says.

"Ok. Ok. Umm..." I start giggling, "Never have I ever... laughed so hard I peed my pants."

He takes a sip.

"Ew! Nicholas Gates! Why would you admit that?" I say as I break out in laughter again.

"To be fair, you asked the question, so don't ask something you don't want to know the answer to."

"Still, ew! You are cleaning that chair when we're done."

He laughs uproariously, "I didn't say that I peed my pants right now! I alluded to the fact that in some point in my life it may have happened." I roll my eyes, and he continues, "Ok, my turn. Umm, never have I ever gone streaking."

I laugh, "Do I look like someone who would go streaking, Nicholas?" He just laughs, and I continue, "Never have I ever been trapped in an elevator."

He takes a sip, "It was the worst experience of my life. Pretty sure that may or may not have been how I peed my pants in the first place anyway," he says laughing again, "Ok, hmm... I am running out of things to ask."

"Ok, I'll ask another one." I pause to think of another. "You are right, I am running out of things to ask too. Umm…never have I ever broken a bone."

He takes a sip. "I was in third grade, riding my bike, trying to show off to my friends. I tried to do this cool Evel Knievel jump, which probably was only like two feet high to begin with, and I crashed terribly. Broke my right arm."

"Oh, poor Nick. I have been fortunate that I have never broken a bone. I have come close, though, since I have been out here."

"Ok, my turn. Never have I ever dined and dashed."

I take a sip. "Grace Baker! I am so disappointed in you," he says as he hiccups.

"Ok, to be fair, it was my stupid friend's idea, and I felt so guilty I pretended I had to go make a phone call so I could go back in and pay the actual bill."

He starts laughing uproariously once more, "That is such a Grace Baker thing to do!"

"I know, I know." I pour more wine into my glass. "I am such a square. I don't deny it. Hmm. Let me think. Ok, I got it." I start to chuckle, "Never have I ever sent a juicy text message to someone it wasn't meant for."

He takes a sip, "That was actually a really funny story. I had this bet with my friends that I lost. I can't even remember what it was about. They made me wear a woman's bikini, and I was supposed to send it to a girl of their choosing. Unfortunately, I sent it to the wrong contact. It just happened to be my aunt who had the same name of the girl they wanted me to send it to. I got yelled at big time for that one."

I start laughing hysterically. "There is so much I didn't know about you, Nick. You have so many funny stories."

"Well since you asked a juicy one, I think it is only fair I ask one in return," he says as he hiccups again. "Never have I ever… received a nice note in a book before."

I look up at him, surprised he would remember that. I take a sip of my wine, and he smiles in response. Maybe, just like I had been holding onto it for comfort, he had been, too. That one small innocent moment that happened before our lives changed forever.

Clearly out of ridiculous questions to ask one another, we just sit there in silence drinking our wine. After a few minutes, I look at my glass, "You know, for the last few hours I almost forgot all of this was happening. It has been so long since I laughed with someone. It feels… normal. I forgot what normal feels like."

"I entirely agree," he says with a hiccup.

"You never told me how you survived last night…" I was waiting to ask at the right time, but when is the right time to ask someone that?

He looks down, almost like he is ashamed. "It isn't some story of heroism or anything, it really was just a byproduct of being in the right place at the right time."

"I'm not tracking what you're saying."

He sighs, "It had been a while since we had been near a town, so I decided to explore. See if any of the stores had anything left. We had never encountered them during the day, and I had no way of knowing a storm was coming. I didn't even know how dark it was outside. I was in the liquor store when I heard the screams, and I just hid. I didn't know what else to do. Not my proudest moment. I ended up falling asleep underneath the counter, and I woke up when I heard you guys fighting. I didn't even know everyone else had been killed." He pauses, "I just don't even know what this world has come to."

"Do you want to tell me about them? Will talking about your friends help?"

"Honestly, I didn't really know them. I have been traveling solo for a while, because you can't trust anyone these days. I met them about a week ago, maybe? To be honest, the only person whose name I knew was Ken's."

"I am sorry, Nick."

"It all works out in the end, I guess. I mean, after all, they brought me up here."

We exchange a smile, but I can't wait any longer. "What is it like out there? I have to know."

He gets quiet and just stares at me for a few moments. "It's bad, Grace. It's really bad."

I get choked up. "Is it all gone?"

He looks down at his glass. "We destroyed ourselves. We blew each other up; left disarray in the ruins. I barely made it out of downtown before we got bombed."

"It is just so devastating."

"Shortly after the bombing, the worst of everyone just came out. It was every man for himself. The media went dark. Honestly, last I heard, the world kind of just blew everyone to pieces." He takes another sip from his glass.

Finally, I find the courage to ask what I really wanted to know. "Are there monsters everywhere?"

"Unfortunately, yes. I mean, everywhere in California at least. That is the only place I have been since the bombings. Just been traveling north up the coast. No one seems to know what they are. They just came out of nowhere. I—I've never seen such destruction, Grace. It's been terrible."

"I really was praying that they were only here."

"With no way to communicate, every place I have been, we just weather the storm and see if the monsters show up. No one seems to know where they came from, or what they want. We were just getting used to trying to rebuild a new life, and then people started getting attacked. I mean, where did they come from? What do they want with us? And how do we fight them?!" He pauses. "Grace, I just feel like, what is there even worth fighting for anymore? We just can't win."

I grab his hand. "Hey, no self-loathing in the cabin—it's a rule. We are better than this. We have to fight. There is something bigger than this; we can't give up."

"But—"

"Don't but me, Nicholas! I am serious. There has to be a reason why I am still here. I feel—I don't know—I feel like I was meant to figure this all out."

He lets go of my hand and places his hand on my cheek. "You look convincing, Grace. I am just tired of running."

I place my hand over his and gently squeeze it. "Ok, then let's not run anymore. Let's figure this out... together."

"Do you really think we are capable of defeating them?"

"I do! Together we can figure them out. Actually, we have no choice, we have to figure it out. What we saw today, that is all new. I don't think we can be here much longer."

He drops his hand from my face. "Ok. We'll try..." He puts his head down on the table, and hiccups. "Grace..."

"Yes?"

"The end of the world suits you..." He closes his eyes and begins to snore almost instantaneously.

"Just what I need... someone who snores," I say to myself. I shake him so he wakes up, "Hey, let me take you downstairs. We sleep in the basement."

He doesn't protest. He clumsily gets up and puts his arm around my shoulder as I escort him downstairs. I lock everything behind me, and I assist him into bed. I cover him with the blanket, and he scoots over as to give me some space.

"I'm just going to do some writing; I'll be up there in a minute." I lie to him.

He falls asleep, and I begin writing in my journal.

Day 621

Today I almost died, again. I went back into town to figure out who the travelers were. Just as I had suspected, they had been attacked by the monsters during the course of the night. A lone traveler remained and attempted to kill me. During the struggle, one of his companions intervened and assisted me in surviving. I guess that is what we call killing people now: surviving. It happens to be an old friend from Los Angeles, and I must admit the company is welcomed. I had gotten so used to being alone that it is refreshing to have someone to talk to besides myself.

I was hoping that the monsters were only in this area, but it sounds like they are everywhere. Nick said that there isn't much known about them beyond what I know, which is practically nothing. They attack during the darkness, they cannot be seen by the human eye, and they make a clicking noise when they are around. They do not seem to be attracted by sound, based on the experience I had when I lost Stephen, which leaves only a few options: sight, smell, or maybe heat signature? Should I tell Nick what I really know about them? Is it safe for him to really know what I know? Will that somehow put him in more danger? I still don't really know his intentions, and I need to be cautious in what I share with him.

I still can't make sense of what I saw today, though. There were the bodies torn to shreds in the town, but then there were the bodies hanging in the trees. The most obvious answer is that we are their food source. That is the most logical explanation. I think the best thing we can do is collectively gather what we know, and apply the good old Papa Baker method. Research, Plan, and Execute. We will have to try doing some tests with animals to see what we can learn. Maybe catch some animals and do different experiments to see what attracts them. We have to be selective in how we conduct our tests, though. Our resources are limited, and the more time we spend outside of the cabin the more likely we are to encounter savage humans or the monsters. We have to determine how we can conduct the least amount of tests, while obtaining the most relevant data. I could really use technology right about now. A notebook and pencil are hardly the tools to analyze and interpret data.

I just feel like now I have a chance to figure this out, because I am not alone. I don't think he plans on being here forever, but maybe he'll be on board to at least try to get a handle on these monsters. Maybe he was right when he said the end of the world suits me. Maybe that is what my purpose has been all along.

Chapter Twenty-One

Before

We get to town and are shocked to see how desolate it is. A complete contrast to what we had seen in Los Angeles. No charred buildings or destruction in the streets. It is just completely abandoned, like everyone around here just disappeared. It is actually very unnerving, like a modern-day Roanoke Island.

My dad finds an alley to park the car in next to the town grocery store.

"We need to be fast, and quiet," he says.

So, we silently exit the car, making sure not to slam the car doors by gently pushing them shut until the lock catches. My dad walks to the mouth of the alley and looks both ways. He turns around and gives us a thumbs-up to show us the all clear. We are practically tiptoeing, trying to be as noiseless as possible. When we get to the front glass door, I am surprised to see that there are no broken windows. Dad peers in to see if anyone is in there. Since there appears to be no evidence of movement, he tries the door handle, and it is unlocked.

He opens the door and has us wait as he checks the aisles to see if anyone is waiting for us. Once again, all clear. There are still a good amount of groceries here. Apparently, small towns didn't feel the need to hoard supplies like the big cities did. We grab as much food with a long shelf life as we can. Canned goods, cereal, oatmeal, cookies, crackers, you know, all the stuff with preservatives that they insisted was so bad for you. It is comical when you consider that all the things people swore were so bad, that would kill you someday, will become our saving grace now.

We run the food back to the car and come back for additional supplies. After food, the most important supplies we can get are first aid items like Band-Aids, gauze, tape, alcohol and peroxide. The last thing we would want to happen is to get an infection on a small injury and die. After collecting as many first aid supplies as we can gather, we grab whatever camping supplies we can find, like lighters, matches, and lighter fluid. Finally, we do one more run to get the most important thing: water. We grab all that remains of the bottled water, because we know we cannot survive without it.

After that, we drive to the local pharmacy, utilizing the same routine. Dad checks to see if anyone is in there, and it is empty as well. We go directly for the important stuff: antibiotics. We have no idea how long we will be in this situation, but we know we didn't want to succumb to something that just required some medicine.

We get back in the truck and drive through the completely deserted town. It has been untouched, and it gives me hope that maybe only Los Angeles had been affected. Maybe there is still a chance of a normal life again after all.

We head back toward the cabin, when I finally ask, "Wasn't that weird?"

"What do you mean, Grace?" inquires my mom.

"The fact that there is absolutely no one up here. There are so many more supplies, too."

"Not really," says Dad. "This is much more of a tourist destination, and this isn't really the high season."

"I know, but it just seems weird how it is like everyone just disappeared."

I see my Mom smile, "They didn't disappear, don't you remember the few times we came up here during the off season?" she asks.

"I guess not."

"Well the town was very much the same, but there were people actually manning the stores."

"She's right," adds Stephen.

"I don't know. It all seems weird to me."

"Everything seems weird to you, because you read all those weird books," says Stephen.

"They are not weird! I don't make fun of you for those dumb video games you play. At least I can continue my hobby during the apocalypse. Sucks to like things that require electricity—"

"Enough. Must we argue like this?" says Mom.

Stephen punches my arm, and I return with a strike in his arm as payback. He is about to hit me again, when Dad interrupts him, "Stephen, stop hitting your sister. You guys will get a chance to fight later, in a more appropriate setting, so save your energy for that."

Confused, we look at each other, "Wait, what? What do you mean we will fight later?" I ask.

Dad just laughs and doesn't answer the question. He begins to have a side conversation with my mom as we drive back toward the cabin. Really, though, what did he mean by that?

Chapter Twenty-Two

Present

I forget that I had slept on the floor. I hear the battery-powered alarm go off, and the alarm is not in its normal spot. As I reach for it, I knock over various items, trying to turn it off before it wakes up Nick.

His head is buried in the pillow, as he mumbles, "I know we have nowhere to be right now, so why in the world is there an alarm clock going off?!"

I finally locate it and mute it. "It lets me know when it is safe to go upstairs, since there is no natural light down here. You can stay down here and sleep. Actually, you should! You need to rest since you are nursing a pretty bad injury."

He groans as he turns onto his back and covers his eyes with his hand, "How can I be so hungover right now that my head hurts more than my stab wound does?"

I laugh, "Your body isn't used to alcohol anymore. Plus, I am sure you are still recovering from the fight you had, and from being stabbed as well. It is like a sensory overload."

I turn on the lantern, and he looks at me. He puts his hand on my cheek and I pull back in pain. I had forgotten that I had bruising and a laceration to my face.

"Looks like you are nursing an injury, too."

"Oh, it is nothing I haven't survived before. Plus, bruises and cuts are good for you. They make you look tougher than you are!"

"I don't think you need bruises to make you look tough," he smiles. "Alright... alright. Show me a day in the life of Miss Baker," he says as he rolls to sit up.

"Well as you can see, we sleep in the basement. Due to your level of intoxication, I was unable to explain it to you better last night."

"It does seem like a weird place to call home," he says as he looks around the room.

"Well I didn't always sleep down here. The night Stephen died, I was so scared that I ran down here to hide. I felt like they were going to follow me home and make it inside. Then, once I was alone, there was an incident when someone tried breaking in, and before he could get in, the monsters got him. I realized that it wasn't a bad idea to have the additional barriers between me and whatever was out there. So, the next night, I moved all the stuff out of here and made it my new room. It's comforting, because I feel like it gives me a fighting chance. Lessens the level of vulnerability."

"Makes sense. I guess the alarm clock makes sense too, then. I have to admit, you have done really well in making this place feel like home. Before the monsters came, it was just us throwing up a quick tent here and there, trying to avoid confrontation with other people. Then once we had to worry about monsters too, it was about trying to find abandoned buildings to hide in. For the last few years, I have been constantly moving and seeking shelter. I can't even describe how exhausting it is to live like that. But you really have figured out a way to make a life here. It's nice."

I begin to look around the room as well. "Well I can't take the credit. Coming here was all my parents' idea."

"I would have liked to meet them. They seem like really good people."

"They were the best!" I stand up, "Now come on, we have work to do."

I do as I usually do and open each door with stealth as I check the following room for disturbances. Slowly making our way to the main living area, without any issues. Another night without being found.

He sits down on the couch, and I walk over beside him. "So, I was thinking about maybe developing a strategy," I say, putting my hands on my hips as I slip into planning mode. "I think it is time we try to figure out how to defeat these things."

He looks at me innocently, "You really think we can?"

I begin walking back and forth before looking directly at him. "I mean, honestly, what do we have to lose? At least we can try to live a more pleasant life. Or we die. Either way it's a win-win I guess."

He looks at me confused, "I don't know what to make of that statement. If that is a win-win for you, I'd hate to see what a lose-lose is."

I just smile and neglect to answer. We spend the rest of the day sharing about our experiences coming across the invisible beasts. Like my dad always said, you need to be able to identify the problem and know what you're up against. Nick and I spend hours discussing what we had seen and learned with every monster encounter over the past couple years. You can only talk about that kind of stuff for so long, though. So we begin talking about each other and catching up. I didn't remember most of the details from our drinking game last night, which probably is a good thing. I know for sure he didn't remember most of the conversation because he drank substantially more than I did.

I think we both feel this need to stay true to who we were before. We didn't want to forget the people who mattered the most to us. He never got the chance to say goodbye to his family either. He said his family had been on a vacation in Europe when the bombings started. He had been able to talk to them before the power went out, but they were literally a world apart, and he has no way of knowing if they survived. No one really knew which other countries were destroyed. It was heartbreaking to watch him speak of the uncertainty. I would much rather be in his position, though. Not knowing whether your family survived would be hard. It would be even harder knowing you have no way of reaching your family if they are still alive. But at least it allows for hope. I find that in this new world, hope is what you need to keep pushing forward. It is the exact reason why I am so compelled to find a way to destroy these creatures. It is the hope of having some sense of peace that is making me not give up.

I find myself getting frustrated with him, though. Listening to what he has been through is nothing in comparison to everything I have experienced. I am trying to be supportive, after all he is seeking comfort in sharing his fair share of tragedies. Yet, the more he divulges, the more I don't understand why he appears so devastated. The majority of people he had lost along the way were accomplices. They were not people he really cared for, or even loved, they were merely travel companions. I know it is unfair to judge anyone for how they perceive and react to various traumas in their life, but a part of me feels like it is unfair. How is it that I have lost so much more than him? The longer I listen to him share his feelings, the more it makes me upset that he had read my journal. Namely, how can he feel it is appropriate to discuss what he has interpreted as loss, after clearly reading what real misfortune is? It almost seems selfish trying to gain sympathy from me. Despite these feelings, I have to put them aside, because I know I need him now. If I am ever going to be successful in beating these monsters, I need a partner. Maybe I am just being unreasonable.

The time comes for us to go downstairs and call it a night. When we get down there, I begin looking for books to read. After spending so many months not talking, I find myself getting tired of the constant conversation now.

He sits on the cot and looks at the shelves. "Grace?"

"Yes?"

There is a slight hesitation, "Do you mind if I read your favorite book tonight? I have been meaning to read it since you told me about it."

I look over at the shelf and see it resting on its side. "Of course!" I grab it from the shelf and hand it to him. He opens the book, and I see him smile. I forgot that I had left the note inside.

"You kept it," he says as he looks at me.

"Of course I kept it. That was the nicest thing anyone has ever said to me."

He smiles, "I was actually really nervous writing it. So corny, right?"

I laugh, "The corniest! But why would you be nervous?"

He looks down at his feet, which are dangling off the cot. "Because you weren't like all those other girls. I knew how to impress all of them, but you were different. I didn't want to make an ass out of myself."

I laugh, "Who said you didn't make an ass out of yourself?" I see him smile, "And of course I was different. I didn't have an IQ below 70."

He lets out a quiet laugh once more, "You know what I mean. You just kind of did your own thing, and I thought it was cool."

I give him a surprised look, "Cool? I don't think that is a word I have ever been associated with before," I say with a giggle.

After a brief silence he says, "I just can't figure you out, Miss Baker."

"I can't even figure myself out, so I would stop trying if I were you. We have other things to worry about now."

He grins, "I guess you are right about that."

"I am usually right." I pause, "Well, get acquainted with Mr. Thomas, I think you will like him!"

He looks down and begins to read. I grab another book off the shelf. When my family and I first got to the cabin, I didn't have many books, but I have been able to gather some during my supply runs. Slowly I have been able to establish a new library for myself throughout the years. After all, what else is there to do now?

I attempt to start reading, but I can't help but think about what Nick said. Maybe I am being too hard on him. Who am I to judge someone for feeling the way that they do? I may not comprehend his need to talk about his feelings, or his incessant requests for me to divulge mine, but we are not the same person. I am sure if he recognized my upbringing, and how we were instructed to always repress our emotions as a method of control, he would think it was peculiar. He was never one to be like the other guys in town, and I should be embracing what always made him unique.

I guess the more I contemplate it, maybe he is behaving in this manner to try to offset my sorrow. After all, he knew what I had experienced with the loss of my family. Perhaps, it is just some attempt to help me push forward and help me focus my energy on something else. It is natural to step in and provide comfort to those who are suffering. Maybe he felt that sharing what had happened with him would allow me to transition my negative energy and help him through his sadness. Who knows what his intentions really are, I just have to be more accepting and considerate.

I look over at Nick, and he is so engrossed in the pages that he doesn't feel my eyes on him. I look away and back down and continue to read. If we are going to be successful then I need to be more open-minded, and a lot less stubborn.

My mind is finally free, and I begin to read. We sit on the cot, just reading our books together, until we both drift off to sleep.

Chapter Twenty-Three

Before

I clumsily walk into the dining room as I let out a long yawn. I look over at my dad, and he is reading an old military book at the table. The book is discolored and bent on the edges. Ever since we came up here, his daily newspaper briefings have been replaced with old books that he used to read while he was in training. I sit down at the table, as my mom hurriedly walks around tidying up the kitchen. I look around and I don't see Stephen anywhere, so he must still be asleep.

It has been a few weeks since the world ended, and up here it doesn't feel any different. For everything my dad warned us about, we hadn't encountered any of it yet. We haven't had people trying to attack us in the streets or trying to steal whatever we have. It really feels like time has stopped, and things are as normal as you could imagine for everything going on.

Due to the lack of excitement around here, it has actually been really interesting learning more about my family. We were always a close-knit unit, but I have realized there is so much I don't know about them. Like, I knew my mom and dad met when they were teenagers, working together at the local supermarket. But I never knew that my mom had always wanted to be an astronaut. She told us how much she dreamed of being able to see Earth from space, and how much she wanted to work for NASA. Unfortunately, she had been in a bad traffic accident as a teenager which gave her vertigo. Her dreams were shattered because she knew she would never be capable of fulfilling her dreams.

I also got to learn a lot more about my dad and his military experience. Without specifically going into what roles he played on his missions, he did share some really cool information regarding his training. I had no idea that Uncle Chris and Uncle Mike were actually his friends from the military. They have been around since I was a kid, and I would have never known that they went on so many missions together. Apparently they were in the same BUD/S class, and everything they had to overcome during training made them lifelong friends. He even told us about the time when Uncle Chris and Uncle Mike saved his life on one of their very first deployments together. The stories he had been sharing were remarkable. I realized just how much my dad had seen and done over the years, and it made everything make more sense.

Some of the best things that came out of our new living situation was learning more about my brother. I knew he was into baseball, and the typical boy stuff, like video games. I knew that he had played collegiate baseball for LSU, which I guess is a much bigger deal than I thought. What I didn't know, though, was that he had a chance to play in the minor leagues with strong potential for the majors, and he turned it down. Apparently, he sat down and talked to my parents one night about how he didn't like what it was doing to him—the constant state of competition—and decided he wanted to pursue other avenues. I just always thought he never got scouted. But it was a conscious decision, that apparently my parents were one hundred percent behind. That made me respect my family on a whole new level. We supported each other and made each other better, even if we didn't understand each other's decisions.

I love these moments of being able to talk about the life we had before. The first few times, it made me sad, but now it is just entertaining to get to know my family in a whole new light. Sometimes I take the few books I still have and read out loud to my family at night. Or sometimes, we play board games, and try to come up with new games of our own. What amazes me the most is that we are still finding ways to be a normal family. We laugh with each other, we still have family meals together, and we have become closer as a family unit.

We are so lucky as a family to have a dad that has the survival skills that he has. I think the only reason we have any sense of normalcy is due to the skill set he possesses. He has been teaching us so many essential survival skills. The stuff you would expect to learn given these circumstances. Like how to make fire using sticks and rocks. Even though we have fresh water, he knows we will run out eventually, so he took the time to teach us two different ways to purify the lake water. He showed us what to do with water purifying tablets because that is the easiest, but those were a limited supply and should be used more for emergencies. He also taught us a way we could use a heat source to purify the condensation into drinking water, and he constantly reminds us to leave pots outside to collect rain water so we can spare our trips to the lake.

One of the more interesting teaching moments was when he showed us how to identify poisonous berries from edible ones. And even though we have knives and a few guns, he also showed us how we could make spears using sticks, if we ever needed them. He said that was helpful when it came to fishing. He is a wealth of knowledge when it comes to these unusual living arrangements.

While we are getting used to this survival mentality, I miss modern technology so much. I never was one of those people who was constantly on my phone, but I realize now how nice it was to always know what was going on. I miss being able to scroll through my various apps to keep myself entertained. I miss being able to listen to my favorite music when I was feeling melancholy, or happy songs that I used to sing along to. I miss talking to my friends. I was always kind of a loaner of sorts, but I do miss my best friend, Sarah. I wonder if she is still alive. We had one of those friendships where we didn't talk every day, but every single time we saw each other it was as if we picked up right where we left off. I always loved hearing about all her adventures. She was completely opposite of me. She always lived in the moment. While I was someone who had to tediously plan every single thing ahead of time, she was someone who would just get in a car and drive. I always admired that about her. I like to think that when she took that road trip before the bombs went off, that she was so far away from the cities that she made it. Sometimes I even imagine that all her expeditions prepared her for this new life, and that she is still just living each day in the moment. I really do miss her so much.

It is not just having no access to friends and the outside world, I also hate not having running water, showers, or toilets. There are so many things I took for granted in my old life. The water situation is difficult, but having no electricity is the worst. We have lanterns and candles, but I miss things that require refrigeration. I miss food like fruit and yogurt parfaits, ice cold drinks, and cheese. I think I miss cheese the most if I am being candid. The weather hasn't been too bad, but I know there are going to be days when I miss air conditioning too, and nights when I miss the comfort of centralized heating.

Yet, taking into account all of that, we are organized, and we have a good regimen. Dad had some supplies stocked up in the basement in case we ever had to come here in an emergency. He had collected some of those emergency preparedness kits with the absolute necessities. However, that is what we would use if we actually ran out of real food. He insisted that we hold off on using those supplies until that was all we had left. So, we rationed our food to last us six months, if we eat only what we had picked up from the store. We did notice, however, how bad we are lacking protein. Dad figured out if we learn how to hunt and fish, that the rationing of food would last us at least a year, which actually is pretty good for a family of four. Fishing is easy. We had been doing that for years. Hunting is something entirely new to me. Dad had taken Stephen a few times to hunt big game, but he wanted my mom and I to know how to do it, too.

Since we have been here a few weeks, and there seems to be a level of peace in this area that was unexpected, he decided to take the family hunting so my mom and I would know what to expect. He spent all day yesterday explaining it to us. That we had to be quiet. We had to conceal ourselves. He also insisted that the time of the day mattered and that we would have the best luck early in the morning.

Shooting was no problem. He had taken my brother and me to shooting ranges as kids, because he wanted us to be able to defend ourselves. He also wanted to make sure we understood that a firearm is dangerous if not handled properly. He always instilled in us that you treat every firearm as if it were loaded, that you never put your finger on the trigger unless you intend to shoot, and to be sure of what you are aiming at. It is an appreciation for the power of the firearm, while acknowledging the responsibility that comes with it.

So finally, the day has come when we all are going to try our hand at hunting a live animal. It is early morning, and it is cold enough to see my breath.

We are wearing our darkest clothes to try to blend in with our surroundings. I have to admit, I like the way the forest looks in the dawn. It is my favorite time of the day to be out here. The way the sunlight barely seeps through the trees, and the mist hugs the floor of the forest. There is a calmness that comes with nature this early in the morning. The birds are chirping as they awaken the rest of the animals. There are no sirens, or cars honking with impatience. No humming of power lines, or roaring of engines as planes fly overhead. The sounds of my childhood have been replaced with the soothing sounds of nature that have brought peace in such troubled times.

We proceed through the forest, exploring for the best place to hunt. It feels like we have been walking for quite some time now. I feel myself getting restless. I am about to tell my dad that we should rest here, when he stops and points toward the left. Just beyond a row of trees, I can see a gorgeous meadow. It has tall light green grass with random flowers in bloom. The sun is shining down on it as if it were a beacon from a lighthouse directing us to come into shore. It is perfect. As we get closer to the meadow, I can hear the sound of water running nearby. There must be a river close to us, which means there should be animals nearby too.

Dad has us hide in the trees just beyond the meadow, and really it just feels like a waiting game. We sit concealed in the trees, and I continue to take in all the sights and sounds of the forest. I am beginning to learn to appreciate everything around me. It allows me to have a feeling of meditation and helps calm my nerves. After some time, a lone deer walks before us. The reddish-brown coat offsets the white around its face. Large antlers crown its head, and its ears flicker with each tickle of an insect. The way the deer saunters through the meadow with each hoof alerting the forest creatures to its presence makes it appear very majestic.

I really do not want to do this now. Every part of me wants to tell my family that we don't need to kill these animals to survive. Why does such a beautiful creature need to be killed just for my own survival? But, I know I need to shoot it; I know it will not go to waste. As if my dad can sense that my hesitation was due to my sudden repudiation of hunting, he leans over and whispers in my ear: "I know it is hard, but you got this, Grace. The deer will sacrifice his life so we can continue to survive. Aim, slow trigger press, and control your breath. You can do this."

I take a long deep breath. I close my eyes, and I bring the rifle up to my cheek and align my sights. It is easy because it has some kind of scope on it, and a red dot to show me exactly where I am aiming. I take a deep breath once more, aim for the center body mass, and slowly pull the trigger back. BANG! The firearm goes off, and the deer falls to the ground.

"Good job, Grace! Hell yeah!" Stephen says as he is walking over to give me a high-five.

We walk over to the deer lying in the meadow, and it is not moving. I feel dreadful that this gorgeous creature had to die on my behalf. This is the first time I have ever killed a living thing, and I know it will not be the last. I am sure it will get easier as time progresses, but I hope it doesn't. I do not want to be indifferent in my quest for survival. I hope that I always see the value in life. I am sorry you had to sacrifice your life for me, deer, I think to myself.

Chapter Twenty-Four

Present

Grace, honey, it's time to wake up.

I open my eyes and turn to see my mom sitting on my bed. She looks very pretty. Her blonde hair perfectly styled away from her face, with minimal makeup making her emerald green eyes stand out.

Yawning I say, "Why are you all dressed up?"

"There is a surprise for you downstairs! So, hurry up and get dressed." She stands up, looks down at me, and smiles before turning away and walking out the door.

I slowly sit up and look at my phone to see the date: July 7. There's nothing special on July 7th. Definitely not my birthday. Confused, I walk into the bathroom, grab my toothbrush, apply just a touch of toothpaste, and begin to brush. I finally look at myself in the mirror and I look sick. I put my free hand up to my head to feel my forehead. Doesn't feel warm. I lean in closer as I continue brushing, and I see a mark on my hairline. Where did that come from? I also notice a fresh scratch on my cheek. Did I run into something yesterday? I finish brushing my teeth, spit out the excess toothpaste, and take a gulp of water to rinse my mouth.

I walk out of my room and begin descending the stairs. I can hear my family laughing and talking in the kitchen. There are big mylar balloons everywhere with congratulations written all over them, and a huge vase of red roses on the kitchen table. Next to the vase is a bottle of champagne. I stand there looking at everyone, and they just continue to stare at me with giant smiles.

"What is the celebration for?" I say as I walk closer to the table. "Congrats for what?"

My dad walks toward me. He feels so much taller than normal. He is also dressed for a special occasion; wearing a nice polo collared shirt and slacks. He puts his hands on both my cheeks and smiles at me for a moment before saying, "Your mom and I are so proud of you, Grace. You amaze us every day." He then pulls me in for a hug.

I see Stephen sitting at the table, and he is smiling at me too. I have no idea what is going on, or what they are so proud of me for. Dad lets me go, and I hear a familiar voice in the living room.

"Who is in the other room?" I ask, "I didn't know we were having company today."

My family laughs in an awkward unison.

"Baker..." calls the familiar voice in the other room. Since my family is not the least bit helpful, I turn and go toward the living room. When I get there, it is empty. I stand there, closely observing the room, trying to determine where the voice came from, but no one is there. The room is dark, lit only by the ambient lighting from the kitchen. I attempt to turn on the overhead lighting, but when I flick the switch nothing happens. The big sectional couch is in the center of the room with no one sitting on it. I look down toward the hall. Still no one there. That is so weird, I could have sworn I heard someone in here.

Click-click-click-click. That familiar sound fills me with unease, like I know what comes next. It sounds like it is coming from behind the couch, so I walk deeper into the room, but I still don't see anyone. Click-click-click-click. I peek over the back of the couch, and nothing is there. Click-click-click-click. It sounds like it is coming from behind me now. I turn around and all the light is gone from the kitchen. I am now standing in the darkness. Click-click-click-click. I hear it in the kitchen now, so I run back toward the table as I scream, "Mom! Dad! Stephen!"

As I cross the threshold to the kitchen, I see it's been replaced with the forest. Still standing there, smiling at me, is my perfect family with no idea of what has happened. In a full sprint I run toward them. Click-click-click-click. As I reach my hands toward my mother, she is abruptly pulled from my grasp, back into the darkness. I stand shocked and terrified. Click-click-click-click. Suddenly, both Stephen and my father are simultaneously pulled into the forest in opposite directions. The table, balloons, and flowers are all gone now, and I fall to my knees. In my ear I hear click-click-click-click.

I let out a loud scream, and I feel something shaking me. Grace! The shaking continues. Grace! Wake up! It is dark. I feel my body tense up, and I feel the sensation of hands on my shoulders. I open my eyes, and I am not in the forest anymore. I am sitting on the cot, with my legs crossed and my arms tightly wrapped around my knees. I look up and Nick is standing there, with a look of concern.

"Grace, you were just having a nightmare." He sits beside me as he places his arm around me, "You're safe. I am here. Just take a deep breath."

I don't know what it was about the level of comfort that broke me, but I turn and dig my face in his shoulder and begin to sob. I have never had a breakdown like this, but I can't hold it in. He runs his fingers through my hair to comfort me, and he does not say a single word. He just lets me cry in peace. It is like everything I had been holding back for the last few years finally hit me. My entire world had changed in an instant. I was having to fight horrible people just to survive. I was killing people to prevent them from killing me. I was running from monsters, trying not to be torn to shreds. I had gone so long without the presence of my family, and I was trying to be strong for them. I never had time to mourn them. I didn't have the chance to give them a burial. I didn't get to say my goodbyes. They were snatched away from me and all I could do was run away like a scared little girl. I wasn't given the opportunity to process everything.

Here in this room I am constantly reminded of all that I failed to do for them. I couldn't save them. It is my punishment to relive those moments over and again. But now at least I'm not alone. Nick is here, and I don't have to be scared anymore. He can help me get through this. I finally stop sobbing, and I pull my head from his shoulder.

I look at him and sniffle, as he looks at me and smiles. He takes his hand and wipes the tears from my cheeks and leans in to kiss my forehead.

"You're ok, Baker. We'll figure this out."

I smile, "I know. That was long overdue. I apologize for the mess on your shirt."

"I didn't know Grace Baker could actually cry. Do you want to talk about it?"

I let out a small laugh, "To be honest, I didn't know I could cry like that either… No, just the same usual dream... I just keep reliving the loss of my family over and over again. It always feels so real, but I am not scared anymore. We are going to fight them. I don't want to run away anymore."

He looks at me with a furrowed brow, "Are you sure you want to do this, Baker?"

I smile at him, "It's now or never. We can't hide in this basement forever."

He pauses then continues, "Well, let's figure this monster problem out then, shall we?"

I grab his hand, "We shall… now get back to sleep. We need to rest if we are going to do this."

He grins, "Yes, ma'am! That is something I have no problem doing."

Chapter Twenty-Five

Before

We get back from hunting, and I am exhausted from dragging the deer home. I never realized how heavy a deer could be, and I never thought about what it would be like to have to take one home for food. My parents skin the deer and divide the meat into what we will eat tonight, and what we will make into jerky later on. That will be tomorrow's lesson: how to make deer jerky.

It is actually incredible to me that they would even know how to do any of these things. Since my new life has started, I have been learning more every day about all the things Dad had learned to do when it came to survival. He is like a walking encyclopedia on survival skills. I am happy that he is such an expert in this subject matter though. I have spent my life with instant knowledge available to me, but I never retained it the way he did. I think that is the difference between having access to the internet and actually having to apply the knowledge in a real setting.

Sometimes, I find myself wanting to ask my dad more about what he used to do in his job. I know he was in the Navy, and I know he had a top-secret clearance. I never really thought to ask him, but now as I see how good he is at all these survival skills, I am beginning to see him much differently. He has always been ridiculously strong, but that comes with the territory. He is so smart that I always just assumed he had some kind of inside job, figuring out some kind of intelligence maybe? But in this new world, I am starting to wonder if maybe he was involved in something more exceptional.

Looking back, my parents were always secretive about everything that came with his employment. Whenever we would ask, they would dismiss our questions saying it was adult stuff that kids didn't need to worry about. He was always gone on long deployments, too. Months at a time, on some secret mission, in who knows where. I know there were a few close calls, though. I remember a couple times Mom was extra worried and upset that Dad wasn't able to check in when he was supposed to. Not to mention all the times he came home with injuries: broken bones, cuts, and impressive bruising on his face.

But he has been opening up more since we have been here. He has already shared so much new information, I don't want to pry any further. I don't want to ask more questions that may lead him to shut us off completely. He will tell us more when he feels it is prudent to do so.

I am sure I am just reading into it. However, with everything that has taken place, nothing really surprises me anymore. I wonder if Mom knows all that he has done? Is she keeping secrets too? Would he still be so secretive now if I tried to ask? To play it safe, I think it is still best to reserve my questions for later. After all, we have a long road ahead of us and a lot of time to kill. It will all come out in due time.

Despite whatever my dad may have done for work, he is still my dad. No matter what bad things he may have seen or done as part of his job requirements doesn't matter. I want to know more, but sometimes parents protect us by hiding the horrors they have seen. Nothing will ever change how I feel about them, regardless of what they know.

Even now, with all these thoughts racing through my mind, as I watch them prep the meat for dinner tonight, I can't help but be reminded of one of the trips we took to Yosemite when I was a kid. Despite everything we have witnessed the last few months, I still only see them as my mom and dad. I can picture that Yosemite trip perfectly in my mind. Back when things were easier, and life was completely normal. Back when I had no idea that any of this was destined to happen.

Chapter Twenty-Six

Present

We skim through my notebook multiple times. For the sake of my privacy, I went through it, and Nick jotted down miscellaneous notes that pertained to monsters themselves. Even though we both know he had already read what was written in there, it was easier for me to find the things that were important to the investigation. After all, now more than ever I have to follow Dad's instructions. Research, plan, execute.

First, we would try to figure out what they are, if that was even possible. If that isn't an option, then we need to determine their strengths and their weaknesses. We have to figure out what they are drawn to, what they want us for, which we both decide is probably for food. That seems like the most logical explanation after all. Why would animals kill us if it were not for food? We need to discern whether there is a way to protect ourselves from them. We need to determine if they really only come out at night, and if so, then why?

"Ok, so the best guess, since we were in different areas when they arrived, is that it happened about six months after the power went out," Nick says. "Does that sound about right?"

"Well, looking through my notebook, it was day 227 that my mom was taken, so a little more than six months. So, yeah, close enough," I respond.

"Ok, so let's organize these thoughts. We'll have a section for possible causes, strengths, weaknesses, possible ways to hurt them, and available weapons."

He takes a large sheet of paper and draws multiple columns.

I continue, "So, their strengths are obvious: camouflage, strength, razor sharp claws, and they are large enough to lift humans off the ground. Their only obvious weakness at this point is daytime. They have to be capable of being killed. All animals can be killed somehow, right?"

"It doesn't make me feel good that their only weaknesses are daytime and potential mortality," Nick says as he taps the pencil on the table.

"I mean, without proper testing, that is all we really know. Oh! Don't forget the clicking noise they make. I would count that as a weakness as well because it alerts us when they are near."

He puts his pointer finger in the air, and then points at me. "That is true! I didn't even think of that. Good point, Baker."

He looks very childlike right now as he continues to scribble notes on the paper. His hair is disheveled, like he just woke up, and his sweater is torn. He is taking copious notes, like a focused student preparing for the big exam. His notes are full of random phrases with branches leading to other thoughts. Like a mind map of various theories and possible explanations.

One factor still mystifies me, though. Why can't we see them? Does it have something to do with the darkness? Is it that they aren't truly invisible, but rather camouflaged among the shadows and the trees? There are so many reptiles that can mimic their environment and change their color to prevent being attacked by a predator. If they are some kind of reptile then it is absolutely plausible that they would have this similar ability.

"Grace!"

I come out of my trance, "Sorry, I zoned out for a second."

"Well, obviously. Maybe we should take a break. We've been at this for hours now."

I look at him, "Has it been hours already?"

He pulls up his pages of notes and flips through them, showing me the material, "I would think that is a safe assumption."

I begin to chew on my pen, "I just need to solve this. I hate not having a solution to a problem."

"Baker, you don't have to be the one to figure it all out. We're a team now. We'll find the answers we are looking for."

I grab the notes and begin flipping through them. "I know, but the sooner we figure it out, then the sooner we will have a real life."

He reaches out and yanks the notes back from me. "I completely understand where you're coming from, but you can't find a solution if your brain is fried."

I look down at the mess of papers on the table, "I guess you are right. It does seem like we could use a break."

"Finally! She is willing to take a break," he says with his hands up in the air like he's saying Hallelujah.

I stand and walk over to the cabinet, grab a bottle of whiskey, grab two glasses, and put them on the table. "I think we earned a couple drinks today."

He grabs the bottle and proceeds to pour the whiskey, "A girl after my own heart. That is the best thing you have said to me all day!"

We clink our glasses. "Here's to our loved ones. Those who are lost and those who have died," I say, smiling softly. Nick grins too, and we drink. I sit down again as Nick leans back in his chair. I pause for a moment before saying, "Nick, after a lot of reflection, I have realized that I can't continue to be so stubborn. While I was raised to conceal what makes me vulnerable, it is only fair that I let you in to the mess that is my head. I am ready to talk now. I want to tell you about them—my family. What we went through. What they went through to keep me alive."

His eyes widen, "Grace—are you sure? I know how hard it is."

I interrupt him, "Nick, I do. It is important to me. You were right, we are in this together."

He scoots his chair closer to mine and grabs my hand. I take a deep breath, and I look down at the table. It is too difficult to look him in the eyes. He had read my notebook. He knows the horrors of what I had been through. But I feel like he deserves to know it first-hand, even though he said he didn't need to hear it from me. It just seems like it is the right thing to do. I am ready to cleanse myself of these memories that have been weighing me down. It is one thing to write about them, but to tell another person about all the horrors you've experienced is scary, yet necessary and somehow therapeutic.

I begin with the first time we encountered them. Not because it is terrifying, but because it was the night I lost my mother. She was the most beautiful soul, and I am so blessed to have had such a wonderful woman raising me. It is a memory that haunts me every day and night.

It had been about six months since we had radio silence on what was going on in the world. We had adjusted to our new life. We had come so far already. Our old lives were a distant memory, and we were finding our rhythm in this new existence. We had a routine and did our best to stay healthy. We had learned how to find supplies, make fires, and hunt small forest creatures for food. Like all the stories I had read, we had learned how to have a new normal in a post-apocalyptic world. It was almost like I was finally feeling some kind of happiness again. I wasn't longing for what I had in my life before this one. With each passing day it was like the people I had known were just a figment of my imagination and were not real. It allowed me to cope with their absence. I was no longer crying myself to sleep picturing the life I had always wanted for myself. I was finally getting comfortable with the new normal. I was finally embracing this new version of myself. The woman I had been before seemed so weak and unsure of herself. In this new reality, I was finding strength I never knew existed. I was loving the person I was becoming, but I was also sad there was so much evil in the world that had to be vanquished. There didn't seem to be a clear line between good and evil anymore; it had become blurred with a rationale for our behavior. I never thought I could take a human life, especially considering how I felt killing a deer for the first time, but I did it to save others. I really did feel like my mom had been right. That it would all work out in the end. I just didn't realize I would lose her so soon.

It was a particularly nice evening. I remember because it was late summer, when the days were long and the air didn't cool once it got dark. While we were foraging for supplies a couple weeks prior, we had found some stuff for s'mores in an abandoned cabin nearby. A long-forgotten treat from a world before this one. I had grabbed the graham crackers, marshmallows, and chocolate and had thrown them in my bag. I planned to save them for a special occasion. But the day was so nice, and it had been so long since we had any encounters with savages that I guess we got complacent. So, we decided to make a small fire in the yard that we would put out before it got dark, just in case there were strangers around in the forest. We lost track of time, carried away by sharing our favorite memories of each other. Stories of our extended family we would never see again, and remembering the times when it seemed like we were always in a state of celebration. For the first time in a long time, we really felt like we were just on a family camping expedition. For a few hours that night, we didn't think of anything but the stories we were sharing. We laughed like we didn't have a care in the world. But life decided to show us just how wrong we were.

It is funny what you remember when something traumatic happens to you. I can recall how we sat around the fire, as day turned to night. I remember taking a deep breath, looking up to the sky, and seeing how many stars were just beyond the tops of the trees. It was beautiful. The black sky glistened with the diamonds in space, and I just smiled. After six months of being in this environment, I never got bored with my surroundings. I was always finding new ways to admire the beauty in the simplicity of nature. It made me feel so small in the grand scheme of things. I enjoyed taking the time to really look at the stars, smell the trees, and feel the clean air on my skin. For some reason, on this particular night, I was completely engrossed in it.

Dad walked into the cabin to get something, and it was just Mom, my brother, and me. The fire was almost out; just a single log remained. Stephen had just finished telling some embarrassing story about me in my childhood, which was his favorite thing to do these days, and we were laughing hysterically. In the distance I heard something I had never heard before. A faint sound: click-click-click-click. Mom and Stephen were still laughing and did not hear it. But my smile faded as the sound got louder. Click-click-click-click. I scanned the trees but didn't see anything. I started looking all around me to see if I could determine where it was coming from. Click-click-click-click. Their facial expressions changed from laughter to concern; I could tell Mom and Stephen could hear it too. They both began looking toward the forest, trying to figure out what they were hearing.

Click-click-click-click. "Do you kids hear—" mid-sentence my mother was lifted off the ground, floating like a human balloon. As I was trying to process what was happening, something ripped through her blouse and I could see the blood pulsating out of the wounds in the light of the fire. She let out a cry, and then whatever had her pulled her violently backwards into the forest as if there was an imaginary harness strapped to her body. Her hands and legs began flailing as she let out the most horrendous scream of desperation.

My father came running out in a full sprint, his face full of confusion. I stood with my hands over my mouth, staring into the forest that had swallowed my mother whole. Stephen stood there pointing, and before we could speak, the sound erupted again. Click-click-click-click. Without hesitation, I grabbed Stephen's and my dad's hands and dragged them behind me as I sprinted for the cabin. Whatever it was, it was close. Click-click-click-click. I didn't look back; I just ran.

I am pulled out of my memory when I feel Nick squeeze my hand, "Oh, Grace. That must have been terrifying. I don't even have the words to say to you."

I feel a tear roll down my cheek, and I quickly wipe it off. "It happened so fast we couldn't even fathom what we just witnessed."

I continue looking away, when I feel his hand under my chin gently turning my face toward him. "I promise we'll figure this out. We owe it to your mom, your dad, and to Stephen."

I look down, grab my notebook. "I can still see it. That is what I dream about every single night. That same incident, just rotating between my family members."

After a brief pause, he says: "I see it too, Baker. Trust me, I see it too."

Chapter Twenty-Seven

Before

Grace, it's time to wake up.

I open my eyes, and I am not in my room. I am in a tent, inside of a sleeping bag. My groggy eyes slowly begin to focus on my mom, who is looking at me. "Honey, Dad made breakfast. Come get some food."

I look over and everyone is already gone. I let out a big yawn, and then exit the tent. It has been a few years since we last visited Yosemite. Dad thought that since he has been gone so much for work, he wanted to do something special for us as a family.

When I look toward the table, I see Stephen is sitting there, and dad is grilling something on the camping grill. It smells like bacon. He knows bacon is my favorite. I walk over, and he looks at me and smiles.

"Took you long enough to wake up, sleepy head," he says, and I hug him.

Mornings in Yosemite are always so cold. Even with my big jacket on, I can feel myself shivering since the sun is still hidden by the trees. I join Stephen at the table, and I see there is already some hot chocolate for me.

"Don't think you are special. Mom already made me some, I just already finished it," he says.

I roll my eyes at him as Mom says, "Ok, children, let's behave. We have a long day ahead of us."

Stephen then punches my thigh under the table, and I punch him back. "Mom, Grace hit me!"

"Mom, he hit me first!" I say in response.

"Kids, stop it. I've raised you better than to actually act your age," says my dad.

I stick my tongue out at Stephen, and then he sticks his out at me. I don't know why Stephen always picks on me. I am ten years old already. I can defend myself. Plus, what is a fourteen-year-old doing picking on his little sister anyway?

My dad puts the bacon on the table, along with some eggs and some pancakes. We begin to eat our hearty breakfast before the day's events.

"So, kids, I thought we would go hiking to see those waterfalls today. Then maybe after we get home, we could walk to town and maybe get some ice cream, what do you think?" My dad asks.

"That sounds so fun!" I respond.

"Hopefully Grace doesn't slow us down," Stephen says.

I shoot him a mean look. "Oh, Stephen, stop being so hard on your sister. You know she just wants to be like you," says my mom.

"Mom! That is so not true! Why would you say that?" I protest.

"Well if you guys can get along, we were thinking of making this an annual trip, what do you say to that?" asks my dad.

Both Stephen and I show our delight. The truth is we don't get to see our dad much, and when we do, he always has some kind of project for us. He is always trying to challenge me mentally, develop my critical thinking skills. He gives me various problems that I have to solve. With Stephen, he focuses on boy stuff, like how to fight and how to hunt. I don't know why he feels like he needs to teach us this stuff, but whatever time I have with my dad, I cherish.

We continue to eat breakfast and have a regular family meal. The forest around us is so beautiful and peaceful. Sometimes I wish this was what life was always like. Just my family and me, all together, and camping. I think life would be better if it was like this. A girl can dream, can't she?

We finish breakfast as we make small talk. Stephen is talking about all the extra training he has been doing for baseball. His coaches think he has a lot of potential and maybe will even get a college scholarship if he really puts effort into it. I would never tell him this, but he actually is very good. I think he has a real chance of getting that scholarship. My parents have been trying to get me involved in sports, too, but I am so clumsy and I get hurt too much.

When breakfast is done, we clean up, get dressed, and get ready to go hiking. I have never been on a real hike before, and I am excited. I know it is just walking, but I am looking forward to seeing the waterfalls, and seeing what kind of puzzles my dad has for me along the way. Usually, when we do some kind of new activity as a family, he asks me various questions on the spot to see if I can think of solutions quickly. Now that I am older I am getting better at it.

It is so serene out here. It is the middle of the day now, and the sunshine feels really good on my skin. I am starting to sweat and have already removed my jacket and tied it around my waist. I'm listening to my parents talk, and I continue to take in everything around me.

Suddenly my dad stops, "Grace!"

I stop and look around but don't see why he's calling to me, "Yeah?"

He begins to point in front of us. "Pretend that you see a bear cross our path a few feet in front of us; what do you do?"

"Oh come on, Dad, do we need to do this right now?" asks Stephen.

"Yes, we do. There is a rock you and your mother can sit on. Take a quick break." Stephen rolls his eyes as my mom ushers him for the impromptu break.

"Well?" asks my dad.

"Ok. You never run away."

"Ok, that is a good start, continue."

I begin canvassing the area and see a large boulder just off to my right, so I walk over to it. "I would slowly walk over to this rock, and stand on top of it so I look bigger than I am. Then I would talk loudly and calmly so that the bear leaves me alone."

Dad smiles, "That was an easy one. Here's the twist now. There are no rocks for you to climb on, and you are about to be attacked."

I put my hand up to my chin, "What kind of bear is it?"

"Very good, Grace. I was trying to trick you. Excellent question because there is a difference in how you would react. It is a grizzly bear."

"Since I have a backpack on, the best thing to do is just lie face down on the ground and play dead."

"Not too bad at all." He walks over and hugs me, and then we walk toward Stephen and my mom.

"You are getting very good at these puzzles, hun," says my mom.

"That was an easy one. Not so much a puzzle, but basic human survival," responds my dad.

Stephen rolls his eyes as he and my mom stand up to continue our journey to the waterfalls. I like when Dad surprises me with easy puzzles because it makes me feel like I really am making him proud. I really do hope we end up making this an annual thing. I like being out here. I already love everything about this place.

We continue making our way along the trail, and the closer we get to the waterfall the more crowded it becomes. It is surprising to see how many people are here. I know we are getting close because I can hear the water crashing on the rocks. Finally, just through a clearing in the trees I can see the waterfall. It is much prettier than I had imagined. It is huge, and the way the water cascades off the stone is beautiful. As we get closer, there are stone steps, allowing us to climb up toward the waterfall. We are so close now that the mist from the water is starting to get me wet. But the water feels refreshing on such a warm day, and I don't mind.

"Oh, kids, isn't that just lovely?" my mom says as we get closer to the waterfall.

"It is so pretty!" I respond.

"Watch your footing, kids, the stone may be slippery," says my dad.

We finally reach the top of the trail and it is picturesque. It actually looks exactly like what I would see in a magazine. The waterfall is so loud as it hammers the rocks and water below. We stand looking at it for a second, and then Mom pulls out a camera from her backpack.

"Ok, everyone, get together so I can take a picture of you guys," she says.

My dad, Stephen, and I all stand together. "Ok, on three!" she says.

"Excuse me, ma'am," says a stranger wearing a baseball cap and a sweatshirt that says Yosemite on it, "Would you like me to take that for you so you can get in?"

My mom smiles at the older man. "That would be great," she says as she hands him the camera.

She walks over and stands next to my dad, as Stephen and I are on the ends. The man says, "Alright, on three! One, two, three," and he snaps a picture. He hands the camera back to my mother, "You have a beautiful family. Safe travels!" He walks away, and we all just stand there taking in the beauty of the waterfall. I could get used to this.

Chapter Twenty-Eight

Present

After spending the day combining our knowledge from previous experiences there are papers and drawings all over the table. We collectively agree that the best approach is to do systematic tests to see what they are drawn to, and what they hunt. It is going to be a tedious process. We don't have the resources to do all the testing we want to, but we will focus on one experiment at a time. We decide that it is safe to assume they only come out at night. Neither one of us have ever encountered one during the day, nor have we heard them. So, we break our testing down into a few essential categories, and we will start from there.

Based on our encounters we decide that we must examine smell first. They seem to attack both humans and animals, but is there a way to disguise our scent? Nick had shared with me one particular incident when he spilled gasoline on himself accidentally, and he was the only one spared in the massacre.

He stated it had been a few weeks since his first encounter with the monsters. He was by himself, and at this point he had no idea if the monsters were even real. He said he had not even been able to process what he saw the night he lost all his friends, and he had convinced himself that it didn't really happen.

He had found an abandoned truck and decided he would try to siphon some gasoline from it in case he needed it for something. He made a makeshift home in an abandoned business nearby that he was able to gain access to. It was his first attempt at siphoning gas, and he said he ended up spilling it everywhere. It sprayed on his shirt and all down the front of his pants.

It was already dark outside, and he could hear people talking. He stayed quiet because he didn't want them to know he was near, and he didn't want them to steal the gasoline he had worked so hard for. He could see the group walking together down the street. They had no idea he was there. Then he felt a sense of unease, like something was in his presence. Then he heard the source of his discomfort coming from behind him. Click-click-click-click. He looked all around him, trying to determine the source of the sound, but he could not figure out where it was coming from. Click-click-click-click. He thought it was coming from right behind him, so he just stood there and listened. That is when he felt something breathing on him. He turned around to see what it was, but nothing was there. Click-click-click-click. Suddenly, he felt a giant rush of wind as he looked toward the group. There, a female was hoisted up above the ground screaming at the top of her lungs, and all her friends darted in different directions. Unsure of what he had just witnessed, he ran for his life.

"It is like it passed on you because you smelled bad," I say.

"Well I wouldn't say I smelled bad, let's not be mean."

I laugh, "Ok, the monster thought you smelled bad."

"I guess that will have to do. It makes sense though. Would you want to eat something that didn't smell appetizing?"

When he said that, it reminded me of when Stephen was killed. We had been in the lake all day, and I was holding the fish we captured. I remember that I had a particularly strong fishy aroma in my clothes. I probably smelled worse than Stephen on the walk home, because I had waded deeper into the lake that day, while Stephen mostly stayed near the shore. I had always thought it had been because I ran, but maybe somehow the fish masked my scent.

We decide that we will hunt some small animals and leave them out. We will leave one with no effort to mask the smell. We will take another animal and cover it in gasoline, and we will take one more and try to replicate that fish aroma. Our plan is to attempt to hunt all rabbits, because they would be the easiest to transport. Plus, it would give us a more consistent and reliable variable in the experiment. It isn't much of a start, but we figure it is at least a good try for the first trial run.

We know it is not the world's best plan, but we have to start somewhere. It is hard enough to hunt these animals, especially when they are being used for science rather than sustenance. But we both agree that of all tests, this is the most important, because it allows for us to be in the open, hiding in plain sight, if it all goes according to plan.

We decide that phase one is to determine if we can disguise our smell. Next, we have to establish what their weakness is. They must be some kind of animal; after all, they are hunting us. And if they are animals, that means we can hunt them in return. There are so many inquiries plaguing my mind. For instance, why did they leave shreds of bodies in the trees? Was that some kind of nest? Is that their way of keeping left-overs for later? Is it their way of marking their territory? If this is their nesting area, does that mean they are always present? If they don't come out during the day, does that mean they are purely nocturnal? If they are nocturnal, where do they sleep during the day? Where do they hide?

Where does one really even begin with this kind of research? This is going to be a lot of trial and error. We know that we will have to be patient, smart, and most importantly, we have to be rational. Yes, we want to learn how to destroy these things because they murdered everyone we care about. Yes, we are in constant fear of being shredded alive; feeling every tear of their razor-sharp claws. But, for the sake of our family, we have to separate emotion from purpose. If we are not able to figure this out, then we will never be able to live on for our family. Nick is right; we have to do this for them.

With a slight sigh, "Well, it is time to go down to the basement," I say.

Running his hand through his disheveled hair, he says: "I hope you are ready for tomorrow. We have a long day ahead of us, Baker. Well, a long few days ahead of us."

We walk down to the basement, locking everything behind us. I go to sit on the cot like I always do, as Nick starts to lie down on the floor. My mind is racing just thinking of all that can go right and all that can go wrong tomorrow. I keep reviewing all the details in my mind. I know I need to get some rest, but it is hard to sleep with all these thoughts racing through my brain.

After a few moments of silence, Nick says: "We're gonna be ok, Baker. If anyone can figure this out, it is you. This is going to work. Just trust yourself."

And for the first time in as long as I can remember, I fall asleep without a single nightmare.

Chapter Twenty-Nine

Before

Camping was much more enjoyable when I was a kid. I remember wishing that we would always be like that. A family together, without everyday responsibilities. Just enjoying whatever life threw at us. Now I have grown to despise it.

The truth is, even though I wasn't longing for my old life anymore, it has been almost a month since the world was extinguished. While the time with my family is nice, I miss modern-day luxuries. I miss long, hot showers. I miss watching Netflix and listening to music. I miss working out for fun, rather than necessity. I miss coffee. Oh, how I miss coffee. I miss the peace of sleeping. The first thing that goes when you are thrust into an apocalypse is sleep. You are constantly on edge. Every little sound alarms you because you don't know what potential horrors await you.

I don't think I would have survived had it not been for the preparation that my parents had instilled in me. Looking back, it makes sense that Dad knew this was going to happen someday. Why else would he have invested what little time we had together as a family into secretly training me and Stephen?

When I was about thirteen, he gave me the most ludicrous puzzle I ever had to solve. I walked into the garage and, like our usual sessions, there were papers scattered all over the table. The whiteboard was blank and ready for my notes.

I walk over to him. "Ok, Dad, what is the puzzle today?"

He places his hand on my shoulder. "We are switching it up and getting creative today. You have to defeat a monster. All that is available are the notes on the table. You have no one but yourself. How do you defeat the monster?"

I look at him with a perplexing stare. "Wait, what? What kind of monster?"

He points at the papers on the table, "You know the drill, Grace. Research, plan, execute."

I take my hand and smack my forehead. "You're killing me, Dad."

He looks down at his watch. "You have one hour. If you solve the problem, we will go out and get some ice cream."

"Ok, Dad, I am on it." He walks back into the house.

A monster? What kind of puzzle is this? I begin to peruse through the notes, and I find a list of strengths and weaknesses. Strengths: large, fast, sharp nails, fangs. Weaknesses: large, animal, sunlight. Seriously? What a perplexing riddle. But, a puzzle is a puzzle and Dad always has his reasons.

I walk to the whiteboard and I make a list with the strengths and weaknesses. I go back to the table and start looking at the notes once more. I see a page that states the weapons available: rifle, knife, fire. Well that doesn't help much. I walk over to the board and list the weapons anyway.

I start writing additional notes: If it is large, make yourself larger. The larger the monster is, then the easier it is to kill because it is a larger target. If it has sharp nails, make sure you don't get close. If it is weak in sunlight, try to draw it out in the daytime. If daytime is unavailable, maybe fire will work. I continue to write down the various thoughts that come into my head.

Finally, my dad comes back. "How's it coming along?" He asks.

I respond, "I think I'm done."

Surprised, he says, "Ok, Grace. Enlighten me."

I walk over to the whiteboard and then turn to face him. "Well based on the notes, it is some giant animal with razor-sharp nails, that can't be out in the sunlight. So based on what was provided, my solution would be to: 1) Make myself bigger. So if I can find something I can stand on, maybe the roof of a building, that would take away the aspect of being overwhelmed by the size."

He nods in agreement, so I continue. "And 2) If whatever it is has sharp nails then I do not want to be close to it, so using a knife would be completely out of the question. I would want to use the rifle because that allows me to be at a safe distance away when I try to take him out."

He smiles in approval. "And finally, 3) If sunlight is a weakness, then I would try to draw this monster out in the daylight, but if that was not an option, maybe set a fire to disorient him, and then use the rifle to take him out," I finish confidently.

My dad starts clapping. "You are such a smart girl, Grace. How long did it take you to figure out your plan this time?"

"Only about ten minutes. One of these days, you'll have to give me a puzzle that is actually difficult, Dad."

He walks over, hugs me, and kisses my head. "Oh trust me, you will get a chance to be stumped one day. It would appear as though our exercises are really allowing you to develop your solutions to our problems much faster."

I look up at him. "I don't know why you would even want me focusing on this monster stuff, it isn't even real, Dad."

"Trust me, honey, monsters do exist, in one way or another."

A brief moment of silence hangs in the air before I interrupt it. "So are you going to take me for ice cream or what?"

He laughs, "A promise is a promise, go get your brother."

Chapter Thirty

Present

When I open my eyes, it takes me a moment to get my bearings. For a moment I thought I was in my old room, in my old bed, but when my eyes adjust I can see I am in the basement. I never sleep this way anymore, completely flat and sprawled out. I am surprised when I feel an arm around me, and I see a hand intertwined with mine. I guess sometime during the night Nick came up here to lay with me. I wonder if I was tossing and turning, or if he just could not sleep on the floor. Regardless of his reason, it makes me wonder what life would have been like had the world not endured annihilation.

I gently unwrap my fingers from his, and place his arm on the bed. I try to get up with minimal movement not to disturb him. I walk over to the shelf and grab my notebook, and walk over to the corner. I slowly slide down the wall to sit down, turn on the flashlight, and start writing.

Day 625

Well after much reflection, Nick and I have decided that it is time to try some experiments to see if we can determine an effective way to fight these monsters.

I think we both realize we want to stop running; we want a chance at a normal life. But what does a normal life even mean now? Are we just going to go around hunting monsters as our normal routine? Is this something that we will have to face for the rest of our lives? Constantly just trying to survive and not get eaten by whatever is out there? I think I just realized that I don't want to be scared anymore. If we can't figure this out then we will never be able to leave. We will be destined to spend the rest of our lives here. What if there are more out there? What if there are more survivors? There has to be more than this place, right?

So that being said, we have decided to go ahead and take a scientific approach. We both agreed that there was no reason to determine if they came out during the day, because if they did we definitely would have been dead already. So, we are moving on to the next thing: smell. Based off of our separate experiences we both feel like maybe they are attracted to a certain smell; like any animal stalking its prey. We are going to grab a few animals, disguise them with different scents and see what is left over. Once we determine the smell factor, we can expose ourselves during the actual trials, and hopefully catch a better glimpse of what we are up against. This will either end up being the most courageous endeavor ever, or the stupidest and most deadly decision we ever make. It really is life and death now. If for some reason I get killed today, and this is my last entry, don't let it be in vain. Whoever may read this after I am gone: Take this and figure out a way to find the peace that we are so desperately seeking. Wish us luck!

I close the notebook, and when I look up I see Nick just sitting on the bed watching me.

"Didn't want to interrupt you, Shakespeare. You ready to do this?" He asks.

I put the notebook on the shelf. "This may be the stupidest thing we could possibly do, but what do we have to lose?"

"Yea, worst case scenario, we are just shredded to pieces by some giant, invisible, human eating monster. I mean, that is how I always planned to go. Am I right?" He says with an awkward laugh.

I point at him. "Actually, now that you mention it, I think I remember you telling me that exact thing back on the café patio all those years back, so yea, we're going to be totally fine," I say with a chuckle.

Despite the sarcastic banter, I know deep down inside we are both terrified. This is so far out of our league of expertise. I feel like we are little league baseball players now trying to play in the World Series. We have no way of really knowing what is going to happen, or if we can even really do this. After all, who is to say that this experiment will even work. I was no longer solving a puzzle with my dad's guidance. These were dangerous murderous beasts that had already destroyed everyone we care about. Failing was not an option. We are planning an entire operation on the fact that whatever these creatures are will be drawn to dead animals. There is a probability that they just like the hunt, and they want to be able to stalk their prey before they pounce. There are so many uncertainties. However, we won't know unless we actually try. You have to start somewhere. Today is the day that can change our lives forever.

Chapter Thirty-One

Before

Looking back on all those lessons, I don't know why Dad had me focus on the most unrealistic problems. Really? Monsters. We all know monsters don't exist. Unless the monsters were actually a metaphor for humans. Undoubtedly, humans are really who we must fear. Humans act in iniquitous ways; humans act purely on emotion; humans hurt and kill one another for amusement at times. Needless to say, after what happened in the pharmacy yesterday with Rick and Bob, it was a stark reminder of the evil that will present itself in this new world. That is why Dad said that Mom and I need to learn how to defend ourselves, and we could not put it off any longer.

We have been fortunate because we haven't encountered more people like those repellant savages. But it was Dad's training all those years that allowed me to fend them off without getting hurt in the first place. The muscle memory of computing solutions for potential problems allowed me to scan my environment to determine a way out. There was no hesitation and no feeling of fear, because the training kicked in. I was able to weigh the risk versus the reward in a calculated manner, and it gave me a sensation of unforeseen strength. When it finally came to applying my training, I emerged almost unscathed. The injuries were minimal for what could have transpired had I not reacted in the manner in which I did. Now it is time to train my body, just like I had learned to train my mind for so long.

Mom and I meet with Stephen and Dad near the fire pit.

"Ok, Susan... Grace... like I said, what happened yesterday was just the first of many encounters we are going to come across. It is important that you girls know how to fight in case we are separated somehow," says my dad.

As we stand there in the forest and I listen to my dad describe what our training will entail, I am pulled back to a different world in my imagination. I picture a boxing ring in the middle of an old gym. The lighting is poor, and there are trophies and plaques aligning the walls. The air is sultry, and there are giant floor fans circulating hot air. As my dad speaks, detailing every move and the importance of never letting your guard down, I can quietly hear "Eye of the Tiger" playing in the background.

I feel a punch on my arm, and I am brought back to reality. "Hey!" Stephen interrupts. "Did you hear Dad?"

"Grace, you need to pay attention. It is important," he says.

"I was paying attention," I respond.

"No, you weren't. You were humming that song from the *Rocky* movies," says Stephen.

"I swear I was paying attention," I say with a small chuckle.

"Well either way, this stuff cannot be learned via lecture. It must be done in practical application," says my dad.

Utilizing Stephen, we start the basic stuff. Mainly boxing and throwing in kicks and knees. Basic combinations of jabs, crosses, hooks, and undercuts. It does not seem overly difficult. Much like the brain teasers, this consists of muscle memory. Associating each movement with a number, and then Dad calls out random numbers for me to perform.

"1, 2, 3," he yells, and I perform without delay. "Good, 2, 3, 6," and I perform the movement once more.

Once we get the basic boxing movements, and learn various combinations, they show us how to block hits to prevent getting knocked out. After practicing that for a little while, they show us how to do some leg movements. They have us practice front kicks, use knees in close contact, and conduct effective roundhouse kicks. At this point, my body is already aching just from shadowboxing and performing endless amounts of repetitions.

"Ok, I know you are tired, Grace, but I want you to try to fight Stephen."

Shocked, I look at my dad, "You want me to do what?"

"Grace, you are going to have to fight much bigger people than your brother. The people out there will not be easy on you. They will be trying to kill you. You will never learn if you don't have to apply these techniques in a real fight. You have to be fast, and you can't be afraid of getting struck."

I had been fighting my brother for years, and he always annihilated me. No matter what I did he always overpowered me. Who's to say he wouldn't now?

I respond with a reserved, "Ok."

"Alright, kids, on the count of three… one…two…three...box," says my dad.

We begin to circle around each other. I keep my hands in my guard to protect my jaw. I throw a jab, and he ducks. We continue to go in a circle, and I throw another jab, and he ducks again, but this time he follows up with a cross and hits me right in my cheek, disorienting me. Ok, so we are really doing this, I guess. I keep circling, with my hands in my guard, and I throw a jab and a quick cross, and I finally make contact with his left cheek. He gets closer to me and I throw a front kick, which catches him off guard and causes him to fold forward. I follow up with an uppercut and a left hook, which strikes his right cheek. He looks at me surprised.

"Grace, way to hit! That's my girl!" my dad cheers from the sidelines.

Pissed by the accolades, Stephen stops holding back. He does a roundhouse kick to my side, partially knocking the wind out of me, then does a jab and then a cross, striking both sides of my face, and finishes with a front kick right to my stomach, knocking me on the ground. The wind is completely knocked out of me now, and everything is throbbing.

"That is enough for today, children," my mom interjects.

Stephen walks over to me and reaches out his hand. I grab it and he lifts me up.

"Not bad, little sis, not bad at all." He puts an arm around me and walks me over to my parents.

"You showed a lot of heart today, hun. It'll only get easier the more we train, trust me," says Dad.

I smile, but I am in so much pain. I know it is for my survival, but I really didn't want to have to fight my brother like this anymore.

"Alright, I think we earned ourselves some dinner. Let's go inside and freshen up," my mom says.

Chapter Thirty-Two

Present

"So how do you want to do this?" asks Nick.

"Well," I pause. "I think the best approach is to draw them away from the cabin for sure. Definitely don't need to inadvertently bring more of them close to where we are living. I think we try to find whatever animal we can. I mean, we would be better off with deer, but trying to find three and be successful might be hard. Plus, we can't risk hauling deer too far because we can't waste our energy. I think we are better off trying to find a smaller animal, like rabbits to make it less challenging."

Nick stands up, and walks around for a minute before turning toward me and responding. "Well we know we were in the town last time we saw the monsters. I say, let's make our way toward the town, bring the supplies, and try to draw them there. I am sure you know of some good places for our experiment. I agree that deer would be the best option but hunting rabbits would probably allow us to be consistent with our variables. I mean, for research reasons wouldn't you want the same animal?"

I tilt my head to the side, as I flip through the pages in my notebook. "Hmm. There are a few decent spots, but you are absolutely right. We have to try to hunt whatever we can get that would allow us to use the same animal to keep it consistent. There isn't the excess of wildlife there once was, so finding three deer in one hunting session will probably be too difficult."

Nick walks over and places his hands on the table as he looks at the scattered papers. "I don't know, Baker. There is a lot that can happen here. You sure this is gonna work out?"

I put my hand over my eyes and gently rub them. "No. I am not sure. We have to start somewhere, though. If we can't figure out how to expose ourselves safely, then we can't move any further in the plan. We have to at least try. If this doesn't work out, then we'll come back and regroup, and we'll try to figure something else out."

He stands there looking at me and places his hand on his scruffy beard before letting out a small laugh. "I just can't believe we are even going to try to do this. It's so insane!"

I look at him with confusion, "Why are you doubting this all of a sudden? I thought you were game to try to do this."

His smile fades, "I'm not doubting you—"

I interrupt him, "That is exactly what you are doing."

He walks around the table, and he puts his hands on my shoulders. "Grace, I swear, I trust that you know what you are doing. I—I just want to make sure you are ready to do this."

I pull his hands down from my shoulders, "If you don't want to help me that is fine—"

He looks defeated, "No. I want to be with you, and I want to help you. It is just a week ago I was trying to avoid these things at all cost, and now we are about to try to figure out a way to suddenly be around them. A lot has changed, that is all I am saying."

I put my hands on my hips, "Seriously, if you don't want to do this I am perfectly capable of doing this on my own."

He crosses his arms against his chest, "Oh really? If you really thought you were soooo capable of doing it on your own, then why did you wait until you had me here?"

I now cross my arms against my chest to show my annoyance, "Excuse me?"

He starts walking away before turning and facing me, "You heard what I said. You are always trying to act like you're so incredibly tough. The ruthless Grace Baker doesn't need anyone or anything. She can just do everything on her own. Yet, it wasn't until you ran into me that all of a sudden you had some desire to go out and hunt these things. You know damn well that you need me to help you. So stop acting like you aren't using me in this ridiculous plan of yours."

I am so caught off guard by his sudden outburst, and I can feel my hands starting to tremble with anger. "Oh, is that what you really think of all of this? That I am just using you? My plan is ridiculous now too?"

He opens his mouth to talk, but before he can say anything I continue, "If that's really how you feel, then you should go. You're right. I don't need anyone."

His eyes widen, "Grace—don't."

I walk away before he can finish his sentence. I go down to the basement and into my sanctuary. I sit on my cot. I am so angry. Why would he allow me to make all these plans if he didn't think it was a good plan to begin with? I wasn't using him. Yes, I did need him because I really could not do this without a partner, but I thought we had something special. I really had this feeling that we understood each other, and that we would be able to contribute to making this life better. I should have never let him in. I am so angry that I allowed him to see me in such a vulnerable state. I don't even know him. He is just some guy I happened to know before I ended up here. Really, Grace? This is the guy you had wished was still in your life?

The plan is a good enough one to start out with. I will prove to him I am perfectly capable of this quest on my own. After about twenty minutes of fuming, I walk to the kitchen, grab a canteen of water, and throw it into my backpack. From the pantry I take some granola bars, and then a few packages of gauze and some alcohol wipes just in case. I walk over to the couch, lift the cushions, and remove the rifle.

Nick is standing by the counter, looking at me.

"Don't worry, this isn't meant to be used on you," I say as I sling it on my back and turn to walk away from him.

He jogs toward me and gently grabs my arm, "Grace, wait—"

I turn and look at him, "What?"

"I'm sorry. I didn't mean it."

I roll my eyes, "I think you did mean it. So don't worry, I'll handle this. Just like you said, Grace Baker doesn't need anyone."

I turn and walk away, and I exit through the secret door, leaving him in the living room. When I exit the cabin, it is very quiet. I don't hear any birds or wildlife, just silence. Somehow the absence of sound makes me tense, and I can feel my hands starting to perspire. With every chary step I take, I can feel the sweat slowly dripping down my back, as the rhythm of my heart escalates. It is already starting to feel very warm, and I dread the journey I have ahead of me.

I continue my way down the path toward the town. Stopping whenever I hear any movement. I find it is difficult to focus because I am still mad at Nick. I guess it is good that we had this argument, because at least I know how he really feels about me. I did not survive the end of the world, and fighting off monsters, to get into some high school quarrel with someone I hardly even know. I think it is only fair that when I am done with this experiment today, I should ask him to leave. I don't have time for distractions.

I stop when I hear movement ahead of me just off the trail. I unsling the rifle as quietly as I possibly can, and I slowly walk toward the bush to see if I can get a visual on whatever is making the sound. I poke my head to the side and am shocked to see a deer drinking from a small pond. Screw it, I will use deer like I had originally wanted to. I slowly bring the scope of the rifle up to my eye and take aim. I take a deep breath, and I slowly pull the trigger. The loud bang of the rifle sends birds flying from the trees as the deer abruptly falls to the ground.

I walk over to the collapsed deer, and it is dead. I survey the area to see where I want to put the deer carcass, and I realize that I am close enough to the town that this is an ideal location to conduct my experiment. I walk just past the small body of water and there is a meadow that I immediately recognize. It is the same meadow where I had learned to hunt in the first place, and subsequently spent so many afternoons with my family. Given any other circumstance, this would be a beautiful place. The sun is warm, and in another life, I can picture laying a blanket down and having lunch here. I can picture the warmth on my skin as I lie sprawled out reading a book. Listening to the music of the birds singing in the trees just beyond the meadow, with the gentle sound of running water in the distance. But now this meadow fills me with dread. It reminds me of the times when my family was still with me and I had to learn how to survive.

I walk back to the deer and attempt to move it, but the weight of my backpack and rifle is making it much more difficult and awkward. Every time I bend over, the rifle unslings and falls to the ground. I look around, and the meadow isn't too far. I don't want to utilize too much energy, and it will be much faster if I put the items down. You will be fine, Grace. Just put the items down and you will be back in a second, I think to myself. I unsling the rifle and my backpack, and I put them on the ground. I look around and I don't see anyone. Using all my strength, I begin dragging the deer toward the meadow. I continue to scan the area as I drag the carcass across the forest floor and listen to make sure I don't hear anything. My breath is heavy, and I feel droplets of sweat falling from my face. I feel my muscles starting to spasm, but I need to keep moving. Finally, I make it to the meadow and drop the deer. I wipe the sweat from my forehead with my hand, and I twist my body in both directions to help stretch my back.

I turn and jog toward where I left the items behind. Still a little out of breath, the jog seems harder than it should. I feel my lungs starting to burn with each exhale. With all the noise the rifle made, I push through the discomfort because I don't want anyone to find my stuff. I get to the other side of the pond, next to the tree where I left the items on the ground, and they are not there.

"You lookin' for this, darlin?" I look up and see two men, standing with my old beat up bag in hand. They have my bag, but where is the rifle?

I immediately recognize the voice from that day in the pharmacy so long ago. Suddenly, I'm overwhelmed with anger knowing I should've handled this the first time I came across them. I am shocked to see they have not changed much since our last encounter. Bob is still overweight somehow, but he appears to be balding more and missing more teeth. Rick, on the contrary, seems even thinner than he was before. His hair has only gotten longer and more raggedy as the years passed.

"Rick, ain't she pretty?" He obviously has long forgotten our first encounter.

Rick nods with a gross predator-like smile. He then looks around before saying, "Oh Bob... I think this fine-lookin lady is all by herself..."

I start looking for avenues of escape. I've been here before. Research, plan, execute.

"Don't even think about it," Bob says as he points a long butcher knife at me.

I know I have a knife in my sheath, and at least they don't have a gun this time. I need to think. If I can get behind Rick, maybe I can use him as protection.

They both start to close their distance on me, triangulating on either side of me. Both looking at me like I am a piece of meat, practically drooling. Rick continues to smile at me, as I see Bob lick his lips and wink at me.

"Bob, is it just me or does this look like that bitch who knocked you in the head with an umbrella last year, and stole Pop's gun?"

Damnit, they do remember. I shrug my shoulders, "I don't know what you're talking about. I have never been around here before."

Bob gets closer, knife still pointing at me, as Rick flanks me. Bob is within arm's reach of me now. I jump as he quickly raises his left hand and grabs my face by my cheeks, squishing my face as a grandma would do when you are a kid.

"I think you may be right. How could I forget such a pretty face?" His hands are rough, and I can feel either callouses or blisters on his fingers.

Rick suddenly pushes me into Bob's arms as he spins me to face him, and I can now feel the cold knife against my throat. The savage then wraps his free hand right around my waist leaving no room, as he sniffs my hair and then my neck.

"Oh... yeah... this sure is her. I may have forgotten the face, but how could I forget someone who smells so… sweet?" I feel a tickle as he proceeds to lick my neck with his rough tongue.

Rick starts laughing as he gets closer to me. He's so close I can smell how foul his breath is, which reeks of remnants of old cigarettes and liquor. Just as it smelled the last time I encountered him. He grabs me by my ponytail and forcefully pulls me toward his nose, jerking my head to smell me better.

I have one shot at this.

As hard as I can, I lift my knee right into Rick's groin, and he screams out, "You stupid bitch!" Rick then falls to the ground, as he continues to hold his groin, and curls up into fetal position.

Unsure of what just happened, Bob leans to see Rick on the ground, loosening his grip on my waist. The small space created by his curiosity allows me to grab my knife from the sheath. In one quick backward motion, I stab him in the stomach, causing him to temporarily let go of me. He screams in agony, and I step down as hard as I can onto his foot. He bends over right as I turn around and utilize another knee strike to his face. His body becomes erect, and I front kick him to get some distance. He cries out once more, saying something unintelligible to his partner.

Just then, I hear two loud gunshots, and I see Bob's blue shirt transform into a grotesque purple, as he looks down in confusion. Bob grabs at his chest but falls to his knees before falling on his face.

I turn around and see Nick standing there with the rifle. I look to the ground to see where Rick is. As he is attempting to stand up, I hear two more shots ring out. He falls on the ground face first before rolling onto his back. I can see that he is still breathing, but he is just staring at the sky. Nick walks toward Rick and takes a position in front of me as he approaches the savages. Rick slowly attempts to move. I hear one shot, a quick pause, and then another. The savages are dead.

Nick turns around and places both his hands on my face. "Baker, are you ok?"

"What are you doing here?" I say with relief in my voice.

"I couldn't let you come out here by yourself after getting into a fight. So I figured I would just follow you to make sure you were safe. I was going to give you your space, I just wanted to make sure you were ok. I heard those guys coming toward where you shot the deer, and when I saw the rifle, I knew I had to get it before they did."

I hang my head, "I almost had it figured out, but thank you."

He hugs me, "I am so sorry. I really am. I didn't mean what I said, and seeing you like that was terrifying."

I stay in his embrace, "I'm sorry, too. I can be stubborn, and I guess being alone for so long has made me bad at handling conflict."

He squeezes me tighter. "I shouldn't have let you leave like that. Not now with monsters and crazy people out here. It isn't safe."

I pull away from him. "I know, I realize it was stupid of me to do that."

He looks me in my eyes, "Wherever you go, I go. Until we figure these monsters out. Is that a deal?"

I can see the regret in his face, "If it really means that much—" I say to him.

He interrupts me before I can finish, "It does."

"Ok, then it is a deal. Wherever you go, I go."

He pulls me in once more and just holds me. I should be grateful that someone cares so much for me. I am starting to feel like claiming my independence is no longer necessary. He has a point that we are a team now. We are apocalypse partners, and we have to be considerate of the certitude that if something happens to one of us, we would be forced to be alone. We have to recognize that our decisions truly impact one another. I have to attempt to be less stubborn, and that is going to be an onerous task.

There's a brief pause. "So... I don't want to ruin the moment—"

Still hugging me, he interrupts, "Yes, Baker, we've got our test subjects."

I pull back and look at him. "It's probably not a perfect plan to use multiple kinds of subjects for an experiment, but I think the fact that we have two humans is huge. I'm thinking we can adjust the test a little bit and see what happens.

"What do you mean?" he asks.

"Well now we can put the gasoline theory to test. We can use one of the bodies and pour gasoline on it, and the other one will remain as it is. Then we can use the deer and cover it with the fish smell. That way if it doesn't really work with the deer, at least we have more reliable test subjects for the gasoline. Make sense?"

He thinks about it for a moment and shrugs, "May I make a suggestion?"

"Of course."

"Why don't we just use the humans, and use the deer for food instead?"

I let out a laugh, "I didn't even think of that. That is actually a much better idea!"

He smiles, proud of his observation. I guess having him around isn't such a bad idea after all.

Chapter Thirty-Three

Before

I wake up and my whole body hurts. I gently bring my hand to my eye socket, and it is tender to the touch. I am very confident that it is already bruising, but it does not feel broken. I recognize that these training sessions are imperative. I am aware that with every session, I will become more proficient, and in turn will have fewer injuries. However, the idea of having another boxing match that is so harsh—before my body even has time to heal—makes my body ache even more in anticipation.

I walk to the kitchen and everyone is already awake.

"Oh, hun," my mom walks over to me quickly, "your face is all bruised!"

"Oh don't worry, Susan, bruises make her look tougher," says my dad.

Stephen walks over and just starts laughing, and my mom slaps him in the arm. "Say sorry to your sister."

"I am not going to apologize for kicking her ass because Dad made me do it, Mom," he says.

I interrupt, "It's ok, Mom, really. I'll get him back next time. And you didn't really kick my ass," I say as I roll my eyes.

"That's the spirit!" says my dad.

I sit down at the table and try to have some kind of normal breakfast. We usually mix it up between the different types of sustainable breakfast food.

Who knew Hostess bakery products had such a long shelf life? Today it is good old Twinkies. Sometimes it really grosses me out eating such sweet stuff for breakfast, but I guess it it's no different than muffins or donuts.

"So, Grace. How do you feel your training went yesterday?" asks my dad.

I swallow the last remains of my Twinkie, "It wasn't so bad. I am pretty sore, but I feel like I am getting the hang of it."

Stephen chimes in, "You actually did pretty good. You just have to be prepared for those kicks."

"I agree, you seem to do fine blocking the punches, but you don't see the kicks coming," says my dad.

"Usually, you can see people move their feet before they kick. They kind of angle their other foot in preparation," adds Stephen.

"You know, that is an excellent point. Good observation, kid," says my dad.

"I mean, I know I need some practice," I say, "but overall I think it went as good as it could go. My biggest fault was thinking I had the upper hand and letting down my guard somewhat. I became overzealous."

"You did wonderful, dear," adds my mother, "but I don't like seeing your face so bruised."

"Aww, don't worry, Mom. It'll go away," I say. My smile begins to fade when I see something moving outside the window. I focus on it, and it is clear that at least one person is outside our cabin. "Dad! Something is out there!" I yell to him.

He runs to the window and looks back at us, "Stephen, grab the guns. Susan and Grace, go into the bedroom."

"What? We can help—" I say.

Mom grabs me by the arm, unintentionally digging her nails into my flesh. "Don't argue with your father, come with me," she says as she is pulling me toward the hallway.

I resist her as I look toward Stephen. He is frantically grabbing the old shotgun and checking to see if it is loaded. I see him conduct a chamber check of the weapon, and then he racks the shotgun to load ammunition into the chamber. The familiar yet terrifying sound resonates in the common area, and I know things are dire.

I feel like I need to help, so I plead: "But, Mom—"

"Grace Tiffany!" That is all she needs to say, and I am quiet and obey her demands.

We hurry toward the back bedroom and lock the door. This room has no windows and I now know why Dad wanted us to come back here. Mom opens the drawer and pulls out two long hunting knives.

"Here, honey, take one," she says as she hands me a knife.

If I ever thought that my mother would be handing me a hunting knife in such a cool and collected manner, I would have been dreaming. I always knew my mom was a fighter. I love seeing my mom in this way. Someday, I will be just like her.

My thoughts are disrupted when I hear glass shatter and someone yelling in the living room. Whoever it was outside had made it inside. I can hear fighting and multiple voices.

"Mom, it sounds like so many people."

"Shhh..." she says in a whisper. "You don't want them to hear us."

The crashing sound continues, and there is clearly an all-out fight going on. I can hear furniture being shoved, glass breaking, and various grunts. I cannot tell how many people there are. I put my ear against the door to see if I can hear better. Suddenly, between all the fighting, two gunshots ring out, which causes me to jump. Oh my god, I hope Dad and Stephen are ok.

It seems like this fight is lasting forever, and I feel worthless for not being able to help. I cannot make out exactly what is going on, all I can hear is the sound of a muffled battle. Then, down the hall, I hear thud...thud...thud... thud... Footsteps heading our way. I look at my mom and she hears it too.

Thud...thud...thud...thud...

Each footstep echoes down the hallway as the intruder makes his way to every room, looking for potential victims hiding in the darkness. With each strike of his foot, the sounds reverberate louder and louder, and I can feel my breathing begin to intensify. The heavy footsteps stop, and we look at the door. The doorknob is moving up and down. Someone is here for us.

Chapter Thirty-Four

Present

When I had to drag the deer carcass earlier, I could have never foreseen that I would be dragging two dead humans shortly thereafter. That was such a close call. I had always felt a tinge of regret for not having killed them that day in the pharmacy, because I always feared I would encounter them again. When the monsters came, I took delight in knowing that they had probably been monster meat. I have changed, though. Watching Nick kill them was cathartic in a way. I am glad I got to see them die. I now lack compunction in these troubled times. I took pleasure in watching them take their final breaths, and the desperation on their faces. People like that don't deserve to live. I don't like that I feel that way. I would never tell Nick, either. I do not want him to know how slowly, with each passing day, I lose more of myself. I don't want him to know that with every life taken, I seem to care less about it. I am now at the point that I don't even have nightmares about it anymore. My soul is transforming into an abyss of blackness, and I don't know if there is any coming back from that.

Somehow, during all this carnage, I am drawn to a memory of my very first meeting with Nick. I don't know why this particular memory presents itself, but I remember it so clearly in this moment. It flashes in my mind as if it had happened yesterday, rather than before everything happened the way it did. It was fall; which really didn't mean much in Los Angeles. No huge trees to change colors, or stormy nights to let us know the seasons had transitioned. But there were leaves blowing on the ground, and a refreshing coolness in the air. I had walked into the café wearing my normal fall attire of a hoodie, jeans, and my favorite black and white Chuck Taylor shoes. I walked to the counter, and suddenly this handsome man was standing there. I had been coming to this café for months, most nights of the week, and I would have definitely remembered that face had I seen it before.

Almost speechless, I could feel my cheeks warm as they blushed, and the moment was broken by another employee walking up to him. "Nick, this is Grace. She is our best customer, so make sure you get her order right."

Nick's eyes met mine and he smiled. "I'll make sure to pay extra attention, in that case."

I could feel my cheeks turning more red. "I'm not a big deal, really, I promise."

"I doubt that," he said with a smile. "Hi, I'm Nick." He extended his hand out for a handshake.

I extended mine, "Hi, I'm Grace Baker."

"Oh, we're being formal. Ok, I am Nicholas Gates, in that case." He shook my hand. "So, Miss Baker, what are you having tonight?"

"I'll take a medium hot chocolate with just a dash of cinnamon, please."

"My pleasure."

I paid with cash and then walked out to the patio. The outdoor heaters were lit, along with the bright Edison bulb lights hanging from the trees. I was pleased to see that my favorite oversized chair facing the fire pit was available. I sat down and pulled my book from my bag.

Nick walked out with a giant cup of hot chocolate and began walking toward me. "Ok, I know you ordered a medium, but since you are our best customer and I am trying to leave a good impression, I thought you could use a large. Plus, it is so cold out here tonight. Who knew Los Angeles could actually get cold? But, shhh, don't tell the owners, Miss Baker, I only charged you for the medium."

I smiled, "Your secret is safe with me." I take the mug from him.

He tilted his head and looked at the book in my lap. "*Saint Thomas*? What is that about?"

Surprised by his observation, I briefly paused, "Oh—it's actually the last of a series of books. It's about this guy who senses when bad things are going to happen. He can see these weird beings, so to speak, and he's constantly saving the world. Even though he reiterates the fact that he's just a fry cook."

"Well that sounds very interesting."

"It's actually kind of a bittersweet feeling. This is the first book series I've ever read from the very beginning, and this is the last in the series. So, I already have a feeling how it's going to end! I've been so emotionally invested!"

He smiled, "That's so cool that you like reading so much. You don't really see that anymore. You'll have to let me borrow it so I can check it out. What's the first book called?"

"It's called *Odd Thomas*, and if I still had it, I would definitely let you borrow it. But unfortunately, I let a friend borrow it a few years back, and she lost it, of course, and now it is gone forever."

"Oh, that's rough. I'm sorry, Miss Baker. If I ever find a copy, I'll make sure to save it for you." He turns around, walks to the door, slowly opens it, and takes one last look at me before walking in.

"Baker!" I can hear him calling me from my memory. "You ok?"

I am pulled back into this new reality.

"Yeah, totally fine. Just figuring out how we're gonna work this out."

He looks at me, clearly unconvinced by my explanation. At this point, we had placed Rick and Bob roughly twenty yards from one another in the meadow.

We place one cadaver on the left side of the meadow, and the other one on the right. I walk over to the body on the left and pour gasoline all over it. While I hate wasting such a valuable resource, it is absolutely necessary.

Nick looks at me, "Do you think it'll trick them?"

I stand there with my hands on my hips, "At this point I hope so! We will never find better subjects if this is unsuccessful."

He replies, "Yeah, that was a lucky break."

We take a step back and admire our work. We know there is a chance this will fail, because we are unable to stay and watch it happen in real time. But we look at each other, give a nod, and begin to make our way home hauling the deer.

Today was fundamental, because if this works—if somehow this pans out the way we want it to—we will finally have a way to be safe. We will finally have found a way to try to observe them without being detected. Most importantly, though, we will have discovered a way to reestablish a new status quo. It all starts with this initial phase. I don't know if it was pure luck that those savages came across us today, or if it is simply all happening the way it was always meant to. But I have to hope that this was all for a reason.

Chapter Thirty-Five

Before

The doorknob continues to move up and down, until abruptly, it stops. Maybe the intruder moved on to the next room. My hopes are dashed when there is a huge boom at the door as the person tries kicking it in. The loud noise startles me, triggering a jump in response, but I do not let out a sound.

I turn toward my mom and whisper, "Mom, get in the closet, I'm going to hide behind the door—I have a plan."

Without hesitation, my mom quietly scoots over to the closet, as I hide behind the door. Boom. He tries again and is unsuccessful once more. Boom. Again, the door does not budge, but it won't take much longer before the lock gives way. BOOM! The door comes crashing in, almost striking me behind it. I see the silhouette of a man enter the room as he is backlit from the light beaming down the hall. Due to the lack of illumination in the bedroom, he appears disoriented as his eyes adjust to the unexpected absence of light.

I softly walk behind him, ensuring I do not alert him to my position to maintain an element of surprise. With one forceful front kick, I am able to make contact with his lower body, catching him off guard. He falls to his knees and groans in discomfort. Promptly, I jump on his back and place my hand on his forehead while forcefully pulling back as hard as I can to expose his neck. He is attempting to use his legs to throw me off of him, but without dubiety,

I take the knife, place it on his throat, and cut into it. There is little resistance; like a knife cutting into butter. He tries grabbing me as I feel his nails dig into my flesh. I feel a rush of warmth on my arm, as the blood flows down to my hand. Within moments, his hands drop and his body falls to the floor. There is no more movement.

What have I done?

I hear two more gunshots, and my attention is turned toward the door. What if they come back here? After a few short moments, I hear no more commotion in the rest of the house. But a few brief seconds later, I hear footsteps running toward me. With a lantern in hand, Stephen is the first in the room, just as my mom is exiting the closet.

I stand up, covered in my assailant's blood, and I see Stephen just staring at me. Dad runs in right behind Stephen, but he comes to a halt when he sees the dead man on the floor. I just stand there looking at the blood on my arm, and the way the dull light of the lantern makes the blood look black. My mom walks up behind me, and as she goes to put her arms around me, I jump.

"Honey, it is ok," she says as she hugs me from behind.

My dad walks over and joins in the hug, and Stephen joins in last.

There we just stand as a family, hugging one another over the dead man on the ground.

"Are you ok?" my dad asks.

"Yeah, I'm fine… I just…"

"You don't have to say anything. You did good, Grace," he says.

I continue to stare at the blood all over me.

"Here, hun, let's go get you cleaned up," my mom says as she takes me by the hand and ushers me toward the hallway. "Your father and Stephen will deal with this."

I nod, and as I walk out, I look back at the person on the floor. Look what you made me do. You have made me a monster.

We walk out into the living room and it is a scene straight from a horror movie. The giant glass window separating us from the beauty of the woods is completely shattered. There are misplaced items tossed and resting all over the wood floor. The dining room chairs are turned on their sides. With all the commotion I heard from the back bedroom, I would have expected more people in here, but there are only two bodies remaining. I had never seen them before, and I have no idea where they came from. They look more like travelers than locals. They are wearing jeans and tennis shoes, rather than boots. They must have somehow come across the cabin on their way to town. Whatever had transpired in here, Stephen and Dad handled it with relative ease, it would seem. The burglars have cuts and bruises to their faces, and each one has a gunshot wound to their head. Their eyes are still open, observing our every move even in death, and I find myself just staring at them, waiting for one of them to blink.

Mom escorts me to the bathroom and begins to wipe the blood off me. I sit down on the toilet, as she gently takes a towel to my face. She is focused on getting every little spot of blood. Slowly, she wipes my face repeatedly until it is all gone. She then takes each arm, one at a time, scrubbing the evidence of the crime away. I sit there in a daze, staring at the wall without saying anything.

Finally, I break the silence, "I had to."

She stops scrubbing my arms and looks at me, "Of course you had to. You saved us."

"It was so easy, Mom. Why was it so easy? That isn't normal. Something is wrong with me."

She places my hands in hers. "Oh, my sweet girl. You're in shock, but you did exactly how you were trained."

I stare at her for a moment, "That doesn't explain why it was so easy, though. I am not an evil person."

"Grace." She pauses, and kneels down to look me directly in the eyes, "Grace, my sweet girl, you did what you had to do to survive. You are not evil. Those people who came in here looking to hurt us are the evil ones. You did good," she kisses my forehead, "I am so proud of you."

I feel my eyes swell with tears because I know there is no going back from this. I killed a human being with my bear hands. I did not hesitate. I did what I had to do to protect my mom. I don't regret what I did. I am more despondent knowing that this may be what my future holds. This is what I have become. Why did I feel nothing when I slit that man's throat?

Who am I kidding, though? This sorrow I feel is not because I killed a man, it is because I was perfectly okay with killing him. I should have remorse for acting in such a cool and collected manner, but I don't. I feel like I have already changed so much, because I should be more upset about everything that I just participated in. I did not want this new life to change my moral compass. I always wanted to have those important character qualities that made me who I was to my core. The Grace in the life before this one could have never acted that way. Who am I now?

Chapter Thirty-Six

Present

I could hardly sleep last night. I had so many ideas going through my head. What if it worked? What if it didn't work? How would we know if it was the monsters who ate or took our test subjects? If this doesn't work out, where are we ever going to find other humans to test on? We don't kill to kill, we kill to survive, and I know it doesn't make that much sense, but it separates us from the savages. At least it allows us to feel like we still have some moral code.

I have this nervous feeling in my stomach. That nauseous, yet butterfly-like disruption to my insides. It reminds me of how I used to feel Christmas morning as I was waiting to open presents as a child. I think I am nervous, yet I am extremely excited to see if our experiment actually worked.

After a few days being each other's only companions, Nick had already caught on to my social cues. On days like these when I was deep in thought, he did not try to distract me. He allowed me to be one with my mind as I frivolously scribbled notes in my notebook. It is still hard getting used to the new normal of his presence. Like a long-lost friend who knows your darkest secrets, but who appreciates you for having survived them. That friend who makes you a stronger, better version of yourself. I cannot be certain if I would have ever had the courage to take on this undertaking of fighting these monsters had we not crossed paths. Nick's candor has also helped me grow. He has made me recognize my stubbornness can sometimes be deleterious to our new partnership. Living is easy. Getting used to a world in which kill or be killed is the social norm is actually easier than I could have ever imagined. But there is this underlying fear of trying to fight something you cannot see that I could never shake. That is the hard part. The anticipation of what things might be like if we actually find a way to kill these creatures.

To be honest, this whole thing is absolutely terrifying. The entire plot is either ridiculously absurd or genius. For all the fantasy I had subjected myself to over the years, monsters came in all shapes and sizes. Yet, it was always the humans who we really had to fear. But now, in this world, monsters aren't just a metaphor, they are real. While the humans have lived up to every stereotype I can imagine under these circumstances, we really are living in a world with real, beastly, horror-movie-like monsters. Every creature has a weakness. I keep having to remind myself of that. It's just this time around, the monsters hiding under my bed can't be killed with the flick of a light switch.

It's days like these when I miss my family so much. You don't realize how much you need those people in your life until they are gone. What I would give to have my mom sit on the side of my bed and run her fingers through my hair to wake me up. I can still smell her lotion, and the gentle way she'd say my name to not startle me awake. Grace, honey, time for breakfast. Oh, how I long for that.

What would I give to have my dad challenge me once more? The way he would present a problem and ask me to solve it. I would get so frustrated, but he would constantly remind me, Research, Plan, Execute. There was no problem on the planet that could not be solved with the famous Mr. Baker formula. No matter how many times I could not solve a problem he would remind me what Thomas Edison once said: "I have not failed, I just found 10,000 ways that won't work." Hopefully it won't take 10,000 times to defeat these monsters.

But missing my brother is a different type of longing. Siblings make you strong through adversity. They fight you tooth and nail, with this underlying admiration for one another. They will ridicule you, and do everything in their power to annoy you, but there is an understanding. Blood is blood; you protect each other. Once Mom and Dad were gone, that was absolutely true! It was us against the world. He helped mold me into who I am now. I can almost feel him laughing at me from beyond the grave for admitting that to myself.

Now, Nick is my family. I have to learn to embrace our situation and find the strength in him that I once had with Stephen. I need to find wisdom in him, like I was once able to do with my dad. Most importantly, though, I need to find the comfort in him that I once had with my mother. That is a lot to expect from someone; I would never even ask him to be those things. However, I need to be able to seek those traits in order to keep moving forward. I can no longer live in a life that no longer exists.

After spending much of the hike toward our science experiment deep in contemplation, we are about 100 yards from the meadow when he stops walking. He turns toward me and grabs my hands.

"Baker, no matter what, this isn't a failure."

Taken aback that those exact words came from his mouth after thinking about my dad, I open my mouth, but no words come out.

He continues, "I know you are concerned. You haven't said a single word all morning, and you were quiet all last night. This is just phase one. Trust the process, ok?"

Maybe he will be able to fill those voids I am so desperately seeking after all. I nod in acceptance. He lets go of my hands and turns back toward the meadow. He walks at a faster pace than normal, and I feel a little breathless as I try to keep up.

We slowly continue through the trees, and pause just at the clearing, scanning the area for anyone or anything. Silence. He grabs my hand, and we walk toward our experiment.

Shocked as we get closer, he says, "Well, Baker, I didn't see that one coming."

Chapter Thirty-Seven

Before

It has been a few weeks since we lost Mom, and I am still not grieving. Everything is different. Whatever hope we had that things are going to be alright dissipated when Mom was killed by whatever those creatures are. We have barely left the house since then, and Dad has been taking it even harder. I know he misses Mom, and God I miss her too.

Life sucks. It is like whenever things seem to be going just fine, there has to be another wrench in our plans. I didn't want the world to end. I did the best I could in this life to start over, and why do I have to pay the price for everyone else?

I walk out into the living room, and I see Dad sitting alone on the couch staring at the wall.

"Do you mind if I join you?" I ask.

He looks up at me. "Of course not. Come sit," he says as he taps his hand on the couch.

I study his face. "Are you ok, Dad? I know it has been hard on you these last couple weeks."

He looks at me and then looks down. "You know, I keep replaying everything that happened in my mind. Every little detail you and Stephen told me that night. What I realized is the tragic fact that it is all my fault."

I sit there trying to make sense of what he is trying to tell me. "What is?"

He pauses briefly before replying. "Your mother dying."

I turn toward him and grab his hands. "Dad! There is no way you could've known that there were some crazy beasts lurking in the forest when you went back into the cabin that night—"

He interrupts me, "Grace. Do you know what I did, before all this happened?"

Unsure of what this has to do with anything, I turn toward him more to face him directly. "Yeah, of course. You were in the Navy."

He looks at me, "What did I do in the Navy?"

I pause, "Well, I just know you had really top-secret clearance."

He looks away and back at the wall, "Grace, I wasn't just in the Navy. I was part of DEVGRU."

I look at him confused, "I don't know what that means, Dad."

He looks down at his lap, averting his gaze from mine. "I was part of the Naval Special Warfare Development Group."

I'm still looking at him, but he is avoiding eye contact with me. "Alright... I still don't know what that means."

His eyes are glued to the floor as he speaks, "It means we were part of a counter terrorism unit, that participated in special missions to combat terrorists."

I quietly respond, "I don't know what this has to do with Mom."

After a brief pause, he finally looks up at me, "It means I knew there was a possibility that these monsters were coming."

A long silence passes as I try, and fail, to connect the dots. I try to piece the information together, but he can see the confusion in my face and knows I am not following.

"You know how it goes," he finally continues. "Each country is always trying to find the most innovative ways to fight wars. They want to be able to fight without our own people suffering the consequences. Always seeking new weapons. Well, they did it. The military created a new weapon to combat terrorism, and to avoid American casualties. We didn't know the specifics of how it was created, because that was way above my clearance, but we knew what it was capable of doing. The government concocted these creatures in a lab and said they were the ultimate weapon. That if we released them, the terrorists wouldn't even know they were coming."

I pull my legs onto the couch to sit with my legs crossed so I can continue looking directly at him, "I don't understand."

He grabs my hand, "Grace, WE created the monsters. AMERICANS. They created them in a lab, not even realizing what they were truly capable of. I was part of a mission where we released them as a trial run, and it was exactly how you explained what happened to your mother."

My jaw drops, "But you couldn't have known!"

"But I did know! I prepared you guys for it. I knew deep down that we couldn't control them. There are always consequences to our actions, and I knew we couldn't contain it, and look! Look what it has done!" He puts his face in his hands.

Finally, the severity of what he has just confessed hits me like a ton of bricks. "So you are telling me that this entire time we have been up here, you knew there was a chance that there would be monsters released into whatever was left of society?"

He nods his head up and down, while holding his face in his hands. Angry, I stand up and face him directly. "Dad, did Mom know?"

He looks up at me, and it is the first time I have ever seen my dad with tears in his eyes, "Grace, if these things are like anything I saw in Afghanistan, it is not going to be alright."

I raise my voice, "I didn't ask you about Afghanistan, Dad! Did you tell Mom?"

He quietly mumbles, "Yes."

I start pacing back and forth. "So let me get this straight. You knew there were monsters out there, and you didn't think to tell us?" I stop and stare at him. "Wait, does Stephen know? Am I the only one you didn't think to share such consequential information with?"

He looks up at me, "No, he doesn't know."

I start pacing back and forth once more. "How could you not tell us about all of this? Especially considering everything going on? I knew something was happening when I heard you talking to Mom on the way up here regarding how you purposely were training Stephen and me. Like we were just part of your stupid government experiment! Training us for something we wanted absolutely no part of."

He looks at me with pleading in his eyes. "It wasn't that—"

I interrupt him, "Not to mention you just let people get attacked by whatever these things are—"

"Grace, honey, it is a lot more complicated than that," he says before I can finish.

"No, sounds pretty simple to me. They went too far," I say angrily. "And you just stood by and watched it happen." I can't bring myself to meet his eyes, but I can feel them piercing me. "You didn't even try to stop this from happening." I turn my back to him.

"I didn't know what to do—" he says.

I turn around, and my eyes dart to his now, and my voice begins to rise again. "Are you kidding me right now? You didn't know what to do? I don't even care about what happened in Afghanistan. How about you should have been honest with us in the first place? What the hell were we doing out at night if you knew there was a chance they could have been out there?"

His voice is trembling now, "If I had known that they released the monsters, Grace, I swear I would have never let anything happen to your mother."

I stand there looking at him now, "So for all of the training, planning, special missions, and ridiculous things you have subjected Stephen and me to, you never once thought: Hey, maybe I should tell my kids now that there is no power, huge man-eating monsters that the government created may be out on the loose hunting us."

For the first time, I see utter defeat in his expression. He doesn't look like my dad right now; he looks like a young child who was being scolded by his mother and was waiting for his punishment. "You are absolutely right. I should have known. Like I always instilled in you kids: Failing to prepare is preparing to fail, and I failed you." His voice begins to tremble. "I failed you kids more than I can ever express, and I failed your mother. She didn't deserve this. She didn't deserve to be taken from us like that. She was an angel—she put up with everything all these years." He looks away, and I see the tears rolling down his cheeks. "I messed up, and I know there is nothing I can ever do to make it up to you kids." He appears contrite in his admission.

Despite my anger, seeing my dad like this is too much for me to handle. I will never understand why he decided to keep such valuable and necessary information from us. It kills me knowing that there was a chance we could have prevented all of this from happening. A million thoughts are racing through my brain. Especially wondering if my mom even realized what was happening that night. When she heard that clicking in the woods, did she know what was coming for us? Did she realize what was about to happen? It is all so much to try to take in, but right now I have to set my anger and devastation aside.

After a few minutes, I finally sit beside my dad on the couch and grab his hand. "Well, first… first we need to address the problem."

He looks at me confused.

I continue, "If this is what you think it is, then we need to figure out the problem."

He sits erect, and places his other hand on top of mine, "I see what you are getting at, but—"

I shake my head. "Saying 'but' is not describing the problem. If this is truly what you think it is, then we need to apply your method."

He squeezes my hand, "It is not that simple, Grace."

I squeeze his hand in return. "You told me that every single problem I will ever encounter begins with researching and identifying a problem, planning a method to tackle the problem, and then executing the plan. Did you not tell me that?"

He looks away before looking back at me, "Well, yes—"

I shrug my shoulders, "So, if this is what you really think it is, then let's start planning. You obviously have some idea of what they are, and possibly how to defeat them. So it is time to put all that work we have done together, and make a plan."

He smiles at me, "I have never been prouder of you, Grace."

I give him a soft smile, "I am only doing what you have trained me to do my whole life. This is the mission now. We can be sad, or we can do something about it. Mom would want us to fight these things. Not just sit around and sulk."

He gently touches my cheek. "Thank you for getting my head back in the game, honey. I needed it."

"Of course, Dad. We are a team now."

He stands up and faces me. "I haven't told Stephen yet, please don't say anything. I know he is going to take this news even harder than you did. I just need to figure this all out, and gather everything together. I will figure out a plan, and then it will be easier to tell him."

"Of course. We will make it through this, I promise."

I stand up and walk away from the couch. I am still so infuriated, but I have to put it aside for now. I had to get him to focus on fixing this because we can't afford to be sulking; there is too much at stake. I am trying to make sense of everything, and acting like I already forgave him makes me feel nauseous in a way. How can I forgive him? How could he have kept such important information from us? I know we are all that we have left, but the thought that we could have prevented this is heartbreaking. Mom could still be here right now if it weren't for him. He should have warned us. There is no going back now. I don't think I will ever forgive him.

Chapter Thirty-Eight

Present

I stand in awe as it appears our experiment worked. I tend to doubt myself in these types of situations. It is natural to have feelings of incertitude when actually implementing a plan you have created and obsessed over. I feel myself getting exuberant, but quickly remind myself that it is too early in the process. There are still so many factors we need to further explore before we can determine if the experiment has truly been successful.

"We can't get too excited," I say.

Nick pulls my arm, "Baker! We did it!"

He continues to pull me toward the meadow, and all that remains is a single body. As I look at the meadow, I can see remnants of one of the cadavers scattered over the field, while one lone body remains intact. As we get closer, I can already smell the odor of gasoline.

"Wow... just wow," I say in disbelief.

I immediately sling my backpack onto the ground and pull out my notebook to record the results. Rick is exactly how we left him. The more I study the body, I realize there are no scratches and no bites. All that seems to be present is the rigor mortis and expected over-night decay. I continue to walk the meadow, stopping to investigate the remaining pieces of Bob, which wasn't much.

Nick comes beside me. “Ok, Baker, what do we do now?”

I pause, put my pen to my mouth and bite on it. “If I am being frank, I didn’t think this would really work. I hoped it would work, but the chances of it were slim. Now we need to decide if we want to try another trial, or go all in and assume the gasoline is a safe deterrent.”

“What does your heart tell you?”

“I think my heart tells me that we have to go all in and can’t waste what little resources we have. The fact that we now have two instances in which gasoline deterred them from attacking is enough for me. Once can be a fluke, but twice is a pattern.”

“You know what this means?” He asks.

“Yes… we are going to need to find more gas,” I say with a chuckle.

“Exactly.”

Being so close to town affords us the ability to go see what is left at the old gas station. We both know it is a long shot that anything would remain, but we have to try. I place my notebook back in my backpack, and we begin to walk toward town.

We finally make it to town, when I notice clouds forming on the horizon. We cannot afford to get caught in a storm today. I point to the unfortunate development, and Nick moves his head up and down in a yeah, I saw that type of way.

We make our way through town as we always do, constantly checking our surroundings, not saying a single word to one another. You never know who is hiding within these deserted walls. It is a constant state of sprinting, maintaining your breath so you can listen, and when there is no sound, sprinting again. We finally get to the gas station, and I already feel ridiculous for suggesting it. The chances we would find gasoline here are slim to none.

We slowly enter the shop and scan the area. The mirrors hanging in the corners that were once used for cashiers to see if people were shoplifting are worn and dusty, but they allow us to see that it is clear. The shelves are mostly bare, leaving nothing but old maps and souvenirs. We walk behind the counter, and into the abandoned employee break room. It consists of a few tables, TVs that most likely showed surveillance footage in real time, and broken vending machines.

We decide to leave, and as I am turning the corner around the counter, my backpack gets stuck on an empty metal display. At first, I feel a slight tug, but my momentum carries me forward. Bewildered, I turn around and see Nick looking at me with a smile on his face.

"Baker, look at your clumsiness paying off," he says as he points down to the ground.

Beneath the counter is a single door leading to some secret compartment. There is no lock, and the door seems very large and heavy. Nick cautiously opens it, and we just stand there and listen for a second. Complete silence. He takes a flashlight and illuminates the room. Much like our sanctuary at the cabin, the door opens to a flight of stairs. It is some kind of basement.

I am about to go down when he puts his arm up and stops me. "Let me go first."

Rather than my usual objections, I allow him to go first. I am right behind him as we descend the stairs into the unknown. When we get to the bottom, he is already scanning the room with his flashlight to see what awaits. It is a storage room, but it had been turned into a place for someone to hide in. There is a cot, much like what I have, and old food lining makeshift shelves. Whoever had prepared this place didn't seem to survive long enough to use any of it. It looks like nothing has ever been touched. As I get closer to what appears to be the bedroom, I see a dusty picture frame next to the cot. I bend over and pick it up, wiping the dust from the frame. It is a young man with his wife and his infant child. What happened to you? I bring the frame close to my chest, placing both hands on it as if I were giving this lost family a final hug goodbye. After a moment, I place the frame back on the ground just as I had found it.

"Grace!"

I am startled by Nick's voice, and the fact that he is calling me by my first name. I quickly turn around and see that he is standing on the opposite side of the room. I rush toward him to see what he has found.

"What is it?" I eagerly ask.

He turns his head to look at me, "We can't be this lucky."

Confused, I am about to see what he is talking about as he takes the flashlight and points deeper into the corner. There I see about twenty red canisters used for transporting gasoline. He's right. We can't be this lucky. I run over and start frantically grabbing them one by one.

"Nick! They are all full!"

Chapter Thirty-Nine

Before

It has been a few days since my dad opened up to me about the monsters. I am still trying to digest it all. I still feel so angry. He should have never kept such a secret from us. I know he wasn't the one who created those monsters, but he was complicit. He stood by while they used those creatures as tools of war. There is no way they could have only been weaponized for who they were intended for. Innocent people have been killed, just like my poor mother.

I have never seen him so vulnerable before. He wasn't acting like the man I had looked up to my entire life. Suddenly, he seemed like he was on the verge of breaking; as if he were a small crack in a windshield, moments away from splintering past the point of being able to be fixed.

His impromptu confession made me realize why we were always so prepared for everything. Why he began training me to solve puzzles that seemed improbable. It also reminded me of that time he made me solve a puzzle about monsters. Had he already been exposed to these things all the way back then? That was so long ago. How come he never actually warned us before then?

The time had come for us to make another supply run, but I think he actually wanted to do some scouting for his plan. We had avoided it for as long as possible, but eventually you need to go out there and hunt. Although, what are we hunting now? Food? Savages? Monsters? Dad refused to divulge what his plan entailed. He just said he would tell me once he had it all figured out. He insisted that he fix this on his own. Apparently, the art of being stubborn came from my father.

It is early in the morning, and we've gathered supplies to survive whatever will be thrown at us today. After all, who really knows what to expect anymore? We woke up early, so we could head to town at dawn. Since he hadn't told Stephen yet, I figured that is why he was not more forthcoming about the venture.

The town is quiet as always, and Dad seems to be exploring it more than usual which is what I had expected. I notice he is paying particular attention to the clocktower and insists that Stephen and I keep watch while he goes to examine it. Rather than arguing, we just sit down and wait for him to come back.

"What is he doing up there?" Stephen asks.

"Who knows, probably looking for supplies."

Stephen shrugs his shoulders, and after a few moments, he asks, "Grace, do you miss Mom?"

Angry he would even ask that, I respond, "How can you ask me that? Of course I miss Mom."

He kicks his feet on the ground, "I miss the way she smells. It's like even though we lived through an apocalypse, she still had that specific smell."

I start laughing, "I know exactly what you mean. Like even though we hardly bathe anymore, she still smelled like that lotion she would use. I don't even remember the name of it anymore."

"She didn't deserve to die that way," he says.

"I know. I hope she didn't suffer."

"Do you think she did?" He looks at me, and I finally, for the first time, see how he's hurting too. "Do you think she even knew what was happening?"

I grab his hand, "I really hope not."

"I'm glad we were having such a good night, you know? Like at least her last night was fun and she was laughing."

I feel my eyes filling with tears, "She's not really gone, you know. She'll always be with us as long as we keep talking about her."

He puts his arm around me and hugs me, "We still have each other, little sis. We'll be just fine."

Our moment is disrupted when Dad exits the clocktower, "Ok, kids, let's go get some food now."

Quietly I ask, "Did you find what you were looking for?"

He looks at me with a half-smile and places his hand on my shoulder. "I think this will work; it has to."

Stephen looks at us with a perplexing gaze, "What are you guys talking about?"

Dad opens his mouth to respond, but I cut him off. "Oh, just something we were talking about the other day. Nothing important." This wasn't the time or place for him to have to confess his sins.

Stephen looks at me, and then at my dad, and then back at me. "Alright, if you say so."

We head toward the meadow just as we always do. It is a little later than we had planned to go hunting, but we go ahead and set ourselves up, and we begin the game of waiting.

Since the monsters had arrived, there have been fewer animals for us to hunt. I don't know if it is mere coincidence or directly linked to their presence. Usually by now we would have already seen deer and rabbits, and heard squirrels dashing up and down the trees, but they seem to have all fled. Maybe we are the dumb ones for staying behind.

Based on the sun's placement in the sky, it is already past noon when a deer finally appears. It is Stephen's turn to shoot our meal. He is a natural at it from all those years hunting with Dad growing up. He does not hesitate the way I do. The deer would appear, he would take aim, and without a beat the deer would be down.

This is a particularly large deer. Per usual, Stephen takes aim and shoots, and the deer is dead. The idea of having to haul the deer all the way back home is already making my back ache in anticipation. Dad grabs the two front feet, Stephen grabs the hind legs, and we switch between the three of us on the haul back.

We have been so focused on hunting and then hauling, that we have not been paying attention to the sky. Out of nowhere, dark clouds emerge above the trees, and we are plunged into a gray gloom. Lightning strikes a tree, slicing it in half, and thunder roars in the distance, startling me. Suddenly, we realize the danger we are in. Can we make it home in time?

"Dad, they just come out at night, right?" I ask.

He hesitates, "I don't know, Grace. We only deployed them at night."

Stephen, confused, looks at me, "What are you guys talking about?"

We all begin to jog. We are close enough to the cabin that we should be fine, but still far enough to be concerned. With every passing second, the sky seems to become darker and darker. I am plagued with the sensation that everything that could go wrong will go wrong right now. The anxiety is causing me to feel sick, but I cannot stop now. I have to keep up with my family.

The forest is dark, and it is hard to see now. The clouds have removed all ambient lighting from the sky, and it feels like we are running blind. Every lightning strike creates a glow just bright enough to distort our vision once it is dark again, preventing our eyes from adequately adjusting.

"Maybe we should leave the deer," Stephen says worried.

"No, we're almost home. We'll be fine," responds my dad.

I look to the sky and see more fingers of lightning above the trees, followed by a loud roar of thunder. I feel my body tense up. We are extremely exposed. With every lightning strike, I find myself looking deep into the forest on both sides of me to see if there is any movement. I just have this feeling of panic, like something or someone is watching us maneuver through the trees.

Click-click-click-click.

No, it is not real. It is not there. It is just my imagination.

Click-click-click-click.

Stop it, Grace. You are freaking yourself out for no reason.

Click-click-click-click.

I am frantically looking around, but I cannot focus with the commotion of the storm.

Click-click-click-click.

"Do you guys hear that?" asks Stephen.

"Wait, you can hear it too?" I say worriedly.

Click-click-click-click. It sounds like it is coming from behind us. Click-click-click-click. Oh god, it sounds like it is right behind me.

Stephen and Dad drop the deer, and we sprint as fast as we can. We cannot be far from the cabin now. We have been running for what seems like forever. I hear a noise behind me, and when I turn, I see that the monster has grabbed the deer. It is elevated off of the ground, and with a flash of lightning I can see that its coat has changed from brown to a dark burgundy. Maybe that will save us.

"Kids, don't stop, we are almost there. I need you to push."

Click-click-click-click.

I look at my dad, and I know he hears it, too.

Click-click-click-click.

Stephen yells, "I see the gate!"

Click-click-click-click. We are now running at a full sprint. A clash of lightning to our left, and another roar of the thunder. Click-click-click-click.

Don't stop running.

Dad slows down and pushes Stephen and me in front of him. Click-click-click-click. We are only a few yards from the gate. Click-click-click-click. It is behind us. I look back and see my dad stopping to turn around.

"Dad, what are you doing?" Stephen yells.

Click-click-click-click.

"Take care of your sister!"

"Dad, no! Come back!" I scream, as Stephen pulls me by the arm.

Click-click-click-click.

Dad stands there, turns around, and looks at us, "I love you guys, and I am sorry for what I've done—now get through the gate! I have this!"

Stephen is tugging me forward, "Daddy, no! We're almost there! Please don't give up! I need you! DADDY! Don't leave us! I am so sorry! I forgive you! Come back!" I scream with tears falling down my cheeks. Stephen is now dragging me to the gate. All my strength has left me.

Click-click-click-click.

"Leave my kids alone, you asshole!" my dad screams.

He is swiftly lifted into the air. In the sudden brightness of the lightning, I see him throwing punches at his invisible adversary. Fresh tears in his flesh are exposed by his ripped clothing, as a waterfall of blood gushes down his back. I turn away, and Stephen and I are in a full sprint through the gate as I hear my dad yell out one final intense expletive.

We make it to our secret entrance, and then inside of the house. We stand there just listening; waiting to see if the monsters will try to find us in here. I cannot believe I just witnessed another member of my family gruesomely murdered at the hands of these creatures. I look at my brother, and I come to the heart-rending realization that, in just an instant, all that remains of the Baker family is the two of us.

CHAPTER FORTY

PRESENT

I cannot believe it. How are we this lucky? It would seem providential to locate a place such as this, but what are the chances? It is extremely dubious that this shrine of indispensable supplies even exists. I feel the need to pinch myself, because it all seems too good to be true.

"We would've never found it if you weren't so clumsy. Good job, Baker."

"This can't be real. I must be dreaming."

"You aren't dreaming. We finally have a stroke of good fortune. You did good here." Nick confidently places his hands on his hips, taking in our success.

I look at him. "It just seems that everything is falling into place, and it makes me doubtful."

He laughs, "Not everything has to be doom and gloom. Sometimes good things happen to good people."

I roll my eyes, "Not in this world. Not anymore."

"Baker, you are killing me. You can't be so pessimistic all the time. Sometimes things just work out."

"I guess you could say I am just waiting for there to be a catch."

"I know, but trust the process. Things are working out because we have a solid plan."

I just stand there looking at the gasoline, and then back at him. "I'm sorry. You are right."

"Well, I'll be damned. I never thought I'd hear Grace Baker tell me I was right about something. It's a win for all men left in this world!" he says as he smiles.

I roll my eyes again, "We're going to have to plan a way to come back. No way we can carry all those canisters back with us. Plus, we could really use the food and supplies they stocked up."

"Well it's been hidden this long; I think we'll be ok."

I remove my backpack from my shoulders and fit a canister inside it. I grab an additional canister to hand to Nick, and then I take one more to carry. "Three will have to work for now, and we'll come back tomorrow."

"Sounds like a plan."

We climb the stairs and exit the basement. I am alarmed by how dark it has gotten. I turn and face Nick, and I can see his concern.

"Maybe the storm will pass?" he says.

"We have to get home."

"Should we just stay here? There are enough supplies to last us through the night."

"I've never been anywhere besides my house when they were out. I don't know how safe it is."

"Well I managed to survive being in the liquor store that one night." He did have a point.

"But they had other people to eat. Now it is just us," I say.

"I don't know, Baker..." He looks at me and then continues, "If we are going to leave, we have to move fast."

"We have enough time. We will make it."

He gives me a reluctant smile as he acquiesces to my plan. I shut the door and move the counter back to conceal the hidden basement. We exit the gas station, and the clouds are caliginous in the distance. It is hard to determine what time of day it is, and it looks like there will be a downpour any minute.

We cautiously jog through the town, remaining silent. The sky continues to get darker, and I feel a sense of dread. We get to the mouth of the forest, and I realize we are running out of time. Nick and I exchange a worried glance, and we both pick up our pace from a jog to a run. He was probably right. We should have stayed there. I just didn't feel safe, and now I have most likely put us in tremendous danger.

We don't slow down. Rather than taking a route off the beaten path, we have to get home as quickly as possible, so we take the direct path home. I feel my lungs start to ache. We are about a mile away from the cabin now, and I feel light rain drops on my head. We are almost home; we need to keep running. The wind begins to howl, but somehow through all the noise, I can hear movement in the trees ahead. I abruptly stop as if my internal emergency brake had been activated.

My heart is throbbing, and I am trying to control my breath to listen. Beyond the tree, I can clearly hear something rustling in the path ahead. I try to conceal myself behind the tree, and Nick does the same. We both stand there, motionless, listening intently to what may be up ahead. I feel heavier droplets of rain now, and it continues to get darker. Very soon it will be nightfall. We did not need this disruption.

Click-click-click-click.

Oh my god. We're too late. This is it.

It is coming from beyond the tree. Click-click-click-click. It is so close to me now. It sounds like it's right next to me. I look at Nick and he points to my hand. I look down, and in my grasp is one of the red gasoline canisters. Why did I not think of this before? I hastily remove the cap, trying to be as quiet as possible. I take a deep breath, lift the canister up, and pour the gasoline on me.

Click-click-click-click. Now it sounds like it is coming from behind me.

Oh please let this work. I look over at Nick as he pours the gasoline on himself. I continue to hear rustling in the bushes. How many of them are there? You are going to be fine. You conducted the test, and it will work. Just remain calm, that is all you can do now.

Click-click-click-click. It is so close now. I try holding my breath, but now I feel like I can actually hear how the rapid beating of my heart has intensified.

Click-click-click-click. I feel a sudden warmth on my shoulder, and I am unequivocally petrified. I feel like my heart is literally going to fulminate in my chest. It's here.

Don't move. Hold your breath, Grace. Don't let it be made aware of your presence. Oh man, is this how it ends?

Click-click-click-click.

I don't know how much longer I can hold my breath. Whatever it is must be standing right next to me. No longer do I just feel its breath, but I can feel the actual warmth of its body. I turn my head toward Nick. I mouth, "It's here." His brown eyes look black as if he had just seen a ghost, and a look of terror emerges on his face.

The rustling continues, and I turn my head toward the sound. A raccoon darts out from behind a tree, and I can feel a gust of wind as the monster leaves me and rushes toward the animal. The raccoon's movement is interrupted, and it is lifted into the air. Its legs continue to move as if it is still running. Immediately, blood pours down the body, as I watch the monster slice into the raccoon's flesh.

Click-click-click-click. Suddenly, the raccoon is pulled deep into the forest beyond our sight. We stand there listening. No rustling. No clicking. We look at each other and sprint toward the cabin. This is our only chance; we are out of time.

Chapter Forty-One

Before

I wake up screaming, and Stephen runs into my room.

"Grace! Grace! You're fine!" he says as he sits down next to me.

"I am not fine! They are both gone! Mom and Dad are both gone. If they can't make it through this, then how are we supposed to?"

He looks fatherly. "Grace, have faith in yourself, kid."

"I am never leaving this house again." I pull my knees up to my chest and bury my face.

"Don't be stupid," he says, probably rolling his eyes. "You know that's not even an option."

"I just want to be alone," I say muffled in my knees.

I feel him pat my back in attempt to console me. "Fine, but no self-loathing. That isn't allowed here."

I finally look up. "Excuse me?"

"You heard me. No self-loathing in this cabin; it is not allowed."

He gets up and walks out of my room. I roll up into a ball on my bed and just try to remember all the good things about my parents. Was I going to forget things about them? Was I going to forget what they were like? How long would it be before I forgot how my mom smelled, or the sound of my dad's voice? Overcome with grief, I begin to cry.

The fact is, in another time and another place, I would have time to mourn. In this new reality, that is a luxury no longer afforded to you. I spent my whole existence trying to be more independent; trying to be an adult. I enjoyed my freedom. But this is never what I wanted. I needed my parents. I needed them to feel safe. They were my crutch; my backbone. I don't know how I can go on without them.

There is a natural expectation that our parents will pass on before us, but not like this. I wasn't ready. I still had so much to learn from them. I was just scraping the surface of getting to really know them. Not just as my parents, but as who they were as people. There is no way Dad had taught me all the lessons he intended to through his puzzles. There is no way I could ever feel comfort again the way I did with my mother. How am I going to live in this world of uncertainty without their guidance? I feel completely astray.

I have been crying for hours, to the point that I have no more tears left to cry. I walk out into the living room and Stephen is asleep on the couch. As I get closer, I see that he is holding a picture in his hand. I gently take it from him. It is a picture from a camping trip we took to Yosemite when we were kids. It was the first time we went there as a family and had gone hiking to see the waterfalls. It was such a memorable day. I look closer at the picture, and it is evident how untroubled we were back then. We were a regular family, embracing the company of each other. That was before we knew what was going to happen. When I was still full of enthusiasm and believed I had my entire life ahead of me.

I slide the picture back in his hand, and I realize for the first time that he is mourning, too. He is trying to be strong for me, but we need to be strong for each other. Dad trained us to work in conjunction with one another. He prepared us to take care of one another if anything were to ever happen to him and Mom. Now that training needs to be put into practice.

I walk back into my room and pick up my journal.

Day 262

I have now seen both my mother and my father ripped from my hands by the clutches of these monsters. If it was not bad enough that we had to endure the apocalypse, now I had to endure watching my parents torn to pieces in front of me. If it were up to me, I would never leave this cabin again. I would stay in my room and just die a happy life here. But, even though I hate to admit it, Stephen was right. That is not an option.

No matter how distraught I may feel, I have to keep living for Mom and Dad. I have to be strong for Stephen. We need to keep pushing forward. All that is left is the two of us, and we must figure out a way to keep on living. I am scared, and I am weak. I have constant nightmares, and I just wish for once we could have a break from all the horrors of this new world.

Stephen was frank but he was correct: there is no self-loathing. We must play the hand we were dealt. Life may not have been kind, but we have survived for a reason. From this day on I refuse to be weak. I refuse to be scared. If this is our new normal then it requires adjustment. We know what we must do. We know how to keep safe. We have to keep on living. We have to, for Mom and Dad.

I close my notebook, when I hear movement in the other room. I walk out and see that Stephen is awake.

I look down at my feet and begin twisting my fingers together. "So, I am sorry for being such a bitch earlier."

He yawns and looks at me, "Well you're always kind of a bitch to me."

I smile and sit on the couch, "I didn't expect us to lose Mom and Dad so close together, you know?"

He sighs, "I know, little sis. It is not going to be easy."

"I think Mom and Dad always trained us to be dependent on each other. That night we drove up here from Los Angeles, I heard them talking about it."

"They did. They told me. They wanted to make sure we could take care of each other if anything were to happen to them."

I roll my eyes, "Of course they did. I just miss them so much."

"I am not going to lie to you. It's going to be tough without them. But we'll manage. Come on, we're Bakers! It's in our blood to overcome whatever's thrown at us."

"I just—sometimes I wish the monsters would just take me, too. What is the point of surviving if I just have to witness everyone I love die?"

He takes a deep breath, "Grace, you may be a pain in my ass, but understand this: You were always going to witness Mom and Dad die."

"That isn't what I meant—"

He interrupts me, "I know, but it is true. Of course you weren't anticipating everything to happen the way it did, but your parents should die before you. That's just the way things are meant to happen."

I pause, "Stephen, I just thought I had more time is all."

"We always think we have more time. I guess we just have to be thankful we got to spend the last few months with them the way we did."

"I guess you are right."

"Come on, kiddo. Let me make you some dinner."

He gets up and walks toward the kitchen. It is in this moment I realize how much we are supporting each other. Not just me being strong for him, or him being strong for me, but as a package. We need each other. The only way we are going to survive this is with one another, just as my parents had planned.

Chapter Forty-Two

Present

I lock the door behind me. What just happened? I am trying to process everything. It was right there. I could feel the large presence prowling behind me. I felt the breath on my cold, wet body. Was it trying to figure out the smell? Could it sense me there too? Could it see me? Was it the gasoline that saved us, or was it just the luck of another creature being there?

I am distracted from my thoughts when I feel Nick's arms around me. "That was a close call, Baker. I thought we were goners."

"I messed up, Nick. I messed up so bad."

He gently pulls me around so he is looking at me, "What are you talking about?"

"I messed up. You wanted to stay in town, and I forced us to come back here. I almost got us killed."

"You had no way of knowing—"

"But I did. That is exactly how my dad died. I should have known better. I'm just so stubborn. I keep making the same mistakes over and over again."

"Look, we all make mistakes. You thought we would make it home in time," he says as he tries to comfort me.

"But I completely ignored your concern, and you could have died because of me."

He begins shaking his head with dissent, "If I really thought it was a bad idea, I would have told you. I am just as culpable in the decision as you were. Stop being so hard on yourself all the time. We are in this together, you know?"

I feel myself begin pulling away from his grasp but suddenly feel comfort in it. I am quiet for a moment before I reply, "I could feel it breathing on me."

He releases me from his embrace, "I could tell." He takes his hand and tucks a piece of hair behind my ear, "Do you want to talk about it?"

"Not really. We are just lucky, I guess."

He looks at me, "It wasn't luck, Baker. You figured out a way for them to not attack us." He takes his finger and taps my forehead, "Your giant brain saved us; not luck."

I smile, "But it was you who figured it out first."

He chuckles, "Now, that really was just luck."

I walk over to the table and throw my backpack down. I smell horrible. "I'm going to try to clean up and get this gasoline off of me."

I walk into the bathroom and open the cabinet to see what's left for bathing. Without running water, normally I'd go to the lake once a week for a thorough cleaning. After all, supplies were scarce. We had stocked up on soap immediately after the bombings and were able to grab a few years' worth of baby wipes, if used sparingly. We had also grabbed more than enough dishwashing liquid, knowing it could serve as double duty for cleaning ourselves. Today it would have to be dishwashing liquid for the gasoline.

I stand in the bathtub, and I stare at the shower nozzle. What I would give for a long hot shower right now. I pour the liquid in a washcloth and begin rigorously scrubbing my limbs. I begin rubbing so hard, my skin turns from a pale white to a light pink. With each movement of the cloth, I can hear it in my head: Click-click-click-click. I rub harder. Click-click-click-click. In a daze, I can't stop scrubbing my skin, trying to cleanse myself of the day's terrors. Finally I stop, sit down naked in the shower, grab my knees with my arms, and begin to sob.

A few moments later, I hear a knock on the door. "You ok in there, Baker?"

I sniffle, "Yeah, I'm fine. Be out in a minute."

I feel like I am starting to lose myself every time something like this happens. Every encounter takes a little more of me. The problem with living a post-apocalyptic existence, is nothing can really prepare you for how harrowing it is. You know things are going to be divergent, and that people are going to be abominable. That is expected. But I never knew it could really be this bad. There is this constant feeling of apprehension. You never feel safe. You are always preparing yourself mentally to have to fight someone or something. You are constantly on edge; every single moment of every single day. There is no relaxing. Sometimes I wish we would have all just stayed in Los Angeles when it was bombed, because living like this is not living at all.

Now, though, I cannot let myself have these thoughts. Nick and I are a team, and if I give up hope then he will give up hope. We need to be strong for each other. Just like Stephen and I were strong for each other when Mom and Dad died. I have to put on a brave face for him. He needs me.

I finally come out of the bathroom, and Nick is just lying on the couch, staring at the ceiling. "What's wrong?" I ask as I sit down on the couch next to him.

"Nothing. That was just a close call. I thought there for a second that I was going to lose you."

"Oh, come on, I'm hard to kill. You should know that by now."

He sits up, "We just have to be more careful. I don't want anything to happen to you."

"Nicholas Gates, we are going to be fine. Here, now that we figured out phase one, we can move on to phase two. It'll all work out."

He just looks down and smiles, "Well considering what happened last time I doubted you, I think I will just take your word for it this time."

I let out a quiet laugh, "Yeah, I guess I need to work on my manners a little bit."

He raises his eyebrows, "Is that your way of apologizing?"

I shrug my shoulders, "Baby steps?"

He laughs, "I guess that will have to do for now."

We end up spending most of the night trying to figure out the next phase of our plan. After hours of talking about what can go right and what can go wrong, and assessing all that we needed for phase two, we finally decide to call it a night.

Before bed, I catch up with today's events in my journal.

DAY 630

Well, journal, I almost got killed again today. I am starting to lose count of how many times that has happened now. I don't know if our plan to try to kill these things is actually putting us in more danger than is necessary. I haven't been near one in months, and today I literally could feel one breathing on me. In my desire to get rid of these beings, I am becoming more and more reckless, and I can't be doing that. When I saw how dark it was outside, I should've listened to Nick—we should've slept in the hidden bunker/storage room we had found. I dismissed his concern and was almost killed for doing so. I knew better. But maybe we should relocate there temporarily since that is where all the gasoline is. I don't know. That's a small space for two people. Plus, I don't really want to leave here since this place allows me to keep the memory of my family alive.

But while today was the closest call I've had thus far, it did present some answers. 1) We can't see them. I always thought we couldn't see them because it was nighttime in the woods and it's so dark. And despite all my encounters, I wanted to believe it was just my eyes playing tricks on me. But today, it was light enough, and it was so close to me and I couldn't see it; it was literally invisible. How is that even possible? What kind of animal is completely invisible? 2) I don't know if they can see us, or if they purely smell us. But they definitely don't like the smell of gasoline. I don't know if it masks our scent, so they don't know we are food or if they don't like the smell and don't want to eat us. Either way, it's a huge win. 3) It is not that they only come out at night. I knew this after what happened with Dad. But for some reason they don't like the sun. But I guess it isn't entirely strange. Lots of creatures are nocturnal. 4) Still unsure as to whether the creature knew I was there and the raccoon presented itself as an easier means to eat, or if it was trying to figure out what I was. 5) I wasn't sure if it could sense body temperature. Some animals sense infrared wavelengths. But since it ate the dead body we set up for it, temperature must not be a factor.

I was also thinking we need to figure out where they stay. I was thinking of that day I brought Nick home and we saw all those bodies in the trees. Maybe it was some kind of nest? Maybe we can attack them in there? I don't know. Now I'm getting ahead of myself. But all in all, it was a tremendously productive day.

I close my journal, and I can hear Nick slightly snoring. I expected him to fall asleep quickly tonight. I am glad he is here, though. I'm glad that I have someone to help me fight back. I know I had a breakdown today, and that is going to happen from time to time given these circumstances. Sometimes I just want it to be over with. Let them take me. Join my family in the life beyond this one. But I feel like I also owe it to them to at least go out fighting.

Chapter Forty-Three

Before

It has been a few months since Stephen and I have been on our own. Somehow we have managed to keep on going after the loss of our parents. It hasn't been easy, but in the spirit of what they had started, we continue this life like they had established.

We continue our daily self-defense training, but now I have started training Stephen in various puzzles and brain teasers, like my dad had taught me before. We are creating a new normal, and we really have gotten very close. I don't think siblings really get to know each other as well as they should because there is always this secret competition for your parents' affection. With the absence of any type of rivalry at this point in our lives, we're really getting to appreciate one another for our differences.

We are also starting to get a sense of claustrophobia, so we decided this morning that since the weather seems to be on our side, we will go out for a little bit today. We want to explore and see if there are any new people in the area. A sibling outing to check and see what had been going on since we had closed ourselves off to the world.

It is a beautiful day. At this point in time, I have no idea what day it is or what month it is anymore. Everything has become such a blur. The temperature is warm but not overly hot, chilly in the shade but warm in the sun. Birds are singing in the trees, and various little animals are scampering on the ground. It feels like just a normal day in the woods, and it is nice to get outside. We have continued our routine, but I think we have both been scared to really leave the safety and security of the cabin. Both of us know it is possible that with any outing we make, there is a probability that something will happen to one of us, leaving the other to remain in solitude. We have a duty to protect each other because we are all that is left.

We have been walking for a few hours. Reminiscing about Mom and Dad and talking about funny stories we experienced as children. It makes me wonder if things had not transpired in the manner which they did, would Stephen and I have ever been this close? Was this a relationship that was always going to develop? Or was this merely a byproduct of two parentless children trying to survive without them?

"You seem to be doing well, you know?" Stephen says, catching me off guard.

"Excuse me?" I ask.

"I don't know," he shrugs, "you just seem to be taking the loss of Mom and Dad very well."

I slow down walking, "Oh, I mean, I guess you have to, right?"

He stops and grabs me by my shoulder, "But are you really ok, is what I am asking."

I push his hand off. "Obviously," I respond in a sarcastic tone.

He grabs my arm and looks at me, "Little sis, I just want to make sure you aren't bottling anything up."

I stop and face him, "Oh my god, Stephen, is this really the time or place to be talking about this?"

"Relax. Just relax for me," he says, as if exasperated. "I am not trying to fight or argue with you. I just want to make sure you are handling this in a healthy way."

"What? Are you my therapist now?" I feel my arms cross themselves defensively, like a reflex.

He balls his hand and covers it with the other one, "Oh stop it, Grace. I am just looking out for you."

I put my hands on my hips. "I am not a little kid, Stephen. You don't always have to look out for me, you know."

He rolls his eyes, "Why do you insist on being so stubborn? You are the only person I know who takes offense at someone looking out for her."

I stand there looking at him, "I am not offended, I am just saying stop worrying about me all the time."

"Well, you are my little sister. Of course I am going to worry—"

"Shh!" I interrupt, jerking my head to the side.

"Don't shush me."

"No, listen." I point to the bushes off to our left, "Do you hear that?"

The rustling continues, so we quietly proceed closer to the source. I point to some bushes just off the path, and as we get closer, the sound gets louder. Cautiously taking one step at a time, we try to be as quiet as possible. From behind us, we hear the familiar and terrifying sound of a shotgun being racked. In this environment the sound is ear-splitting.

"I wouldn't do that if I were you," says a voice.

I turn around and see a large male. He stands about six feet tall with an old beat up trucker hat. His black hair is to his ears, and his clothes are dirty and torn. He is pointing a shotgun directly at me. It is very unnerving to be staring down the barrel of a shotgun. Coming from behind me, I hear the voice of a female.

"I told you they would come look for us, Carl," she says as she gets out of the bushes.

"You sure did, sweet thing," he responds as she walks toward him. She is much smaller, probably about my height. Her hair is in pig tails, and her arms are covered in bruises.

"What do you want from us?" asks Stephen.

"Oh come on, this can't be your first rodeo," says Carl as he gets closer to Stephen.

Research, plan, execute. Two of them, two of us. One has a shotgun, and who knows what the female has. All we have are knives. Carl obviously has the advantage.

The girl gets closer to me, "You guys look too clean to be hangin' out here in the wilderness. Where you stay at?"

"I don't know what you're talking about," I respond.

Irritated by my response, she grabs me by the neck, "I said where do you stay at?"

"Take your hands off of her!" yells Stephen.

Carl redirects his aim and is now pointing the shotgun right at Stephen's head, "Like I said before… I wouldn't do that if I were you."

Chances are if I do something to this girl, then Carl will divert his attention to us. He might shoot me, but at least Stephen will have an avenue of escape. I have to try something, if I don't, we are both dead.

Before I can make my move, I suddenly hear a shotgun blast. I look over with the girl's hand on my neck, and I see that Stephen and Carl are wrestling over the shotgun. I front kick her to the stomach, causing her to release her grip from my throat. I take one jab to her nose, a cross to her cheek, and, with all my might, a hook to her temple. She is completely dazed and clumsily falls to the ground. I hear another shotgun blast go off. I look to Stephen, and they are still wrestling over the gun. So in a full sprint, I run over to Carl and jump on his back. I take my knife from its sheath. With one swift motion, I drive my knife into the side of his neck, causing him to drop his grasp on the shotgun. He raises his hand onto his throat as I jump off his back.

Stephen dives for the shotgun, chambers a round, and shoots Carl point blank with the shotgun in his torso. I see movement where the girl had been, and she is running full speed toward Stephen. He chambers another round, shooting at her. The buckshot strikes her in the torso, and she flies backward before falling onto the ground.

We just stand there looking at the two people we had killed, before looking at one another. Every time we go outside, are we going to have to kill people or be killed? What I would give to go back in time before all this happened. I don't want to do this anymore.

"You can handle it all by yourself, can you now?" Stephen says with his eyebrows raised.

"Oh, shut up, Stephen. I had it under control."

We head back toward the direction of the cabin, and I cannot help but feel this is what my future will always be like.

Chapter Forty-Four

Present

Miss Baker, it's time to wake up.

I am startled awake, when I see that it is Nick. I must have fallen asleep in my chair again.

"Sorry to wake you, but we're closing, and I didn't want someone to take your stuff."

"I am so sorry! I can't believe I fell asleep." I look down at my watch and it's almost 11:00 P.M.

He hands me my laptop. "I grabbed this when you fell asleep so no one with sticky fingers could steal it."

"Thank you so much—" my phone rings. Unknown caller. Might be work. "One second," I say to Nick. "Hello?"

Static.

"Hello?" I'm about to hang up.

Click-click-click-click.

"Hello? I'm sorry, I don't understand," I say.

Click-click-click-click.

I take the phone from my ear and put it on speaker so Nick can hear. But the call ends.

"What was that?" he asks.

"I have no clue. Thanks again for watching my stuff. I didn't realize how tired I was."

"Oh, no problem. You know how L.A. is, people always helping themselves to other people's belongings."

Click-click-click-click.

What is that noise? I shift in my chair as I search the patio for the source of the clicking. "Do you hear that?" I ask Nick.

"Hear what?" He starts looking around.

"I don't know, it is some kind of clicking sound." I continue to look around as we remain there in silence, listening.

Nick glances around too, "I don't hear anything, Baker."

Click-click-click-click.

"There! I just heard it again."

Nick stands there for a moment, "I'm sorry. I still don't hear anything."

Click-click-click-click. It's coming from behind me. I turn to look, but nothing is there. I turn back around, and the setting has changed. I am still sitting in my chair, laptop in hand, and Nick is standing in front of me, still in his work apron, but now we are in the forest.

Click-click-click-click. Scared, I start looking for where the sound is coming from.

"Miss Baker, you—" before he can finish his sentence, he is lifted into the air, as huge cuts slice through his white, collared shirt.

I let out a scream and cover my mouth, and he is pulled back into the trees and out of sight. Standing there in shock, I am unable to move.

Click-click-click-click.

I can't move. Grace! Move! You have to run.

Click-click-click-click. I can feel its breath. Click-click-click-click. Without warning, I feel a sharp pain rip through my abdomen as I am lifted off the ground. I have never experienced pain as excruciating as this. The claws penetrating my skin are like razors, and every small movement of my body sends shock waves to all my extremities. I try to scream but I can't draw the breath to do so. I look down, and I can see that my light-colored jeans are red with blood. I then feel the sensation of sharp teeth piercing my neck as something begins to tear into my flesh with its mouth. It is eating me alive.

I feel my body shaking.

"Grace!"

I let out a scream, as I open my eyes and realize it was another nightmare. Nick is facing me, and his hand is on my shoulder to wake me up.

"Grace, you were having another nightmare." He looks at me with a concerned expression.

I cover my eyes with my hands. "I am so sorry I keep waking you up like this. I know it is getting out of control. I need to stop journaling before bed. It's making me crazy."

"Do you want to talk about it?"

I shake my head no. "Do you mind just lying with me?"

He scoots closer to me on the cot, wraps his arm around me, as I put my head on his chest. This is the first time I've had a dream in which he was there and got hurt. For all the nightmares I have had, I have never had one where I was actually the victim either. It felt so real. The pain was so agonizing that I honestly felt as though I was going to lose consciousness. I have felt fear, happiness, and sorrow in my nightmares, but never physical pain. I don't know what that means. I am deep in thought when I feel him kiss my forehead.

"I know I keep saying this, but we're going to be ok, Baker."

Are we? I pull my head off his chest and turn onto my back. "Nick, I'm sorry for always waking you up like this."

He turns to face me. "I have had nightmares too, it is totally understandable."

I look toward him, "I just don't understand why they are getting so bad."

He looks into my eyes and begins to run his fingers through my hair, "If I had to guess, I would say it has to do something with the fact that we are actively trying to fight these monsters. Your mind is constantly trying to figure out what might go wrong."

"Is this what our lives are going to be like? Just constant nightmares and fighting?"

"Is that what you are worried about, Miss Baker? Come on, now. You know that isn't what life is going to be like."

I take my hands and put them up under my head. "I am just tired of being scared. I am tired of running. I am tired of losing everyone I love."

He grabs one of my hands and envelopes it in his. "Life is what you make of it, Grace Baker. I mean, I'll be honest. When you first told me that you wanted to fight these things, I thought it was all talk. I thought it was something to get your mind off of whatever you were dealing with. I admired your motivation, but I never thought it was something we could actually do. But look where we are now. I mean, is it all absolutely crazy? Of course it is!" He pauses momentarily, and then continues, "But, all those doubts I had initially, they're gone. I really think you have a way of figuring this out. It will be alright."

"I want to believe you."

He places his hand below my chin and gently pulls my face toward his. "Have I ever let you down?"

I take a deep breath. "No. Not really." I pause, "Well, only if you don't count that time you let me rush out of here angry and alone," I let out a laugh.

He smiles, "Well played, Baker. I had that one coming."

"It's ok, I know what you mean, though."

He sighs, "So, please, just trust me. I'm not going to lie to you, this isn't going to be easy, but we will figure it all out. We have survived so much already, and we will make it through this. There is light at the end of the tunnel, I promise."

Something about his confidence caused me to capitulate his reasoning. Maybe he was right and we would make it through this.

Chapter Forty-Five

Before

I sit on the couch staring at the wall. I don't remember the last time I ate, and I cannot recall the last time I got adequate rest. Yesterday everything I was fearful of became a reality. One by one I have watched my family get taken from me. The cabin is silent. There are no muffled voices of my parents talking in the other room. No sounds of footsteps down the hall. The sounds that once filled this place no longer exist. There is no more laughing, no more discussion, and no more reminiscing. There is no more training, and no more learning essential skills for my survival.

I look around as I sit on the couch, and I realize that this is my own personal hell. How do you continue in such a solitary life? This is how people go insane, right? Eventually the silence will become torture. I know I need to find the will to keep living, but I am bone-weary and debilitated.

I don't know how long I have been sitting here, but finally I grab my notebook and begin to write:

Day 440

The cabin is so quiet. Yesterday I lost my brother, and now all that remains is me. I used to like being alone. I loved the peace that came with the quiet. I loved being able to be at one with my thoughts. There was a time and place when I would put my cellphone on "do not disturb" and just cut myself off from the world. Now, though, the silence is a reminder of all that I have lost. It is that constant state of knowing my entire family is dead. Each loss has been more tragic than before. I don't know how I will recover this time.

What I hate most is knowing that there is no escape from this. I know that every day I wake up, I will be praying that all of this was just a horrible nightmare. Each morning I will be forced into the reality that there is no one left. How can I stay here only to be reminded of all that I have lost? Yet, where can I go? What is still out there? This is the safest place to be, and even then it is far from safe. We have had to fight off monsters and people, and somehow made this place a fortress. Nowhere I try to go will have something like this place. I would have to start completely from scratch, and I don't even think that is feasible at this point.

I will never understand why these monsters didn't take me instead. I know I am suffering from survivor's guilt, and it will plague me for a long time. But I just don't understand why they had to be taken. I wasn't faster than my mom, dad, or Stephen. As I sit here thinking of all that has gone so wrong, I feel like the only reason I am still here is because they sacrificed themselves for my survival. Sometimes in the quietness of my thoughts, I wish they would have just taken me instead. What is the point of surviving when that is all you are doing: surviving. I will never know laughter again. I will never know the comfort that I once had. I am all alone, and I am absolutely terrified. I feel so melodramatic even writing that, but deep in my soul I feel like it is true.

What makes it worse is that I don't even cry anymore. I tried to last night, but I had no tears left. I have become an emotionless robot. I've come to a sense of normalization with death and loss. I've become ok with not being ok. Where is the girl I used to know? Maybe whoever she was died with my family.

The truth is, I don't know who I am anymore. I didn't even know who I was when all of this started. Things I loved no longer exist. Things I strove to be don't exist. I am just a girl, all alone, trying to survive without being eaten by monsters. It doesn't seem fair. What did I do to have to endure such a cruel fate?

I know there has to be a reason why all of this has happened, but please let me see it! No one should ever have to endure such loss. I am asking for some kind of sign. Please, Lord, why am I still here? Why do I have to do this all alone? Dad, is this your doing from beyond? Is this some final puzzle I am meant to solve? I need answers desperately. I am begging you.

I close my notebook and lay it on the floor. I lie down on the couch in fetal position and listen to my heartbeat. I close my eyes and try to remember better times, but I can't. Every memory I try digging up is ruined by what I have seen the last few months. I know this is temporary, but I wish I could remember just one minute when things were good. I need to find a way to move on, or the depression will kill me if the monsters don't get the chance to first.

Chapter Forty-Six

Present

After my nightmare I don't sleep for the rest of the night. I keep reviewing everything in my mind. Today we need to see if we can determine where they are staying. We need to see if it's accessible, and if we can defeat them somehow. I don't want to have these nightmares anymore. Somehow we have been incredibly lucky so far, and everything has worked out how we wanted. But eventually our luck will run out.

I feel Nick stirring, and I can tell he is probably having a nightmare, too. I put my arms around him, because for all the times he's supported me, it's my turn to support him. He stops moving, and I see his eyes open.

"Getting kind of handsy there, Baker."

I laugh, "It seemed like you were just having a bad dream."

"I didn't peg you to be one to take advantage of a helpless sleeping man. I didn't know you had it in you." I begin to pull my arms away as he holds onto them.

"Oh stop, I'm kidding." He looks at me so innocently.

"Were you having a nightmare?" I ask.

He looks up at the ceiling. "Probably. I don't remember."

Surprised by his sudden reluctance, I pull my arms away. "I understand if you don't want to talk about it."

He turns his head and looks at me. "I really don't remember."

"Can I ask you a question?"

He turns onto his side and faces me as he folds his hands beneath his cheek. "Of course, hopefully I will have an answer for you," he smiles.

I look away, "Nick, can you tell me about the first time you saw them?"

His face changes, "Oh, I didn't think we'd be starting work talk so early." I can tell he's disappointed.

"I just feel like you know my experience, so I want to know yours."

He takes my hands in his and kisses them, then pauses before saying, "Baker, can we not ruin this moment? I'm afraid you won't see me the same when I tell you."

Confused by what that means, I drop it. He takes his hand and moves my hair from my face, tucking it behind my ear, which has become his go-to comfort move for me.

"What's your favorite memory, Grace?"

"Oh man, that is tough. I have been blessed to have so many amazing memories in my short lifetime."

He scoots closer to me, "Can you tell me?"

"Hmm... let me think." I pause for a few seconds, "When I was a kid, my favorite place was Disneyland. It was so expensive, and my parents would plan months in advance. But knowing I would always choose Disneyland, my dad would come into my room and gently wake me up. He'd ask me what I wanted to do that day and without a beat, I'd tell him Disneyland. And then we would go for the entire day, open to close. And I'd be so tired, to the point that my dad would have to carry me out, half asleep. Every time we did this, though, it was so amazing. And for some reason I always thought we took a spontaneous trip to Disneyland because I had actually made the decision for the family. I was special enough that I got to choose what we were going to do. I know it is such a silly memory, but it was everything about it. The feeling like I had a choice in the matter. The being there from when it opened, to right after the fireworks display. But it was one of the few times a year when I got to spend the entire day with my family. There was just something exciting and memorable about the way he would come in and ask me. I always smile thinking about it."

"I love that, Baker." He wraps his arms around me.

"What's yours?" I ask.

He looks away, clearly embarrassed, "You wouldn't believe me."

Taken aback by his sudden shyness, I just smile at him.

He continues, "Let's just say, it was in a place I never thought I'd be, with a person I never thought I'd meet, under circumstances I couldn't even make up if I tried."

We just lie there looking at each other. The fact is, Nick has become my best friend. He is my family now. I am getting so protective of him, too. I couldn't allow anything to happen to him. I no longer see him for his handsome face and charming smile, but rather what he does for me. Being in this situation together has made me realize just how different we are from one another. In many ways he is completely opposite of me. He has this overt kindness and optimism that I will never understand. Despite my obstinate ways at times, he has been patient and tolerant. He accepts me for all that I am. Somehow his presence has made me strong. He makes me unafraid, and he makes me want to figure this out. He took what my family had developed and let me out of the cage that I had built for myself in their absence. He set me free.

I feel butterflies in my stomach. "Nick—" I pause. "I—I just want to say thank you."

He looks at me, "Thank you for what?"

I sit up, and then look toward him. "I'm not good at this, but please—just bear with me."

He sits up with concern on his face, "Are you breaking up with me, Baker?"

I let out an awkward giggle, "No—no. That's not it at all. And wait, what?" I shake my head, "I didn't think this was like that. But—no, that is not what I need to talk about."

He takes his hand to his forehead, "Whew! You had me worried there for a second."

I grab his hands in mine, "I couldn't have gotten this far without you. I know I am not the easiest person to get along with, and I know I can be... what's the word I am thinking of? Unaccommodating, maybe?" I let out a laugh, and I see he smiles. "But, I just want you to know I do appreciate you."

"Grace, I never thought that you didn't—"

"I know, but I can't just expect you to understand me. I need to be willing to put myself out there sometimes, we are all that we have right now." He puts his arm around me as I rest my head on his shoulder, "I just don't want you to think I don't realize how much you have helped me."

I feel his head rest against mine as he says, "You gotta give yourself more credit. Yes, we're a team, but a lot of what we are accomplishing here is because of that stubborn attitude of yours."

"But—" I say.

"No but, Grace. You have a fire inside of you. After all you've been through, it's amazing. I'm only here for the ride. You're the one driving. To be honest, I can't wait to see where you take us."

He kisses my forehead, and I am at a loss for words. It is incredible that somehow we found each other, and how much I think I actually needed him here after all.

I lie back down, and he follows me. I turn my back and face away from him as I attempt to fall back asleep. I feel myself starting to drift off when he breaks the silence.

"It was bad—" his voice startles me.

I turn toward him, "What was bad?"

He is staring at the ceiling again, avoiding eye contact. "The first time we saw them—"

"Oh, you don't have to..."

"I do," he stops for a little bit. "I am a coward. I survived only because I ran."

I place my arm on his chest. "Well, that's what we all did—"

He sits up abruptly. "No, just stop. I don't want to keep secrets. Just... please don't think of me differently."

I sit up as well and look him in the eyes. "Never. I promise."

He looks away from me and down at the bed. "It had been like six months, maybe, after the terrorist attack. We had left Los Angeles right before the bombings, because it was just a nightmare the minute the power was out. It was me, my roommates, and a couple other stragglers. We had traveled to a little town called Morro Bay. Well, one night we were walking down the street, laughing, and I hear it. That clicking sound. At first they didn't hear it, but I did. They said I was being crazy, but it kept getting closer and closer. Then—" He stops.

"You don't have to keep going," I say quietly.

Now his eyes meet mine. "No, I just remember it so vividly. Click-click-click-click. It was all around us, and finally everyone stopped. And right before my eyes, in the middle of this street, Tommy just rose off the ground, like he was... floating. I couldn't see what caused it, but he had these huge cuts to his stomach, and the way he screamed. Oh god, Grace, I can still hear it—"

I know the exact feeling. I put my hand on his cheek, and he places his hand on top of mine.

"Suddenly he was pulled back, and Mark, he was elevated too. And I knew I just had to run. So I ran as fast as I could. And Bryan was with me, and we were running together. Then I heard the clicking again and I knew they were there. And I did the most horrible thing."

"It's ok, Nick. We've all done things we aren't proud of."

He looks at me, and continues, "I knew if I didn't do something, the monster would get me. I punched him, Grace!" He covers his face with his hands in embarrassment. "I punched him and he stopped, not knowing what happened. And I didn't look back, but I heard him screaming and I knew then... I sacrificed him to survive.... Oh my god, I can't believe—"

I stop him. I put my hand over his mouth. "Did you not hear what I just said? We have all done things we are not proud of to survive... but you are here for a reason. We have survived for a reason. We're going to figure this out."

He doesn't say another word. We lie back down and remain silent. He pulls me close and rests his head on my chest. I know it took everything for him to tell me that, and I can't imagine what it was like to relive it. We had done horrible things to get to where we are today, and it makes it even more necessary that we don't screw this up. For all the Tommys, Marks, and Bryans we had sacrificed to get here... we have to defeat these monsters.

Chapter Forty-Seven

Before

I wake up and I am covered in sweat. I had another nightmare last night. Ever since Stephen died a few weeks ago, I have been having nightmares every time I sleep. I feel like I am starting to get delirious with the lack of rest I am getting.

Maybe I had the nightmare because I know I have to go into town today. I checked my supplies and I am running low on medication. I noticed I have been breaking out in hives, and who knows what I am allergic to around here. I don't expect there to be much left in the stores, but I have to get whatever I can.

I am so nervous because this will be my first time going to town alone. No backup to rescue me. No emotional support for whatever I may endure. This will be my first real venture completely on my own. I am beside myself just imagining everything that can go wrong.

I grab my backpack and throw in a few essential supplies. Pull my hair up in my usual messy ponytail. I grab two knives this time: one on my waist, and one in my shoe.

I start making my way toward town and I decide that maybe I shouldn't be on the beaten path. Who knows who is out here, and what might be waiting for me. So I make my way just off the path, out of sight, but close enough to keep my sense of direction. I have no way of finding my way back if I were to get lost out here.

I am especially cautious this time around. It has been a little while since I have been here, and I don't want to risk being seen. I spend about an hour just sitting in the trees on the outskirts of town, listening to see if there is any activity. It seems to be the usual abandoned town that I have come to know so well. Finally, after an absence of activity, I decide to proceed. Nothing seems to have changed, and I don't see anything that seems out of place. It does not appear that there have been any new visitors, either, which is advantageous for me. There are strong gusts of wind through the main thoroughfare of town, which troubles me because I fear I will not be able to hear if someone is around. It is an inconvenience, but I must persevere.

I get to the pharmacy, and it is really down to the bones. I scan the shelves to see if there is anything worth taking, and there is not much to choose from. I go back to the prescription medication behind the counter, and there are still some items that can be useful. Fortunately, I find some antihistamines, so I grab those first. I continue to peruse the various medications still left behind. I am surprised to see that some Vicodin is still on the shelves. Due to the country's narcotics problem, you would think that would have been the first thing to go. So I grab it and throw it in my bag. Finally, I see a handful of Z-Paks, little packets of short-term antibiotics, scattered on the ground so I throw those in my bag, too.

As I am walking out of the store, I see a display with some postcards. For some reason I feel like taking them, so I grab them and throw them in my bag. I also see a display of dusty sunglasses. I take a pair, put them on, and look in the mirror. They are pink Ray-Ban knock offs, but not too bad. I toss those in my bag, too. They remind me of better times.

I walk out of the pharmacy and start making my way toward the mouth of the forest. I am caught off guard when I see a tent in the distance that I had never seen before. I know I should just head home, but my curiosity is getting the best of me. So, I walk toward the tent. The wind is helping disguise the sounds of my footsteps, but on the other hand, it is also making it impossible to hear anything else. As I get closer, I can't hear anything coming from inside. As I quickly glance around to the front of the tent, I am immediately hit with a foul smell. The smell of death.

I pull myself back to the side of the tent, and I take a deep breath in preparation for whatever I may see. I walk to the front of it and see that half of it is zipped open. I look inside and there is a female who is very much deceased. Flies are buzzing around her corpse, and the closer I lean in, the better I can see her wounds. There had to be at least twenty stab wounds. This was done by a human. This woman was murdered. Worriedly, I look around, and I realize what a mistake this was. Someone may be watching me.

Chapter Forty-Eight

Present

We decide that today we're going to see if we're close to the nest. There must be a reason why all of a sudden there are dead bodies among the trees around here. If all goes according to plan, we will be able to attack them in their comfort zone: where they are not expecting it.

We spend about an hour trying to determine what our plan is going to be. We know we have to go back to the spot where we first saw the bodies and scattered clothing in the trees. From there, we have to try to follow the items to see if they lead somewhere. We will bring the last remaining gasoline we have on us for now, and if we find the nest, we can pour it on us and wait until nightfall to determine if this location is their home.

I look at Nick. "Are we crazy?"

Nick tilts his head to the side like a confused puppy, "I guess, if you really think about it, we are."

"Ok, I just had to make sure you realized it, too."

"Baker, I don't know what we are going to find out there, but if you really want to figure out a new way to live, then we have to take this next step. Don't be getting second thoughts on me now."

"I know. I just have to remember that it isn't just me anymore. I don't want you to put yourself in unnecessary danger for some crazy plot I came up with in a notebook."

He points his finger at me, "Correction: what we came up with."

"I just want to make sure you know how dumb this is," I say with a smile.

He crosses his arms, "Oh I know it's dumb, no doubting that. We're trying to hunt things we can't see, without even anything cool, like night vision goggles."

I laugh, "Oh man, night vision goggles would have made this whole operation so much easier. That's some Navy Seal stuff there."

He proceeds to do a few karate moves and breaks into laughter. "It'll work out. Stop underestimating yourself."

I smile. Sometimes I find his cloying nature a little overwhelming, but I needed to hear that today. He was right. Just like my dad taught me. Research. Plan. Execute. We cannot complete the mission without doing our research, and unfortunately this research requires us putting ourselves in a certain level of danger. We had decided that we were not going to live a life full of fear, and how can we ever do that if we are not willing to sacrifice our comfort to do so. He did bring up a great point, though. Why had I never thought of night vision goggles? In such a random comment it made me start to wonder: 1) Hopefully, if there is some sort of military left in the country defeating the monsters is easy for them because of their technology, 2) Did dad have any in the cabin? 3) If so, where would I find them, and 4) Is there a way to make our own night vision goggles? Those are inquiries for another time and another place. I must focus on one mission at a time.

We gather the normal supplies and throw them into my backpack. I leave room for the last canister of gasoline. We will definitely have to go back to town tomorrow and re-stock. I am about to place the supplies on my back, when Nick stops me.

"I can't always have you doing the heavy lifting around here. It is an insult to my Texas roots."

I roll my eyes, "You are still nursing that stab wound to your side. I don't want you putting any extra strain on yourself until it heals."

"Oh stop it. It's just a backpack."

"Fine." I am learning to pick my battles.

I hand over the backpack, and we exit the cabin. I had been so used to having my backpack on me every time I left, that it actually makes me feel uncomfortable to be free of it. Like I am exposed to more danger somehow. It had become a safety net of sorts.

We begin travelling toward the carnage. The air has a dampness to it, and it makes it hard to breathe for some reason. It feels heavy; like the wilderness is trying to warn us to stay inside. The forest is silent, absent of the normal animal sounds, and there does not appear to be any birds fluttering around in the trees. All I can hear is our labored breathing. Every footstep into the fallen leaves and branches seems to echo loudly in the silence.

I feel my nerves get the best of me. I try to focus, but the stillness of the forest makes my worried thoughts so much louder. I continue to revisit our plan over and over in my head; trying to determine if there is something we did not consider. Had we thought of all plausible outcomes?

I am still deep in thought when I look up and see that Nick has come to a complete stop. We are here. I look up in the trees and, just like before, there are body parts scattered within the leaves. I scan the trees to determine where it appears the first trail of body parts begins. It is about three trees to my left, so I walk over, take out my knife, and carve a giant X in the bark. During the hours of darkness it would be hard to see that high in the trees, but this way we will know where our trail begins.

This time around the smell is revolting. The combination of decaying human flesh, old bloody clothing, mixed in with rotting animal parts, is an aroma I will never forget. It burns my nostrils, and I begin to breathe out of my mouth to help minimize the smell. It definitely does not minimize it enough, though, and makes me feel like I am tasting it instead. I take my shirt, pull it over my nose, and create a makeshift mask to cover my face. Much better.

Nick continues to scan the floor of the forest, watching for predators both human and animal alike, while I continue to look up at the tops of the trees. We continue to walk for about ten minutes along a predetermined path. We hit a juncture. The path goes east toward town, and the bodies continue south. I take my knife and, once more, draw an X.

I whisper to Nick, "I'll mark all the trees so we can find our way back to the path."

"Great idea." He points to his head as he smiles, "Quick thinking!"

I continue to mark an X on every tree to give us a secret path through the trees. I cannot believe how many people have succumbed to these monsters. I had no idea so many people had been here to begin with because it always felt so desolate. There are so many parts. It is devastating to see. Suddenly I am struck with the most horrifying thought. What if some of those parts are what remains of my family? Inundated with disgust, I stop and pull down my makeshift mask as I turn and begin to vomit profusely. My body trembles as I continue to dry-heave with nothing left to spew. I fall to my knees and cover my face with my hands.

Nick runs over to me and helps me stand back up. I wipe my face and grab some water from the backpack to cleanse my mouth of the aftertaste of my vomit. I just shake my head, and he gives me a hug.

"You alright, Baker?" he says with his arms still around me.

"No. Not at all," I say with my head buried in his chest.

"Do you want to talk about it?"

I stay silent for a moment. "I just can't fathom the thought that my family may be up there."

I feel him kiss the top of my head, "Even if their bodies are up there, Grace, they are in a much better place. They aren't really there."

I pull my head from his chest and look up at him. "I don't want us to be like these people. I don't want us to end up this way."

He smiles at me, "We won't. I know we won't; I just have this feeling."

I look to the trees once more, and I realize we are standing in some revolting graveyard meant to show how inadequate we are compared to these creatures. Rather than bodies buried in the ground with headstones to pay our respects, the bodies are scattered among the trees to force our respect to whatever it is that had taken them from us.

Chapter Forty-Nine

Before

Grace, you are so stupid!

I am almost in a full sprint as I leave town. Whoever killed that woman was probably watching me the entire time. Why would I be so dumb to expose myself like that? I have so many thoughts racing through my head. How many people were out there? Why did they kill her? Was she by herself? What if they saw me? What if I'm leading them back to my house?

You really are so dumb, aren't you? I am running as fast as I can, but I can feel my cadence already starting to slow down. I sense a sharp pain in my chest, and I don't know if it is from my pounding heart, or if I am actually having a panic attack. I begin to grow paranoid, and I am anxiously looking in all directions while still trying to propel myself forward.

I take deep breaths, but it doesn't seem to be helping. I am breathing so heavily that I feel like I am gasping for air. I am still pushing forward but I know I cannot keep this pace for much longer.

I turn to scan the forest behind me, and the coast seems to be clear at the moment. When I turn back around, instantaneously, I trip. I fly forward, landing on an old tree branch. There is a burst of pain as bark tears into the flesh of my abdomen. I let out a scream in agony, as I feel the blood pulsating to my wound. As I look down I see that I have been impaled by a sharp branch of wood. Every beat of my heart sends shock waves to my stomach, as the blood pumps out of the injury. Taking a deep breath, I attempt to push myself away from the bark, but the resistance is too much. I feel my arms start to shake with adrenaline, and I know I cannot stay here much longer. Once more, I take a long deep breath and close my eyes. As I attempt to free myself from the tree placing both hands on either side of me for leverage, I take another deep breath and push as hard and quickly as I can to free myself. It feels even worse coming out than it did going in. I let out another scream, as I look down and see that I have freed myself. I try to stand up, but now my muscles are in a full spasm and I fall back to the ground.

I feel numb with throbbing pain, and I lift my shirt to expose my wound. It is a hole the size of a golf ball, and the blood is gushing from it. Why did I not bring any first aid supplies? I take off my shoe and remove my sock. "This thing is going to get infected for sure," I say to myself. I put my shoe back on and take my sock to pack the wound. It burns so bad, and I grind my teeth to prevent myself from screaming again.

I can't stay here. I have to keep going; it is not safe. I stand back up, and I try my best to run again. I can't. With every foot strike, I can feel the blood oozing out of my injury. I look around, and I just feel like someone or something is watching me. It hurts like hell, but I bring my pace up to a jog. I have to get home as fast as possible.

I am starting to feel light-headed, but I cannot afford to collapse. I am trying to maintain my composure as I run, all while maintaining pressure on my injury. I look down and I can see that the sock has already started to morph from an off-white color into a dark mahogany. I try to distract myself from my pain, but it is getting absolutely excruciating. With the slightest movement of my body, the blood feels like acid flowing from the gash in my flesh. If I don't make it home soon, there is a high probability I am going to pass out, and then if the people didn't follow me back here, the monsters will have their way with me. I am starting to lose hope, when I see the bushes that lead to my house. Finally, I am home.

Chapter Fifty

Present

I have never traveled this deep into the woods, nor have I ever strayed so far from the path. I have marked at least fifty trees at this point, and it is really mind blowing to see the destruction caused by these monsters. It almost seems like they are hoarding their prey; storing their food for later, the way a beaver does, or how squirrels hide their acorns. It is almost as if they are prepping for a shortage of food supply. Do these monsters know the food is scarce now? Are they prepping for something coming that we don't know about?

A few yards beyond the trees I see a giant rock formation that I never knew existed. Nick taps my arm to follow him west through the trees to try to circle around and hopefully get a better view of whether or not this formation will be an obstacle. At this point, we have slowed down our cadence tremendously to try to prevent excess noise. There is a break in the trees, and as we get closer we can see that the carnage is now all over the ground. It was not like what we had seen in the trees; no longer are there the remains of fleshy body parts. The tattered and torn clothing, stained a grotesque purple, is now interlaced with animal and human bones.

Steadily, we continue through the trees. Now more than ever we have to be careful. As we get closer, we begin to round the rock. To my surprise, beyond the bones is a giant opening. It isn't just a rock formation, but it is a cave.

This could work. If they are all living in there, maybe we can set them on fire? Maybe we can prevent their escape somehow and block them in? But how would we know if they are actually in there at any given time? How would we know they are all in there together? These are questions for after tonight. Tonight our focus is just to determine if this is truly their home. It will be much easier to have a plan of attack if we know where they regroup every day.

I walk over to Nick and take my notebook out of the backpack. Trying to stay as quiet as possible, I take my pencil and write: We need to find somewhere to hide. This location is not ideal. Unlike by the cabin, there are no large bushes to conceal ourselves in. The rocks are jagged and unsuitable for climbing. In a true stroke of Grace Baker luck, this particular section of the woods is bare of anything besides the tree trunks.

We begin walking around, checking for a spot where we can conceal ourselves. We need to find an area with line of sight to the cave to try to pinpoint if that is where they are coming from. The way their feet clicked, there is no doubt the sound will echo within the cave alerting us to their presence. We just can't seem to find a good place to hide. After walking around for about twenty minutes, it is clear that we have to get creative. I take my notepad once more: We are going to have to find ground soft enough to try to dig a hole for us to fit in.

His eyes widen as he reads it. We are running out of time and options. He mouths, "you have to be kidding me!" So I just shrug my shoulders because it is our only option. I am pretty confident it is not going to work, but we have to try.

We spend the next thirty minutes or so trying to find a spot. In the second row of trees, with a clear view of the entrance to the cave, we find a soft patch of dirt. I pull my knife out of my sheath and hand it to Nick. I grab the other knife from my boot, and we begin to dig. Using the knives to soften the dirt, we utilize our hands to throw the dirt to the side. We spend the next hour or so digging, and the hole is just big enough for us to sit in. My hands are raw, and I can feel my muscles starting to tremble from the repeated stabbing motion into the semi-hard ground. My nails have chipped off from making contact with rocks within the dirt. I look down and see that my knuckles are beginning to bleed. How people were ever capable of building graves to dispose of their victims is beyond me; this is hard work. I am fatigued, and I am sweating profusely. The air is still heavy over here, and it makes it that much harder to catch my breath. Finally, we look at the hole and it appears we can both fit in. I take my shirt and wipe the moisture from my face. I look at him, and mouth "I think this will do."

He sits in first, and I go in after. It looked much larger as we were digging. We realize that in order for us both to fit it in, I need to sit on his lap. I feel a little uncomfortable, to be honest. While we had been inseparable since we found each other that day in town, this still feels like a level of intimacy I am not acclimated to. There is a fondness he and I seem to have for one another, but it has grown into something much deeper. There is an appreciation we have for one another, and a level of respect that is undeniable. No lines had been crossed, and what we share is something much more than just friendship. Yet, sitting here on his lap, with his arms wrapped around my waist, makes me nervous. I try to set my feelings aside because we still have a mission to complete.

"Does this feel alright?" I whisper.

"Oh, yes, very cozy. Nothing like feeling buried alive to set the mood."

"You are so dumb sometimes, Mr. Gates," I say with a whisper.

"Oh, stop it, you wouldn't have it any other way, Miss Baker."

I move around to see how much additional room we have, which is not much room at all. It seems we have just enough space to duck down if they come. Are they capable of grabbing something if it is secreted? Is it possible that their nails are sharp enough to drag us out of here?

I get out of the makeshift grave and he follows me, though he seems confused. The shadows of the trees are long, which is no doubt an indication that the sun will be setting soon. I begin to walk toward the cave to grab some of the scattered bloody clothing, hoping if we cover our heads with the gasoline-soaked cloth in conjunction with concealing ourselves in the hole, we will be undetected when they come out to hunt.

I tip-toe to the clearing, and I listen for a few moments. Pleased with the silence, I cautiously take one step at a time to get closer to the scattered items on the ground. I grab a few bloodied garments that are not wrapped around bone and toss them onto my shoulder. I carefully grab as many bones as possible and, at a snail's pace, I walk closer to the opening of the cave. I quietly place the bones in a line across the entire entrance of the cave. Hopefully, as they cross the threshold when they exit, they will step on the bones, crushing them, alerting us that they are coming. It definitely isn't the alarm system we once had in our old home, but it will work for now.

Before I turn to head back to our hole, I listen again to verify there are no new developments. Once again, nothing but silence. As quietly as we can possibly walk, we go back to our freshly dug grave.

The sky begins to darken, which means it is finally time to enact our plan. I can feel myself getting apprehensive as I ponder all that might go wrong. We planned for every possible outcome we could think of between the two of us, but that did not mean we anticipated everything that could go sideways. There are still so many variables that we could not plan for. I have learned that you always have to expect the unexpected when it comes to these types of experiments.

I have Nick pull the canister out of his backpack. He mouths: Are you ready? I nod. It is time to do this. It is time for Phase 2 of our plan to commence. He takes the canister and pours it on me. I look at him in confusion because I don't smell the gasoline. He roughly grabs me by the arm, lifts it to his nose, and sniffs. Frantically, he pulls the canister up to his nose and smells once more. He then brings the canister to his mouth and takes a sip of it.

He looks at me with terror in his eyes. He mouths: It's water! Oh my god. OH MY GOD! It is filled with water, not gasoline! How did we not check before we left today? Seriously, who fills gasoline canisters with water? I would have never even thought to check. How could I make such a disastrous miscalculation?

He drops the canister, grabs me by the hand, and we make a full sprint toward the path we left behind. We are going to die.

Chapter Fifty-One

Before

I somehow make it home without any further incident. I come in through the hidden back entrance and feel a sigh of relief when I lock the door behind me. I walk into the living room and grab a lantern so I can assess how bad I impaled myself. I feel so debilitated, and I know it is because I have already lost so much blood. I want to lie down, but I know I have to try to disinfect this before it gets bad. I am so mad at myself for being clumsy. I don't want to die this way.

I can feel the throbbing as if I can feel the infection spreading in real time. I grab the lantern and head into the bathroom. I lift up my shirt and remove the bloody sock. Immediately, the wound begins to ooze thick, dark burgundy blood. I really did a number on myself this time. First and foremost, I need to stop the bleeding. I grab a towel and apply pressure as I look for supplies to tend to my injury. I grab some alcohol, some cotton pads, and I continue to look for something to close the wound. As I go through the drawers, I am surprised to find an old sewing kit. Grace, you cannot be thinking what I think you are thinking. Do you know how bad this is going to hurt? If I don't close it, though, it will get infected. What other choice do I have?

I take the alcohol and pour it on the needle and thread, and I place it on the counter to dry. I pour alcohol onto the cotton pads, and slowly lift my shirt. I look at myself in the mirror and take a deep breath. Pain is temporary, you got this! I place the pad on the wound and I scream out in the pain. Don't stop, it will only make it worse. I clench my jaw as I continue to wipe the wound while still applying pressure.

I take the needle and thread, and my hand starts to shake. You better sit down for this. I sit on the toilet and take a long, deep breath. I am about to penetrate my skin, when I stop and take another deep breath. Just keep going. The faster you do it, the faster you will be done. One final breath, and I pierce my skin with the needle and pull the thread. The pain is absolutely excruciating. I can feel every tug of the thread as it pulls my skin together. My eyes are watering, and my hands continue to shake. Don't think about how much it hurts; it'll get better. Slowly, I continue, one stitch at a time, until finally the wound is closed.

I coat the wound one more time with alcohol, before applying a bandage. I stand up and look at myself in the mirror. Now I am particularly pale, but I am grateful that I came across those Vicodin tablets in the pharmacy.

I walk into the living room, grab my backpack, and take a few pills. It is hard to believe just how much my life has changed the last few years. I am trying to wrap my brain around how I would have even known how to do this to myself. I am not even sure this impromptu surgery will even prevent the infection. All I am certain of is that I needed to close the wound, and I did whatever I could do to make it happen. I haven't taken Vicodin in a long time, and I can feel it start to kick in. Please work, because I really need the throbbing to stop.

I lie down on the couch, and it doesn't take long for the medicine to numb my senses. I must have fallen asleep because I jump at the sound of banging on what used to be the front door. It takes me a moment, but then I realize someone followed me home.

Not feeling that great, I get up and try to run to the back bedroom and grab the rifle. I feel like I am almost in a state of intoxication, and I know I have to try to snap out of it. I check the chamber and it is loaded. I go back into the living room and remain completely silent. BANG-BANG. I am in no frame of mind to fight someone off right now. Why did I take those stupid pills? Stop worrying; they can't get in here; just remain calm. BANG-BANG-BANG. Whoever it is, he is knocking how I'd imagine police would knock at your door if they were about to break the door down. Just stay quiet.

"I know you are in there. I followed you from town," yells the stranger in a menacing tone.

Just stay quiet. He may have followed you here, but you are safe because he can't get in.

"I also saw the way you fell on that big ol' tree, too. You really should be more careful," he yells once more. "Maybe you should let me in so I can help take care of you."

He can't get in. You will be safe here.

"Do you really want to be in there, all alone, possibly bleeding to death?" he yells almost gleefully now.

What should I do? I can't let him in here. What if he was the one who murdered that girl in town?

"Ok, I see what is going on here. You're scared I'll hurt you like I hurt that woman?" he says, as if reading my mind. "I don't blame you, after all, but you have nothing to fear. Yeah, I killed her, but it's not what you think." He slams on the side of the house in a new spot, causing me to jump. "It was just a misunderstanding, I promise."

The banging continues, and I just sit with the gun pointed at what used to be the front door. The metal siding will protect me. He can't break it down. BANG-BANG-BANG.

I jump once more when I hear a loud thud on the roof. Is there more than one intruder? What if they find a way to get in through the roof?! Is there an attic? Why have I never thought of this before? Another loud thud is followed by click-click-click-click. Oh my god, there is a monster up there. He led them here. Click-click-click-click. What if they break down the roof? I have nowhere else to go.

Click-click-click-click... click-click-click-click... It sounds like there are two of them. The clicking moves from the center of the roof toward the front of the house. Click-click-click-click.

"Listen here," he is now screaming at the top of his lungs, "I have lost my patience. Let me in or—"

Mid-sentence I hear a harrowing scream. They got him. I run toward the basement, lock the door behind me, and run down toward the wine cellar. I run to the deepest corner, and just hide there, like I did after Stephen died. I can hardly hear anything besides the pounding in my chest. I hold on desperately to the rifle, ready to take aim if the monsters find me down here. What was he thinking? Why would he make so much noise? Am I safe here? Will the monsters know I am down here?

My mind is racing in a hundred different directions. How could I be so stupid? I led not only that man back here, but those monsters as well. I have to be smarter from now on.

Chapter Fifty-Two

Present

"Grace, don't slow down!" he screams at me.

Nick is pulling me so hard I can feel my wrist starting to bruise. I am wheezing as I attempt to breathe, and my heart is pounding with pain. I know I can't slow down. I can't try to look behind me. I can't make any more mistakes. I really screwed this one up. The sun has set, and all that remains is the gentle glow in the west. It will not be long until they are here.

We continue sprinting and finally make it to the path. Not much farther now. Please don't wake up, monsters. Please give us more time. I am now drenched with sweat, my mouth is dry like cotton, and I am struggling to breathe, gasping for every small breath. Every time I feel my legs start to slow, Nick pulls me harder to maintain my momentum.

We pass the tree with the first X and I know we are almost home. We are so loud. Every crunch of broken twigs beneath our feet, every branch we slam out of our way still attached to a tree trunk, and every breath is louder than the last. Our time has run out.

Despite my prayers, I hear it. Animals crying in the forest, screaming in their own animalistic terror. The rustling of the leaves above us. Oh please, don't give up now. Run faster. You still have time, you just need to try. But we cannot escape the sound I am dreading.

Click-click-click-click.

"Grace, don't you give up on me!" Nick screams.

Click-click-click-click. It is in the trees to my left. It is loud and terrifying.

"Grace, we're almost there! Just keep pushing!" He is now pulling me so hard that I feel as if I will face plant any moment.

Click-click-click-click. I hear it directly behind me now. We aren't going to make it. There is no way we are going to make it.

Click-click-click-click. Now it sounds like it is on my left again. How is this possible? Are we surrounded? We have to be.

"Grace, I see the bushes! Don't stop, please, don't stop!" he continues to yell.

Click-click-click-click. I am filled with horror because I can tell it is in front of me.

I keep trying to propel myself forward, but now I feel like my legs are running through quicksand. I know I am surrounded, and I am trying not to give up, but I feel my body starting to falter. My wrist is still stinging from the strength of Nick's grasp.

Click-click-click-click. I can't even tell where it is coming from now.

"Grace, don't you even think about quitting. We are almost there. Please, don't give up on me!" he screams once more, but out of breath this time.

Click-click-click-click. Damnit, where are you? I can't see anything now.

Suddenly, like hitting a wall, I collide with an invisible being. It is like a ton of bricks stopping me dead in my tracks. I feel discombobulated, and I feel like the wind has been knocked out of me. I gasp in distress as Nick continues to propel forward, breaking his grip of my arm as I tumble to the ground. I feel heat on my face as it scrapes the dirt and rocks on the forest floor. I try to pick myself up, but I am so dizzy from colliding into the monster that I struggle to maintain my balance. I try to stand up once more, losing my balance again, which causes me to roll to the right. Click-click-click-click. I hear it to my left. Did our collision disorient it, too? Click-click-click-click. I do my best to try to stand back up, and suddenly Nick grabs me and throws me over his shoulder. We have no time to waste. I am so disoriented, but I see the bushes surrounding the cabin. We are home.

He pushes through the gate, through the bushes, and toward the back. Click-click-click-click. It sounds above us now. He puts me down, drops to the ground, opens the hidden door, pushes me in, and follows behind. Click-click-click-click. He slams the door shut and locks it.

Before I can even take a breath, we hear something on the roof. With every step, the sound echoes in the cabin from above. Click-click-click-click. We run to the basement, lock the door, descend the stairs, and make our way into our sanctuary. We sit in silence waiting for it to find us.

After a decent amount of silent anticipation, it is evident that the monsters did not follow us inside. I finally let out a deep breath.

He stands up and looks at me. "What happened out there, Grace?"

I put my hand up to my freshly cut face, and flinch at the tenderness. "I have no idea. It was like I collided into the monster head on, and it must have made it disoriented."

He begins to pace back and forth. "Could you tell what it was?"

I sit there looking at him and shake my head. "It literally felt like I ran into a concrete slab at a full sprint. Whatever it is, it was solid. I don't think I even made it fall back on its heels."

"I wonder why he didn't attack?"

"I think it was just placement. We were running so fast, that maybe it was getting ready to pounce, but just didn't have the opportunity?"

He walks over and stands directly in front of me. "Is your head alright, though? Do you feel like you have a concussion or anything?"

"I was definitely perplexed when it happened, but I don't think I hit my head."

Bending down to my level, he grabs my face and starts feeling for bumps, "Yeah, I don't feel anything. Wow, that was crazy!"

"I still can't believe that happened!"

Nick sits next to me on the cot. "I know, but honestly, who fills gas canisters with water?" Clearly exhausted, he rubs his eyes with the palms of his hands. "It really is absurd; comical even."

I lean my head back against the wall. "It is like the more we plan, the more mistakes we make. I thought I would be better at all of this, but I guess it is a lot easier when your dad is in charge of the puzzles."

"Things like this happen—I think. We knew it was all going to be trial and error at first anyway, right?"

"I guess you're right. I just would have never expected there to be water in there. What a weird turn of events."

He lets out a laugh, "Someday it will make a great story for us to tell."

I just smile at him. He takes his hand and feels my forehead, which is very tender to the touch. He follows my forehead, down my cheek, and to the bridge of my nose.

"You look pretty beat up. Do you want me to clean that for you?" He asks politely.

"I don't have any supplies down here for that. I just scraped my face when I fell, it's fine."

He pulls his hands from my face, "Does it hurt?"

I touch my wounds gently. "Not really. It stung when I fell, but my whole body is aching right now."

"You know, we may have messed up. But we survived them. Twice now, we have escaped their clutches. That's a good sign."

I grin, "I think if we are being honest with one another, it really has just been luck."

He shakes his head in disagreement. "No, it isn't. This is just the first of many. You may see it as a failure, but I think it is a success. I think we are going to be just fine, Miss Baker."

I smile at him, "While I adore your optimism, we still have a long road ahead of us."

"We have to appreciate our wins when we have them. We survived to-night. That is a win," he grabs my hand.

While I could spend the majority of the night debating with him what a win means in my mind, I decide against it. It was a win, no matter how lucky we just ended up being. We live to fight another day.

Chapter Fifty-Three

Before

Well I think it is safe to say that the person who tried breaking in was a fluke. It has been about three weeks since it happened, and I haven't had any more encounters with burglars or monsters. To play it safe, I have transformed the basement wine cellar into my new room. I have replaced the wine shelves with my belongings and moved a cot downstairs for me to sleep on. I find that there is a level of comfort and security down here. While it may be cold, and scary at times, it is in no way as scary as what is out there.

Despite the loss of my entire family, I am starting to feel some sense of normalcy, if that is even possible. I write in my journal a lot now. I find myself having conversations with my family quite frequently, if I am being honest. I don't know if that is a good thing—a sign of healing—or if I am just losing my mind. The silence is what gets me, though. I don't know if hating the silence so much allowed my coping mechanism to manifest itself into very realistic dialogue with my lost loved ones, but it is a likely cause.

Sometimes I swear I can hear my mom and dad calling me from upstairs. There have even been times when I will be reading, and I can hear Stephen on the other side of the door. I can hear their voices with such clarity. The first couple instances, I was able to dismiss it. Initially, it was startling because I thought people had somehow broken into my fortress. Then the more it happened, I realized who the voices belonged to.

I appreciate it now because it makes me feel less lonely. Sometimes it scares me, because it is truly unexpected. I really have no control over it. At first I thought I was going insane, but now I welcome it. I really don't know what to make of it. I don't know if it is truly them speaking to me from beyond the grave. I was never one to believe in ghosts, or that spirits haunt the living. There are just times when it feels so real that it makes me substantiate the theory. After all, I would have never thought monsters exist either. So, why would it be so improbable to believe that my family is still here with me? Without experiencing it first-hand, no one could ever understand what it is like to be completely alone, all the time, in a cabin with nowhere else to go.

Despite my family being gone, I have still tried to keep the routine we had established. I still do my daily training sessions. Now my fights with Stephen have been replaced with shadow boxing and a lot of burpees. I hate burpees so much. I punish myself with burpees when I screw up the combination, or if I find myself not being creative enough with my defense. I still write in my journal a lot and read on the nights when I can't stop the voices in my head. Life has become a bit monotonous in the absence of my family, but I seem to make do.

I guess when everyone is gone, and there is no way to fill your loneliness, you try desperately to keep their memory alive. I spend a lot of time lying down here and just going through some of my belongings. I find that I do that more now as I try to hold on to the few things that used to make me happy.

Grace, honey, you seem so sad today.

I jump at the voice. I know, Mom.

Why are you so distraught today, honey? Her voice sounds calming as ever.

Because I am tired of always being in this cabin by myself. I am tired of this kind of life.

Grace, you are better than that. You are just having a moment of weakness.

I sigh, I know, Mom, but look around! Would you want to spend all of your time stuck in this cabin? Even worse, stuck sleeping in this dumb basement?

There is a bigger plan for you, my sweet girl. You know that, her voice sounds distant today.

I just wish I knew what this bigger plan is. I am getting anxious.

Just keep fighting; things will get better, I promise. Her voice is soft and soothing, just like it always had been.

How can you be so sure?

I am your mother, I just know. Keep your chin up. There is so much to see out there if you are just willing to look.

I miss you, Mom. I start looking around to see if I can see her anywhere, but nothing is there.

I miss you too, dear. Time to get up. You can't stay hidden in the basement forever.

I love you.

I love you too, Grace.

I guess she is right. It is time to try to start my day. Sometimes I feel like maybe I should try relocating. See if the world is really as bad as it seems. Then, I get second thoughts because this place is all that I have left of them. The memories here were made long before the world ended. This is a place where we laughed as a family; where we played as a family; where we got to reconnect as a family. This is all I have left. Then again, maybe the reason I keep hearing the voices of my family members is because I am still stuck in this place trying to move on without them. Maybe it is this cabin that is making me crazy.

I am no longer feeling the guilt of surviving like I did right after Stephen died. I have pages and pages in my journal dedicated to trying to determine why I am alive and they are not. But as cliché as it sounds, I feel like I am destined to solve this problem. Everything happens for a reason, and I think the fact that I survived, after Dad spent so many years preparing me to solve impossible riddles and puzzles, means that maybe I can make things right again. I don't know, maybe I am getting ahead of myself. I have to at least try though, right?

Chapter Fifty-Four

Present

I am trying to fall asleep, but my mind is running in a million different directions. Nick fell asleep quite fast, and I don't blame him. Today was a marathon of adrenaline, and it really takes a lot out of you. I just cannot stop replaying the events in my head over and over again. Always check your equipment; always have a backup plan. What was I thinking? Maybe I am being a little too overzealous about enacting this plot. Maybe the years of reading have made me feel like I am the protagonist in my very own fictional drama, where the good guy always wins. Maybe I am being reckless with our lives because I can't just accept what my life has become. Maybe I am being selfish. I look over at Nick, and he looks so child-like. Am I being irresponsible and not taking his life into consideration? He was right, we had survived twice now, and both times we were in danger because I was misguided and overlooked something. This entire plot may need to end, because I can't risk losing him and being alone again. He has been so supportive; annoyingly supportive if I am being honest with myself. He deserves more than being a pawn in this game of chance. I think it is time for me to put this entire ludicrous scheme to bed. I close my eyes and attempt to finally drift off to sleep.

When I open my eyes, I am in the garage of my childhood house. The sun is shining brightly, and it already feels like it is going to be a very warm day outside. I walk to the table centered in the space to see what the project for today is.

Sprawled across the table are various notes, doodles, and a drawing of a town. I look closer and I do not know what town this is. What kind of project are we working on today, Dad?

The notes are bizarre and speak of monsters. This must be some type of Halloween-themed experiment. I always love Dad's ingenuity for lessons. He walks out of the house into the garage, and he his smiling from ear to ear. The sun is beginning to set and is shining into the garage. I feel myself smile, because the way it is beaming on him makes him appear to have an angelic glow.

My dad always looks so strong and put together. He is fit, but he looks kind. He is hard on us because he knows what is out there. He knows that evil exists, and he is always trying to prepare us for the unknown. His years in the military, with his top-secret missions, led him to insist we were always prepared for anything.

He walks over to me. "Ok, you ready, Grace?"

"Sure am, what problem are we solving this time?" I say as I sit down on the chair beside the table.

"The problem is that there are creatures you cannot see, and you must defeat them. Everything you know about them is written in these notes. Everything you have in your possession to defeat them is in these notes. Your objective is to determine how you will beat them."

"Wait, what? Invisible monsters? Have you been watching too much SyFy Channel in your retirement, Dad?"

He places his hands on his hips appearing like a grown version of Peter Pan. "Grace, you know every mission I give you has a purpose. Let's work this out together."

"You want to work as a team? We never work as a team."

He laughs, "No, you will still be doing all the leg work. I will just be here as you are figuring it out."

I shoot him a glare, but a mission is a mission. I grab the papers and organize them. I walk to the whiteboard and make a chart. At the top I write: How to Defeat Invisible Monsters. Column 1: Strengths, Column 2: Weaknesses, Column 3: What attracts them, and Column 4: Weapons Available.

I take the papers, and I write the corresponding details under the column headings. I take a step back and look at the details. From my peripheral, I see my dad watching me, as he examines the research display.

"I prefer conducting my own research, Dad. What if this information isn't accurate?"

He laughs, "Oh trust me, Grace, a very good source found these facts out for us."

I roll my eyes. "Ok, so based on the chart, these are invisible monsters that only come out at night. Since they attack people and animals, it would be safe to assume they are some kind of animal as well. If they are animal, then they have a brain, and everyone knows the quickest way to kill something is by causing damage to the brain."

"Ok, I'm listening, continue," says Dad.

I put the marker up to my mouth, and bite it. "I don't have any access to real tools? Like night vision or infrared?"

"You know the rules, all you have is what is listed."

I stand there looking at the whiteboard. "Well that seems like a shame. It would be easy if I had the right tools. So, I guess since they don't like the smell of gasoline, that allows you to be present without becoming their next casualty. So it comes down to putting yourself in a place where you can take out their brain from a position of advantage."

He nods his head in approval. "So how are you going to execute this plan?"

I put my hand up to my mouth and look at the chart once more. "I would find somewhere with height. If these things are ginormous, you would want them to feel small, it would make them less intimidating. So somewhere with high ground. You would want to mask your scent by pouring gasoline on you, even though that is highly dangerous and not normally recommended. But based on the provided research, it appears as if that's all that deters them from attacking you. So, despite the inherent harm of pouring gasoline on oneself, it seems that, unfortunately, is what you will have to do. Once the high ground is attained, and gasoline poured on oneself, the person would take them out by shooting them in the head with the rifle."

He's smiling. "All great conclusions, Grace, but what are you missing?"

I look at him, and then look at the chart.

"Grace, you are missing the most important aspect, dear."

I sigh, and then start tapping the marker on the board as I review it. "I don't know what I could be missing. I seem to have covered all the bases, Dad."

He stands up, walks over to me, and looks directly into my eyes. "Grace, my smart girl, what do you do with something you cannot see?"

Again, I just look at him and then back at the whiteboard.

He places both hands on my shoulders. "Grace, how do you make them visible?"

I jump and open my eyes. Can it really be that simple? Have I been living in fear for months when I already knew the answer?! He had given me this riddle as a child and I completely forgot about it. I had already figured this problem out long before any of this happened. I bury my head in my hands because it truly is something we can do. We have all the tools that we need right here. Thank you so much, Dad, for leading the way! I had forgotten what you taught me, but now I know what to do!

I look over and Nick is slightly snoring. I shake him awake, and he throws his hands up like he is going to fight.

"Nick! Nick! It is just me."

He looks at me concerned, "What's the matter?"

"I figured out how to beat them!" It is clear from his expression that he is still confused, so I try again. "Nick! I know how to beat the monsters!"

As if he has finally made sense of what I just said, his eyes widen and a huge smile spreads across his face. "How did you figure it out?"

With a huge smile on my face too, I respond, "My dad showed me!"

Chapter Fifty-Five

Before

Grace, honey, it's not safe here anymore.

I jump awake. I hear my mom's voice clear as day. I start frantically looking around my room to see what she is warning me about. It takes a moment for my eyes to adjust, and I realize that I am in my sanctuary. What is she trying to warn me about? I have been here for about six months now, all by myself. I have not encountered any monsters since the day that guy tried to break in. I have not had any savage encounters, either. I would make my normal trips to town to gather whatever was left, but I have had zero issues lately. I have seen a few encampments pop up here and there, but never any trouble. Why do I feel like it is unsafe now? I continue to lie in my bed and ponder the possible reasons I would have a sudden sense of danger. I have learned to trust these feelings since I have been alone. They have served to be good warning mechanisms; almost as if it were my very own sixth sense.

Mom, why isn't it safe?

Grace, you know why, she responds softly.

Why are you talking to me in riddles? I get enough of that from Dad.

If anyone can solve riddles, it is you, dear.

Mom, I haven't had any issues here. Is something coming? Are more people or more monsters headed toward me?

Grace, you know I cannot answer that for you. You need to figure this one out on your own. Just think about it.

The problem with this sixth sense is that it doesn't really help. It may guide me in a certain direction, but it does not provide me with the straight-forward answers I am often seeking. So, I do what I always do. I grab my notebook and start flipping through the pages. Everything post-bombing is in here.

So I glance through the more recent pages. Did anything stand out about things that I have seen or experienced? I feel myself begin to get frustrated because it just does not make sense. Nothing in here indicates that there are more monsters than before. Nothing in here indicates that the threat has substantially increased. I am safe here. Right?

What do you know, Mom? Why won't you tell me?

You know what you have to do.

Maybe only the cabin is unsafe. Maybe I need to go to town and see if there are new developments. No evidence supports this claim, but why else would I have such a strong feeling in the pit of my stomach? It has to be my imagination. There is no way that my mother is somehow giving me a divine warning. That stuff doesn't happen in real life. Right?

I am so lost. I don't know what to do. Maybe I need to trust my gut on this one. Maybe something even worse is coming. But how would I survive being out there at night without shelter? It would most certainly be a death sentence. Then again, what if by staying up here I am cut off from whatever progress has been made out there? What if there is a way to defeat them?

Mom, is that what you are trying to tell me? That if I don't leave here, I'll be stuck living like this forever?

Go to town, and it will all make sense.

What is possibly in town that I need to see?

Grace, honey, just go. Trust me.

For some reason I need to go to town and see what is going on down there. I wish Mom could have been a little more helpful, but I have to trust this feeling. I am supposed to go there for a reason. It has been months since I made a supply run. Maybe more people are here now. Maybe it is time to leave this cabin.

I know I won't be satisfied until I see what is out there. I grab a few things that I know I will need for my run into town today, and I try to get out of the cabin as quickly as possible. I really hate going on these excursions by myself. I have found that when you are alone in the forest, every little sound makes you tense. You are constantly assessing your surroundings, and you are even more paranoid that something is out there trying to harm you.

So far there seems to be usual forest activity. The birds are singing their songs while fluttering between the trees. Squirrels are dancing up and down the bark, pausing whenever I get near them. A few forest creatures running on the ground, chasing each other playfully. If anything, it seems like an extraordinarily peaceful day today. Under any other circumstance, I would be taking everything in. The beauty of nature's vibrant color palette, and the ways the creatures frolic with each other without a care in the world.

As I get closer to town, the feeling of content fades and I am thrust back into my reality. I am not here for a leisurely hike into town. I am on a research mission. I am here to see if there is a new danger here. I am here to gain a better understanding as to why I don't feel safe anymore.

I conceal myself in some trees that give me a clear shot of Main Street. I am sitting here for about an hour or so, reviewing my notebook once more, when I am startled by the sound of laughter. I put my notebook back in my backpack, and I listen. The laughing continues. Am I going crazy or do I hear what I think I am hearing?

Just past the pharmacy, a group of people emerge. They are casually strolling down Main Street. It is a decent-size group. It is hard to tell exactly who is in the group, but it appears as though there are four males and a female. I wish I had some binoculars to see better, but there are a lot of things I wish I had access to these days. I cannot make out what they are saying, but their body language suggests they are in playful conversation. They are walking in a line, no one checking to see if they are being followed. I feel a sudden tinge of jealousy that they are so calm and happy. I forgot what it was like to just walk down the street, laughing and joking with someone else. I forgot what it was like to not have to constantly tip-toe around and check your surroundings to ensure your safety. They are walking down the street without any concern about anything.

Where did they come from? Do they not have the same dangers where they lived prior? Have I been so cut off from the world that I have possibly handicapped myself from moving forward? Are these monsters only in this region? So many questions are beginning to rapid fire in my mind. Who are these people?

They are now stopped in the middle of town and sitting in a circle. They have some papers in front of them on the ground, and I cannot see what the papers are from this distance. Perhaps a map to determine where they are, or how far they have traveled. There is still so much laughter between them. What is there to laugh about? I want to learn more. I want to run down there and ask them what they know, or don't know. I want to know so bad where they have been and what is going on in the world. Exposing myself to five strangers is just too dangerous, though.

I don't know how long I have been deep in thought, but I am startled when I hear thunder. My trance is broken, and I realize that the sunshine has been replaced with rain clouds. I have to get back home. I don't have much time.

Chapter Fifty-Six

Present

The next morning, I lay out the entire plan to Nick. I tell him about the old clock tower in town, and how that would be the perfect way to have a position of advantage, especially because we could lock them out. I tell him how I was confident that my dad had planned on using the clocktower as well, based on the research he had us conduct the day he died. I tell him how we can draw the monsters to the area and use some freshly killed animals to focus their attention to the tower. Most importantly, though, we need to make them visible so we will know they are coming.

If we had more time, I would have loved to be able to do a few more tests. I prefer going into an experiment having more data to support our actions. But time is not on our side, and we have to act quickly. I tell Nick about the previous missions Dad had me solve regarding invisible monsters, and the few things I could remember from back then. He thinks the clock tower is a great solution because he likes the idea of being behind cover, sheltered from the elements, and having a position of advantage. He is the one who came up with how to make them visible, though. I never would have thought to use paint as a way to show us their footprints. It is an absolutely genius idea.

He is amazed by the way the whole idea came to me, and he believes it was a higher power helping us realize we already knew what to do. I am not a big believer in signs, or holy intervention, but everything about my dream was amazing. What I find even more fascinating is the way the dream came to me on the same night I had decided to give up. I really felt like I was there with my dad, thinking through one of his missions for me. Part of me really wants to believe it truly was my Dad speaking to me from beyond this place, guiding me on this ridiculous quest. God, I miss them so much. Even with them gone, my family still finds a way to make me stronger.

We lay out our entire plan in detail. We know we will have to go to town early to grab the extra gasoline and set everything up. We decide that we will not attempt to do it today, as we are still recovering from the events of last night, but we will do it tomorrow. I make sure that Nick is physically ready because it had only been a few weeks since he was stabbed. He insists that he is up for the task, and hardly feels it anymore. So, we decide that tonight, we will relax and try to enjoy the evening. I think we both know the risk of what we will be taking on tomorrow—one last normal night is the least we can ask for. After all, it may be our final night together.

After we finish all our planning, we make a deal to avoid talking about anything that is going to take place tomorrow. If for some reason this is our last night on earth, we want to actually remember what it was like before all of this happened.

We didn't use a drinking game to share our secrets this time. We just sat there talking and exchanging stories like it was a completely normal evening.

We are sitting on the couch when I look over at Nick, "So what made you even decide to come to Los Angeles in the first place?"

He laughs, "Women. Well, work, and women."

I playfully slap his shoulder and roll my eyes, "Of course that was it."

"Nah, not like that. I grew up in this small country town where everyone knows each other. I think there were fewer than a thousand people in my hometown. I loved the country, but I just wanted something bigger. Then a few people I knew came to Los Angeles and were just getting into the acting thing, and they said I should try it."

I give him a sideways smile, "I don't see you being the type of person who would want to be an actor."

He laughs, "Me neither! It was so out of my comfort zone. But then I kind of liked the idea of maybe getting to pretend to be someone I wasn't. You know—action star. The guy who gets the girl. That kind of stuff, I guess."

I shift my body to look at him. "Why would you want to pretend to be someone you aren't, though?"

He looks away, and then back at me. "I don't know—I mean look at you. You were always so fascinated by what you were reading. Wasn't that because you imagined your life resembling those people you were reading about?"

I look down, "I guess you have a point there."

"It's just when you are in a small town, you feel—well I felt at the time—that there was just so much more to this life than I was ever going to experience there. I mean after all, we legitimately used to play cow-tipping drinking games."

I laugh heartily, "No way! You have to be kidding! That is real?"

He starts laughing, "Yes, cow-tipping isn't just something you see in movies. I have some great stories actually."

I eagerly scoot toward him, "There is no way we are going to bed without you telling me one of these stories. I am completely fascinated."

"Ah, hell, who cares right? I have nothing to hide."

I throw my hands in the air and clench my fists, "Yes! I am so excited."

He laughs, "So have you ever heard of the beer mile?"

I shake my head no, "I don't think so."

"My friends and I decided to do the country version of the beer mile. A beer mile is when you run a lap, chug a beer, and then run a lap, chug a beer, and so on. Well we thought it would be fun to do this with cow tipping."

I take my hand and cover my face, "Why do I have a feeling this is going to end terribly?"

He places his hand on my knee, "Oh, because it does. My friend Mike's family owned a dairy farm, so we were running around tipping cows and chugging beers, when all of a sudden, Mike, who was inebriated at this point, tries to get a head start and runs full speed toward one of the cows. He was so drunk that he didn't see that the cow was turning away from him—"

I put my hands on my mouth. "Oh, please stop—this is going to be gross isn't it?"

Nick is laughing hysterically, "He was so busy watching his feet to make sure he didn't trip, and his hands were extended in front of him—"

"No, no, no—"

Nick starts slapping his knee, "That when he went to push, he pushed the cow's rear end—" he is laughing so hard at this point, "that his whole arm went up you know what."

"That is so gross!" I say slapping his shoulder.

"No, that isn't even the best part," he says as he begins to reclaim his composure. "The cow was so startled by the unexpected enema that the cow kicked him and got him right in his knee."

"You have got to be kidding me!"

Nick wipes the tears from his eyes from laughing, "Yeah, he broke his knee that night, but it was so hilarious. He was so drunk he didn't even realize it was broken until the next day."

I let out a small laugh, "That was not what I was expecting, but I imagine it was pretty funny when it was happening. That sounds… fun, I guess."

He lets out a breath, "Don't get me wrong, it was fun. I just wanted more."

I smile at him, "I get it. Come to California to reinvent yourself. It makes sense. Did you ever regret it?"

"Oh, you have no idea. Los Angeles was a weird place. People were so mean and so into themselves. I felt like a fish out of water, to be honest."

I put my hand on his shoulder, "That sucks to hear, I'm sorry."

He looks at me and smiles, "I was actually considering going home. Then I got this call that I got hired at this café, and then it didn't seem so bad staying."

I feel myself blushing, "Oh, stop it."

"No, I mean it, Grace. I know we hardly knew each other, but just being around you made it feel more real. I wasn't in this sea of plastic robots anymore. It gave me a reason to stay."

I give him a half-smile. "I think we are far past flattery at this point."

He grabs my hand, "I mean, are we though?"

I raise my eyebrows, "What do you mean?"

"Well look around us. Life sucks, right? But what we have is something special isn't it?"

I feel myself getting very shy, "Nick, all we have is each other. We can't be doing anything stupid."

His expression becomes very serious, "You can be so impossible sometimes. Anytime you feel any sense of intimacy, even just emotionally, you push people away."

"That isn't what I am doing—"

He interrupts me, "This isn't a fight, I just want to tell you this. Please?"

"O—ok, go on," I feel my heart starting to beat rapidly in my chest.

He places his hand on my cheek, "I would never do anything to ruin our friendship. Not now, not ever. You mean the world to me, and I need you to understand that."

"Of course I understand that, it's the same for me, I promise—"

He moves his hand to below my chin, "Wherever you go, I go, remember?"

I nod my head up on down, "Of course I remember."

He leans in and kisses my forehead, "Whatever happens tomorrow, we'll get through this together, ok?"

I feel oddly comforted, and don't have the words to respond. He puts his arm around me, and I place my head on his shoulder, as we relax back onto the couch. I listen to him continue to tell me more stories, but I am lost in the moment we had. I have a million and one thoughts running through my head, and I can't focus on a single one.

As I sit there listening to him talk, I'm reminded of when our worries, while they seemed extraordinary at the time, pale in comparison to what we deal with now a daily basis. So much has happened, and we have grown so much. However, it is a relief to see that underneath all the pain, fighting, and killing we have endured, we really are those same people who met in a café all those years back.

I pour us each one final glass of wine, knowing we need to be on our best game tomorrow. It is getting late, and we need our rest.

Nick twirls his wine in his glass, like you would see connoisseurs do before tasting a wine for the first time. Still focused on his glass, he says, "Grace, can I tell you a secret?"

I feel my heart flutter, "I thought we already discussed all our embarrassing secrets."

He takes a sip of his wine. "Remember that book I gave you?"

"Of course I do, you saw it downstairs."

"I didn't find it at the café."

I laugh, "Your secret is safe with me."

He looks up at me, "I went to a used bookstore and bought it for you, because I wanted you to think I found it and remembered."

I look at him, surprised. "You didn't have to do that."

"I know, but I wanted to give you a note, and I remember you talking about it the first time I met you."

"Regardless of how you came across it, Nick, the gesture was something that I will never forget, and I appreciate your honesty."

"Can I tell you another secret?" he asks, half smiling.

I chuckle, "You are just full of secrets today."

"Remember when I asked you what your favorite memory was, but didn't tell you mine?"

I find myself wondering if this was what he was going to tell me before he felt me pushing him away. "I do."

He looks at me. "I'm ready to tell you now."

"Ok, I am listening," I say as I take a sip of my wine.

"It was the first day I met you—"

"Oh stop, you are being ridiculous," I interrupt him.

"No, please, let me finish. The whole town was all sorts of crazy. I didn't get Los Angeles. I was feeling so out of place. I was ready to pick up and just leave and go home. Then, you came in, and you were the first person I talked to that just made me feel happy. The way you hid yourself in the corner, and the way you smiled at me when I'd come out to see you. Right away, I knew I wanted to know everything about you."

"You were right. You said I would never believe you, and I am certain you have way better memories than that one."

"I knew you would kiss it off, but it's true. And even though you think I'm full of it, I just had to tell you in case we die tomorrow." He shrugs and takes a drink of his wine.

I grab his hand, "Hey, you just gave me a pep-talk, you can't turn around and say we are going to die."

"You're right, Baker. No backing out now."

He looks up at me, smiles, and takes another sip of his wine. Our conversation continues for a little under an hour, and we finally head down to the basement. It is hard to believe we are really going to try to do this.

He lies on the cot, gives me space to lie down too, and says, "Make your entry a good one tonight. Goodnight, Grace."

"Goodnight, Nicholas." I take my journal out and begin to write:

Day 635

I read once that, "Extinction is the rule; survival is the exception." I don't remember where I read it, or who said it, but today as I pen these thoughts onto paper, I can't help but laugh. It is strange how the brain fires off random tidbits of information when one is confronted with conflict. Extinction really is the rule, isn't it? Our entire childhood is spent learning about the history of extinct creatures and fallen civilizations, and the eventual species that take their place. Life is one continuous cycle of people thinking that they are untouchable; that they are so much more advanced than the others that came before them. Yet, it is that very way of thinking that has ultimately led to our demise. For some reason, humans always destroy each other. There is always someone or something bigger and stronger waiting to take our place. Complacency is our downfall.

I don't know what will happen tomorrow. Here within these pages, I've documented every experience since my life changed forever. What I realized is that when something ends, something better has to take its place, and I want to be the exception to the rule. I want us to survive. Every being on this planet has a weakness; it is just a matter of recognizing what that weakness is.

My name is Grace. I am the daughter of John and Susan Baker and the younger sister of Stephen Baker. Everything I am I owe to my parents and to my brother. They taught me to be strong; they taught me to be smart; they taught me to never give up trying. It is in their memory that I attempt this venture tomorrow. I refuse to live like this any longer. There has to be a better way. There has to be more to this life. There just has to be a reason that all of this is happening. I refuse to be scared. I refuse to hide any longer. I know in my heart that I would rather die with courage, going out fighting, than live a life in hiding as a coward.

God Bless.

I close the journal, go up to the cot, and close my eyes. But I get back up when I realize I left out a very important part of my story.

And if for some reason I don't survive, then I need to let you know, Nick, that I would not have gotten as far as I have without you. You came back into my life when I was ready to give up. I was tired of fighting. I was tired of constantly looking over my shoulder, waiting to be attacked by a savage human or the monsters. I was tired of running. You reignited a spark that I didn't know could be relit. You have been exactly what I was seeking since I lost my family, and you made me strong again. You pushed me to find a solution. You made me start living again. I know I probably have not given you the accolades you deserve, but thank you for saving me when I needed saving. I just pray that we make it through this, and that we are finally able to take a long, deep breath and see a life worth living again.

I put the journal back on the shelf, and I lie back down. I feel Nick's arms wrap around me from behind. He whispers, "You forgot to write something about me, didn't you?"

I laugh, "Never. I just had something that I felt I needed to reiterate."

"It's ok, Baker. You can tell me what you wrote after we beat those guys tomorrow."

He pulls me in tighter, and I know that there is a probable chance that this might be the last time we lie like this together. For the first time in a very long time, I just embrace the moment. In the short time since he has been back in my life, we had become fighters. We needed each other. We were all one another had in this entire world. I would die for him, and I know he would die for me. But if all goes according to plan, the only thing dying will be those damn monsters.

Chapter Fifty-Seven

Before

I still don't know what to make of that group of travelers I saw. They were walking around like it was no big deal. They were even laughing and playing around with each other. I was so close to them, and I know I should have just run down there and asked all the questions I was dying to know. I should have warned them about what was up here, because they didn't seem to worry about it. I should have maybe screamed or alerted them to the dangers in the forest, but I didn't. What if they were my only chance of getting out of here, and I just let them die?

Mom, when you said it wasn't safe here, were you talking about the people I saw in town today? Are they going to draw more monsters here?

Grace, you know what you must do.

I don't understand any of this. What is it that you want me to see?

What did you see? Write it all down. Then it will all make sense.

I grab my journal, and I begin to write about what I saw. I document everything that happened, and I still do not understand much of what occurred. Is it possible that there is some place that doesn't have monsters? Is that where the travelers came from? Yet, if they did emerge from some sort of new civilization, why did they leave? It can't be that great if they are choosing the vagabond lifestyle. It would seem that if they are embarking on these travels by choice, maybe things are less dangerous from where they come from and they don't even know these monsters exist. Once again, my brain is firing away with questions that cannot be answered here. I should have tried to talk to them, but it just seemed like an unnecessary risk at the time. But there is something about this group that is important; I can feel it in my bones. Tomorrow, I have to go back. I have no other choice.

Mom, I can't get your voice out of my head. You want me to go back, right? Is it that I need to try to make contact with these people? I don't know what you want me to do.

If you look deep inside of yourself, Grace, you know what you need to do. This isn't a quest that I must lead for you. This is all you.

What is it about this group of people that makes me so fascinated? Why, of all days, did I get a warning to leave today; and then when I go to town, I come across a group of people? Whatever it is, I can't fight this feeling that somehow I was meant to cross paths with those strangers.

Ok, Mom, you convinced me. I'll go back.

Chapter Fifty-Eight

Present

The town is empty. There is a chill in the air; the sky is dark and full of clouds, absent of its normal sunshine at this time of day. It is a little before dusk, but due to the cloud cover it feels later than it really is. Our plan is simple. We combined the ideas I had recalled from the puzzles I worked on with my dad, along with our own research. First, we woke early so we could do some hunting. We wanted to draw them to our exact location when we implemented our plan. Since we had to travel with whatever we hunted, we decided to go with small animals, like rabbits or squirrels. After the hunting was complete, we went to the gas station and grabbed a few additional canisters of gasoline. From there, we went to the local hardware store and were pleasantly surprised that there were still gallons of paint on the shelves that hadn't dried yet. I guess at the end of the world, no one is interested in doing renovations. With our animals, gasoline, and paint we are ready for our upcoming battle.

As Nick and I walk through the town toward the abandoned clock tower, we stop every few feet and listen. The leaves are blowing along the street, and I feel like I have seen this very scene in so many scary movies back before the world ended. It actually reminds me a lot of the original *Halloween* movie. The hair on the back of my neck is standing up, and I have goosebumps all over my arms.

We don't say a word to each other, but we have rigorously planned for today. We decided on the clock tower because it gives us the advantage. It gives us the high ground. We are not in the open; no hiding among the trees. We have adequate cover. We trained for this.

We get to the clock tower, and Nick breaks the chain keeping the doors shut. It only takes a few strikes with the butt of the rifle, and the metal chain falls to the ground. I don't recall there being a chain when we came here with dad. Maybe he placed one to keep it secure until we could make our way back. He opens the door, and flashes the inside with his light, but it is quiet. We slowly climb the stairs until we are at the top. We approach the clock face, and we can see there are multiple latches that keep the clock in place.

Nick leaves the latches closed on the top of the clock and loosens the lower ones. He pushes the clock forward, and it gives just enough space to see what is directly below us. He looks at me and smiles.

"I think this just might work."

"Don't get ahead of yourself yet," I say quietly.

He unslings the rifle that we brought from the cabin from his back, conducts a chamber check to see if there is a round in the chamber, and there is. He rests the rifle against the wall, takes a wooden block, and places it between the wall and the clock to give just enough space to shoot down at whatever is approaching.

"Ok, this looks good," he confirms. "Let's go back downstairs and get the rest set up." We grab the bags and descend the stairs. By the time we get back down, it is already getting stormier outside.

"I really hope it doesn't rain." I say looking up at the sky.

"Yeah..." he says, pressing his lips into a line as he looks at the charcoal clouds. "I don't think there's anything we can do about it at this point. We just have to have faith that it'll all work out."

I look at him with despair. "But the rain will ruin everything."

He turns toward me and places his hands on my shoulders. "Don't back out on me now, we got this."

I take a canister of gasoline and I place it next to the door, just on the inside. He looks at me, and smiles.

"The good thing about rain is that the moisture and the cloudiness will help keep the paint wet longer," he says.

"I didn't think of that."

He pulls out two buckets of white paint from our bag and throws a roller at me. "Alright, time to get painting."

We knew that this had to be planned perfectly so that the paint wouldn't be dry when they came. We pour paint around the door and roll it out to create a walkway, leaving a path of exposed asphalt. I have never painted anything so fast in my life, but we know that this is a life or death situation.

We quickly admire our artwork, as the white paint really stands out against the black asphalt. Nick walks over and steps on the fresh paint and takes a couple steps on the asphalt. Just like we hoped—it works! We look at each other and give one another a huge hug.

"Are you ready?" he asks me.

"As ready as I'll ever be. You?"

"Let's do this."

He grabs the bag full of the bait, walks over to the door, and systematically throws one animal out at a time. Our painted walkway is now lined with rabbits on each side. He closes the doors, grabs the chain that he had broken upon our entry, wraps the door handles with the chain, and re-locks it with a lock we brought from the cabin.

He grabs my hand and walks me back toward the clock tower. We couldn't have planned the timing better as the sun is just disappearing in the distance below the clouds. We make it up to the top of the stairs, and he looks at me.

"Ok, tell me the plan one more time," he says.

"It is simple. The smell of the bloody rabbits will draw them to the path leading into the clock tower. When they start eating the rabbits, they will cross the wet paint, and then we will see their footprints. The minute we see the footprints, pour the additional paint on the body to expose the head, then we shoot down at them, hopefully killing them from the safety of up here," I tell him.

"Sounds perfect! You ready for the gas?"

I nod yes. He takes the canister of gasoline, raises it above my head, and says, "Close your eyes and hold your breath," as he pours gasoline on me. I feel him wipe my forehead, my eyes, and my mouth so I can open my eyes and begin breathing again.

"Ok, it's not so bad. Your turn," I say. He hands me the canister, closes his eyes, and holds his breath as I do the same. I put the canister down, wipe his forehead, eyelids, and mouth. "Ok, you can open your eyes now."

I look down at the ground. The paint is set, the rabbits are in place, and we are covered in gasoline. This is it. This is the moment we are going to finally see if we can win.

"Now," I begin to say, "Don't forget when you shoot, Nick, to have the barrel of the rifle just outside of the clock face."

"We will be fine, Baker."

"I know, I just get worried about being covered in gas, and shooting a firearm. We can't risk a hiccup here."

"The rifle is far enough away from our bodies; the muzzle flash has no way of catching us on fire."

"I know…" I pause, "I just want us to be extra safe."

"You have thought of everything. We will be fine. I promise."

"I don't want to jinx it…but—"

Before I can finish my sentence, we both jump at the sound of a woman screaming at the top of her lungs.

Chapter Fifty-Nine

Before

While Nick is upstairs recovering from his surgery, I kill the time by going through some of the items I have collected over the past year. I take the necklace that was given to me for my first communion and I admire it. I don't think it is appropriate to wear jewelry now because I am in a constant fear of someone trying to steal it from me. With everything that has happened, though, I think maybe I need to start having a little more faith in the feelings I get. Whether it is from a higher power or not, I need to keep trusting that faith. I take the necklace and put it around my neck. Now I will always have my family with me.

I continue to go through my belongings, and I come across some postcards I picked up a few weeks ago. Or was it a few months ago? Now I can't remember. I look at the postcard, smile, and decide to write a note on it.

Mom, Dad, and Stephen,

Been enjoying my time up here. Things have gotten back to whatever normal is. I am missing the city, though, and missing the hustle and bustle of downtown. I know I thought I was ready to come home, but I think there is just some stuff I have to take care of here. Just some unfinished business. I miss you guys so much, and I will touch base soon. Love you to the moon and back! –xoxo Grace.

I look at the postcard, let out a small laugh, and place it back in my journal.

I lie down on the cot and close my eyes. I hold on to the cross on my necklace.

I get it now, Mom. I get why you warned me yesterday. You knew I would go to town and I would try to figure out your cryptic message. It was not safe for me to keep being alone. I was losing my sanity, right? That is why you wanted me to find him. You wanted me to not be alone anymore. You knew the only way I would defeat these monsters was if I had someone to help me. That was it, right?

I told you, my sweet girl, that you would figure it out. Life goes on.

But what if he stays here and I forget everything you guys taught me? What if I forget you guys all together?

Oh, Grace, that is not going to happen. There is no way you could forget about us, even if you tried. We are a part of you.

I know, Mom. I am just scared.

Of course you are. You are growing up; life is changing. You can't let us hold you back anymore.

You aren't holding me back though, Mom. None of you are.

Then you need to move on, honey. You know what you need to do.

I don't want to move on. I don't deserve to move on.

Grace, honey, everything has happened as it should. You followed your gut, and now life can start again.

I turn over on my side. I grab the picture of us from Yosemite, and stare at it for a few minutes.

The truth is, I know you aren't really talking to me, Mom. I know when I hear you, Dad, and Stephen, that it really isn't you guys. I have just been so alone for so long. I know the voices in my head aren't real. How I knew that I had to go to town baffles me. It is truly a mystery. I am not a believer in fate, but why else would I have been drawn to town the way that I was? Maybe it was all just a coincidence. Either way, I think it worked out the way it was meant to.

I am glad you are finally realizing it, dear. We will always be with you, even if it is just in your imagination.

I don't want to let you guys go. I miss you all so much my heart breaks at the thought of moving on. We were all supposed to be in this together. I know I imagine you talking to me. I know the voices in my head are truly just my thoughts, with your voices superimposed. I know that had I not used you guys in my head to guide me, I probably would've been lost a long time ago. I am not alone anymore. I can let you guys go. I can let you move on, even though I know you have already moved on from here. I can't help but see the parallels between what I have been experiencing, and the very same thing that happened to Odd Thomas when the love of his life was killed. Without even realizing it, I used my favorite story to cope with my tragic loss. Isn't that what I have done here? I have been talking to you guys for months. Telling you about my day, using you as guidance. Trying to cope with everything that has happened.

We all deal with grief in our own ways, I hear her say.

This whole time it was just me unable to accept the loss. It was just me trying to figure out a way to not be alone. It was me trying to survive when I didn't want to survive anymore. I am so grateful for all that you have been for me. I am so grateful that I had the time I got to spend with you. Mom, you are the kindest, most generous person I ever knew. You were strong, but you were sweet, and someday I pray that I can be the type of mother you were to me.

Grace, I am so proud of you. I love you, baby girl.

I bring the photograph to my chest and hug it. Dad, I will never understand the depth of what you knew. I don't know what you knew about the apocalypse, or what you knew about these monsters, but damn, you were a really amazing dad. You never once made me feel handicapped for being a girl. You made me tougher than most of the boys, but you always focused on my mind. If it weren't for you, I would have never been able to survive. Daddy, you will always be my hero, and I am so sorry that I was so cruel when you told me what you knew. I should have forgiven you right away, and I regret not saying I was sorry.

I hear my dad's voice: Grace, you are a smart girl, and nothing I could have ever done to prepare you would have been successful without you leading the way. You can do this; I have faith in you. It will all work out.

I smile, and then address my brother. Stephen, you are what big brothers are supposed to be. You picked on me to make me strong. You protected me, when I was too scared to protect myself. You helped me pick up the pieces after Mom and Dad were gone. Thank you for protecting me even until your very last breath.

Stephen chimes in: I know I never had the chance to tell you in real life, but I am proud of you, little sis. You are one tough girl, and I only wish I were there to watch you destroy those monsters. They have another thing coming. You will figure it out, I know it.

I am crying now, but I can't stop: It is time I move on. I can no longer hear your voices in the silence. I have to move forward. I will cherish all that you were to me, but life has to go on. I cannot be in this purgatory of feeling like you are still here. If I am going to move on, then I really need to move on. I love you all so much, but that chapter is past us now. Now I have to figure out how to start living again.

We love you, Grace, and we will always be with you. Live your life. Until we meet again.

I close my eyes and their voices are gone. I always knew it was some form of a coping mechanism, but it still feels like I am saying goodbye all over again. I know they will always be with me. Even though it was all in my imagination, everything they said was true. I had to figure out how to start living again, no matter how much leaving them behind hurt me. I had to figure out how to defeat these monsters. I had to put the car in drive and stop looking in the rearview mirror.

Chapter Sixty

Present

"Oh my god, there is someone out there!" yells Nick.

"You jinxed it!"

"We have to do something. We literally just drew them to this area!"

I am about to run downstairs when Nick grabs me by my arm.

"Grace. You have to think this through. She is probably already dead."

I pause. "But—no. No, we can't be those people. We can't just sit and watch innocent people die."

"Ok, but we can't give up our plan. You stay here."

"No! No! I am not letting you go out there without me. We are a team!"

I try to run but he grabs me again, pulling me back. "Grace Tiffany Baker! Listen. I am covered in gasoline. That should be enough that they can't smell me. I will lure them over here, away from whoever needs us, and you finish this."

"I—no—this is a terrible idea." I feel my chest tighten with anxiety.

"Grace, it is the same plan, but I am the rabbit now luring them in for you. You have this. I promise, I will be fine."

"But—"

He grabs me by both of my arms, looks into my eyes, and says, "Please, trust me. I promise you I will be back." He kisses my forehead and then runs downstairs before I can protest.

I should run after him. I should be there by his side, but he is right. We must do this. This will change our entire future. I feel a sense of disgust that I just let him leave. I look down from the clock tower and watch him as he runs out the front door, avoiding the freshly painted pavement.

It is so quiet I can hear my heart drumming away in my chest. I lean against the wall because I feel like I am going to hyperventilate. I close my eyes, and that just makes it worse because I have that sudden sensation of dizziness that comes with vertigo. When I open my eyes, I see that there is a tapestry I hadn't noticed before hanging on the opposite wall.

It looks like it is of an ancient battle, with men on horses and elephants, and dozens of people dead on the ground. It is faded, but well maintained considering everything it has been through. As I stand here looking at this tapestry, I can't help but think that it is such an odd place for a tapestry of this kind to be hanging. I feel like it is some kind of sign.

I look out the clock tower and Nick is nowhere to be found. And then I hear it. That ominous sound I have grown to despise since the first time I heard it: Click-click-click-click. It is so loud that it drowns out the sound of my heartbeat. In my head I can hear the blonde girl from *The Poltergeist* saying, "They're here...." And I know this is it. Oh God, please let this work.

I grab the rifle and aim down at the pavement. Click-click-click-click. It sounds like it is above me. I jump right as I hear a loud bang strike the roof above me. Yes, they somehow made their way above me onto the roof of the clock tower. Click-click-click-click.

Relax, Grace. Relax. This will work. Have faith in your plan; don't doubt yourself now.

Click-click-click-click, it is getting louder.

Remain calm. They will not attack you. They are just stalking their prey and trying to figure out what you are.

Click-click-click-click.

Oh man, please go down there already. I feel my hands starting to tremble.

I realize I smell a familiar scent of iron. I look down and see we made another horrible mistake. The bag containing the animals is still up here. In the reckless attempt to save a stranger, we forgot to throw the bag out. The bag that smells like animals and is covered in blood is lying adjacent to me. I reach in and there are still dead creatures inside. Stop it. Don't worry. Your scent is masked. It just smells the rabbits. You will be fine. I grab the bag and throw it down below me where the other animals are. It is such a stupid mistake, but hopefully getting rid of it is enough to deter them from my location.

I look down and I can see movement. I see a rabbit elevate into the air as it begins to be shredded. Click-click-click-click.

Step on the paint you bastard! Show yourself! I see another rabbit lift into the sky, but still no footprints. "Show yourself!" I scream at it.

Thud-thud-thud-thud. Wait, what is that? Thud-click-thud-click-thud-click. I have never heard this before. Thud-click-thud-click-thud-click. Am I hearing what I think I am hearing? Did it make it inside? Is that the sound of it climbing the staircase? How is this possible? Thud-click-thud-click-thud-click. I stand there too scared to look behind me, still waiting for the monster down below to show himself. It is all in your head, Grace.

Click-click-click-click. I stop breathing, because now I know it is not in my head. Click-click-click-click. It sounds like it is directly behind me. In a moment of terror, I realize that Nick must have accidentally left the door open. If we survive this, I am going to kill him myself. He must have left it open when I forced him to go save a stranger. This is my karma. No good deed goes unpunished. What was I thinking? He was right. There is no way she could have survived being out there. In a moment of trying to, once again, act like the noble person saving strangers, I have ruined what we have been preparing for. You are so stupid, Grace. But how did it make it past the paint without me seeing it? Unless it somehow stepped on the bag I just tossed down onto the asphalt. That can't be it, that is just too much of a coincidence. How it got past the paint is irrelevant now.

Click-click-click-click.

Oh God, Grace. Think. THINK! Plan, research, execute. He doesn't know you are here. He smells whatever was left of the rabbits. You are safe. I close my eyes, and I can see my mom and dad. They are looking at me, and they appear as they did when I was a kid. They are smiling. I can hear my dad in the distance, "Grace, what do you do when you can't see something? You make it visible!"

Click-click-click-click. I turn around and I can feel that it is directly in front of me now. I open my eyes, raise the rifle, take aim, and shoot the hook where the tapestry is fixed to the wall. With perfect timing, the tapestry falls and lands directly on top of the monster. It begins fluttering around attempting to rid its back of the tapestry, and for the first time, I can see how large it is. There in front of me stands a huge creature that is at least seven feet tall, with a very large upper body. I can tell by the way the tapestry is hanging over its head and shoulders. Here is my chance.

I take the rifle, point it at the floating tapestry, take a deep breath, and shoot three quick rounds to what I believe is the head. The creature falls, with the tapestry still draped on top of it. I can see that the tapestry is darkening with burgundy blood. The monster is wounded. I look closer and see the tapestry move up and down; whatever it is, it is still breathing. So I aim once more, and shoot three more times. All movement ceases, and whatever it is, it is finally dead.

One down, one more to go. I run downstairs and peer outside to the walkway. Click-click-click-click. It is still out there. Click-click-click-click. I really loathe that noise. As I walk closer to the door, I see a rabbit body fly into the air and get shredded. Pieces of his little furry body flying everywhere. The monster still has not been alerted to my presence.

I peer down at the walkway and I can finally see footprints. One by one, the white footprints appear against the black asphalt. I am shocked to see just how large they are. I try to get a little closer to see what kind of footprints this monster is leaving behind. It looks as though it has some form of reptilian footprint with three appendages. What kind of monsters did the government concoct in that laboratory?

I cannot delay any longer. I must try taking the shot. Click-click-click-click. I am watching the footprints closely. One by one it is coming closer to the door. Pausing at every snack we left for it to feast on. My concentration is broken when I jump at the roar of thunder and a bright flash of lightning just beyond the street. The darkened clouds open, and a sudden downpour emerges. I have never seen such a torrential downpour, and when I look to the ground, I see the wet paint starting to run. Seriously? Can anything else go wrong?

Click-click-click-click. It is still here. I squint my eyes in an attempt to see through the rain, when I realize that this is not bad at all. Just beside the path, I can see that something is blocking the rain. The rain is pouring down, yet the creature's pure size has created a waterfall effect. The rain has made him visible to me. Click-click-click-click. I see the invisible creature making his way toward me now.

I raise the rifle, and I am just about to take a shot when I see movement in the distance. It is Nick. I point the gun down toward the floor and realize I can't just blindly shoot with Nick in my crossfire. I look down at my feet and see the other paint can. I pick it up, and I can feel that there is still paint inside. This might work. I have one final chance to make this thing more visible. Whatever it is, it doesn't seem to be interested in me, and I can see Nick just standing there trying to figure out what he should do. I can't let him get Nick. The rain will wash away the scent of gasoline, and Nick will no longer be protected. I have to draw him in here.

I pop off the lid to the paint, and then I take the knife out of my sheath. I take a deep breath and slice a huge laceration into the top of my arm. It was not as easy to cut into my own flesh as it had been with others before me. The cut is jagged because the pain is excruciating. Dark red blood begins to gush from it, and despite the throbbing pain, I take my hand and cover it with the fresh blood. I smear the thick red blood on both arms and my face, like some post-apocalyptic war paint. "Come and get me!" I grab the paint can, and I move into the corner and hide.

Click-click-click-click. It sounds like it is in the doorway.

Just wait, you only have one chance at this. Be patient. It is trying to find you.

Click-click-click-click.

Ok, it sounds like it is inside the room with me now. Wait… not yet.

Click-click-click-click.

NOW!

I throw the remainder of the paint on the creature, and it is just enough to show his head. I drop the paint can, raise the rifle, and I take one shot. The creature spins toward me. I take another and then another, and then it falls to the ground. Once on the ground I take another shot, and another, and one more. Finally, it stops moving.

"How does it feel to be hunted, asshole?!" I yell as I choke back tears.

I feel something behind me and I spin around, pointing the gun to shoot.

"Whoa whoa whoa! It's just me!" Yells Nick.

Chapter Sixty-One

Present

I let the rifle hang on the sling, and hug Nick so tight it hurts. Then I realize he smells like gasoline and copper. Blood. I pull back and he is covered in it. I look at him with horror in my eyes as I frantically start pulling up his shirt to see where he is hurt.

"It's not mine. It was her. The girl we heard screaming. I got there too late. I had just found her, and I grabbed her for us to run. Then I heard it. It was there with us. It ripped her right out of my arms, Grace. I couldn't stop him. So I just ran as fast as I could back to you."

I look at him, "Do you think there are more?"

"I don't think so. Not right here at least."

I put my arms on his forearms, "How can you be so sure?"

"I can't be. I just think we would have heard them by now."

"Well it isn't safe to go home tonight," I say to him.

He grabs me by the hand, "Here, let me take you outside. You are covered in blood, and it's not safe."

He walks me out, and the rain has yet to let up. I stand there just letting the rain pour down on me. I close my eyes and tilt my head back, and while the rain is cold, it feels good. I reflect on everything that just happened. So much went wrong, and nothing we planned came to fruition. We made such dumb mistakes today, but that is bound to happen, right? We really are just kids trying to fight this war. A plan is a great place to start, but things do go wrong, and at least we came out on top this time.

As I am standing there letting the rain cleanse me of the sinner this new life has made of me, I feel something touch my face. I open my eyes and see that Nick has a cloth and is wiping my face clean from my blood.

"That took a lot of guts, you know," he says as he continues to wipe my face.

"Everything we planned went wrong. I had to fix it," I say quietly.

He continues to wipe my face, "I'm sorry I left you here to handle this on your own."

"Well, I am sorry I sent you to go save a stranger. I guess we're even."

He smiles at me, and then grabs my hand to walk me back into the clock tower. When we get inside, I look down to see what remains of the creature I just killed. The paint does not do much to educate us on what these creatures are.

"What do you think it is?" he asks.

"Honestly, I have no clue. I mean, look at it. It's just a round head. No ears, or anything. Before the rain washed away the paint, I could see it had big reptilian feet, though. They were huge."

"So weird. Should we drag them outside? I think I would feel better if they were outside when we tried to sleep," he says.

"I entirely agree with you on that!"

I bend down and begin to feel the creature on the ground. The skin is rough with what feels like minimal coarse hair, and is already cold to the touch. I am closing my eyes to try to imagine what I am feeling and it doesn't make sense. I stand up to help Nick lift the body, when the sudden pressure of the weight causes my arm to begin throbbing. I am suddenly reminded that I had just cut my arm open.

I let out a sharp cry, and Nick rushes over. "I completely forgot about that! Here, let me help you."

He begins looking around the room for something to wrap my arm with. After lifting a few items on a shelf, he finds an old rag. He walks over, and begins to wrap the rag around my wound, just tight enough to help the bleeding stop.

He smiles at me, "Here, that will do for now. If we can get these things out of here, then you can finally get some much-needed rest."

It takes a while, but we eventually drag both bodies out, which is no easy task. They are so heavy and have to weigh hundreds of pounds. Although, no clicking can be heard, and the silence is such a sweet sound. We place their corpses just outside the path covered with paint, lock the doors, and walk back upstairs.

I sit down on the ground. "We have to see if we can find something that allows us to see them better next time," I say. "Something we can cover their entire bodies with; maybe grab more paint from the store. That way we really know what we are dealing with."

He shakes his head, "You are always focused on the next challenge. We won today, Grace. Let's chalk this up to a victory and get some rest. We will worry about whatever we need to worry about tomorrow. Ok?"

"That seems fair enough. Should we take turns keeping watch?" I ask.

"Yes, we should. I will keep first watch, since you ended up fighting them all by yourself. Gotta redeem myself somehow."

I laugh, "Yeah, who knew I would be the tough guy around here?"

He laughs, "I did."

As I am sitting on the ground, I look up at where the tapestry once hung, and it looks like something is wrong with the wall. I stand and get closer to investigate. When I look closer, I can see that there had been a hole cut into the wall, and there is a makeshift wood cover to conceal it. I take my knife and wedge it into where the wood meets the wall. I slide the knife in, and with just a little bit of pressure, the wood falls off.

Inside, I see a metal box. I pull it out, and when I open it, I am shocked at what I see. On top of the items is a note.

Grace,

If you find this letter then things did not go according to plan, and I fear that this is a fight you will be doing on your own. I pray Stephen is still by your side. The truth is, I am hoping it is all a fluke. That whatever got your mother isn't really what I think it is. This note is just a contingency plan. The back-up plan to the original plan. Today I intend to prepare you guys for the possible battle we have ahead of us. I am ready to tell your brother what I know, and it is time we work together as a family to hunt these creatures down. Ever since your mother was taken, I have been planning a way for us to survive. I have been fortunate to have the tools necessary to fight these monsters, and it is time we put all that training to good use. However, if somehow we get separated, this will allow you to fight them without me. One always has to be prepared for the unexpected, and that is why you are reading this note.

I know this is the only place you will come to fight them if you have to. You have always had an eye for things that didn't seem to fit in, and I know you will notice that something isn't quite right about the tapestry. I cannot afford to leave these items out in the open, because I do not want strangers to find them. I have kept the other pair of these goggles in my backpack if we were ever to come across them on our travels. If we ever get separated, then I know you will find these other ones here. If you are screaming at me for not giving them to you sooner, please don't be mad at your dear old dad, Grace. This was never the plan. After your reaction to the news, I felt hesitant to tell your brother. I had to figure out a way to make this all work, so we could solve this, and then maybe somehow I could come clean to him too. I am supposed to be here with you. We were supposed to be doing this together as a family. This was only Plan B. I knew we had to keep our supplies in different places; I knew we had to be smart if we were going to win.

Alas, if our plan did not come to fruition, and you are reading this note, just remember that things in life have never been easy. With every challenge you have ever been introduced to, you have overcome it. Things never go according to plan in life. Remember all that you learned: Research, Plan, and Execute. You got this! Love you to the moon and back.

—Dad

Beneath my letter, I see another one addressed to Stephen.

Stephen,

I know if you are reading this letter then you are with your sister. I know I have always been so hard on you, but it is because I love you, son. I have been doing all I can to prepare you to be the man I wish I could have been. I am hard on you because I needed you to be strong. I needed you to be able to take my place if anything ever were to happen to me.

You are a great young man, and you have definitely lived up to my expectations. Hell, you exceeded them if I am being honest. This is not the future I had planned for any of us. If you are reading this, then I have failed you guys. I have left you to live on your own. I know I have always asked so much of you, but please be easy on your sister. She has always tried so hard to be like you. She needs you now more than ever. She needs you to protect her. She is smart, and she will help you get through this, but I need you guys to take care of each other. She'll need your guidance. I know this is a lot to ask of you, but I wouldn't ask if I didn't think it was possible. You have made me so proud to be your father, and I regret I am not there to see you guys through this mission. I love you.

–Dad

I fold the letters and lay them next to me. Tears are streaming down my face, and it makes me wonder what this battle would have been like if his plan really worked out. I wish he could have been here to witness Nick and me adapting to the unexpected. I think he would have been proud of us.

Inside the metal container is a pair of night vision googles, and some items that look like grenades. There are also some pieces of old crumpled paper. I pull them out, and they are some of the notes of the research we had done back when I was younger. He saved them for this very moment. The last thing I find is a photograph of my family. It was the last time we were at Disneyland together so many years ago. I bring it my face and kiss it. I turn it around, and on the back, he wrote: The Baker Family before monsters existed. No matter what happens, we are all in this together.

I feel Nick behind me. I turn around and dig my head into his shoulder. He holds me tightly, and I just let out a sigh of relief. We did it. We beat the monsters. We beat them without even using what my dad had left behind for me.

"Grace, do you mind if I ask what that was?" He says breaking the silence.

I look up at him. "It was a box my dad left behind for me to fight these guys."

"That's what I thought. Is that what I think it is in there?"

"Which part?"

He looks toward the items. "The night vision goggles?"

I let out a laugh, "Yeah, he thought I would find it before we had to fight them."

"Well I guess if we could fight them without those, from now on it'll be a breeze."

I just look at him and we both start laughing. Yes, it will be.

Chapter Sixty-Two

The Morning After

I wake up to light filling the room and the sound of birds chirping. A sensation that had long been forgotten from months of sleeping in a silent basement. I feel an arm wrapped around my waist, and realize my hand is intertwined with his. I go to move, and I feel him grasp me tighter.

"Not yet," he whispers. "Just a few more minutes."

For the first time in a long time I feel peace. In no way have we won, but this is the beginning. This is the first of many battles, but I feel optimistic. I feel like this is something we can really do. We have a chance at starting over. I am no longer afraid.

We continue to lie there for about an hour more, but before I know it, it is time to leave. I move again, turning to face him. Every part of my body is in pain after sleeping on the wooden floor, but it is worth it.

He looks at me and takes his hand to wipe my hair off my face. "Grace, I screwed up."

"What do you mean?"

"When I ran out last night; I left the door open."

I laugh, "Oh you did? The monster that made his way up here didn't give me that impression at all!"

"I was just trying to get back here so fast I didn't even think about it."

I smile, "Nick, it is ok. We both made mistakes. We survived. That is all that matters."

"I have a good feeling about this, you know. I think we are going to be able to survive this," he says as he runs his fingers through my bloody, knotted hair.

"You know, I was just thinking the exact same thing."

"We did good; you should be proud of yourself. You improvised flawlessly. I am so proud of you."

We both smile as he stands up. "Hey, let me check outside and make sure everything is good. I'll be back, ok?"

"Are you sure you don't want me to go?" I ask as I sit up.

"Yeah, I am sure."

He walks down the stairs, and I sit on the ground, just listening, because old habits die hard. I glance over to where he had been lying, and I see a piece of paper that is a little bloody. I grab the piece of paper, and it is a note.

Grace,

In my last note, the world was so different. Today I write this not knowing what tonight will bring, but I just have to tell you that how I felt all those years ago when I saw you for the first time is how I feel now. I keep telling myself that there are no coincidences. There is no one I would want to endure the end of the world with but you. I want you to know that you are what keeps me going. You kept me alive all these years. Everything you were back then only resonates now. Your strength is something I can never replicate. Remember that time we made a deal that you would protect me from the monsters hiding in the storm drains? I guess somehow I always knew Grace Baker would protect me from monsters someday. I can't wait to start this new life with you. I love you.

—Nick

My eyes swell with tears as I read those words. I look up and I see Nick watching me read it.

"Corny?" he asks.

"The corniest," I say with a sniffle.

He walks closer, "I mean it, you know."

"I know. I still have your other letter," I say, as I pull a ragged piece of paper from my pocket. "I brought it for good luck."

He grabs the letter and smiles at me. "I can't believe I wrote this to you on the day the world ended. But I am glad I did. Knowing I told you this made the end seem ok. I was happy you knew someone loved you."

"Loved me?"

"Loved you then, love you now, love you always." He looks at me, grabs my face with his hands, kisses my forehead, my nose, and then gently my lips.

He smiles, "I've said it before, and I'll say it again, the end of the world suits you, Miss Baker. I always knew if we were going to survive this, it would be because of you."

Epilogue

Day 1011

It is hard to believe this, but we are finally relocating! It turns out that while we were figuring out how to defeat the monsters, apparently so was what remained of the U.S. Government. Dad was being honest when he said they were created as a way to combat terrorism. The problem is, when the power grid was destroyed there was no way to keep them in captivity. So in a cruel turn of events, they began hunting the very people they were supposed to protect.

There are now about a dozen colonies across what remains of the United States that are full-functioning cities again. They have limited power, clean water, food, housing, and are just trying to utilize people's strengths to rebuild. The best part is that they have hospitals! No more homemade sutures for this girl!

We spent a lot of time trying to figure these monsters out. Since we knew they were created in a laboratory, it allowed us to be a little more open minded as to why they were the way they were. They seemed to be like most animals, when you really broke it down. Just really big, scary, man-eating, invisible animals.

I told Nick about how one time in a science class, we were learning about the human eye and eyesight, and how you are able to see things. I had vaguely remembered a lesson about how certain color hues and light frequencies cancel each other out and make them impossible to be seen by the human eye. Maybe when they were concocted in the lab, they were able to somehow replicate these forbidden colors. Who knows?

The government still hasn't explained in detail to us what they are, but I hear they do have a more in-depth explanation at the colonies of where they came from, and I am eager to find out. However, knowing what I know about them from what my dad told me, it would be safe to assume they will not be forthcoming about how they actually were the ones to create them in the first place. I guess it would make sense to keep that under wraps when you are trying to form a new civilization.

After our F.E.P. (which stands for First Epic Battle, which Nick named, obviously), we ended up successfully killing about twenty of them over the last couple of years. It was so much easier with the tools Dad left behind. Being able to mask our scent and use night vision really did make killing them a breeze. It was not until we had the night vision that we finally got to see what they looked like. But the goggles had seen better days and were not the best quality, so really all you saw was an overall creature in size, and not the specific details. The first time Nick saw one through the googles he said, "I think they somehow mated a Grizzly Bear and a T-Rex together in that lab. What freaks!" I still laugh at that description, but I had to agree that it really was the best way to articulate what we were seeing. But it was true that being such a large target made it easy to kill them once you could see them, of course. We were even able to destroy their entire nest one night. It turns out the grenades Dad left behind were actually flashbangs that the police and military use as a distraction. We threw them into the cave, which caused them to exit the cave all at once, and we were able to pick them off as they tried to flee from our man-made sunlight. We ended up killing seven that day.

After that, we hardly saw them anymore. It was a good six or seven months afterwards when we finally saw one again. It was during that battle that an old Army tanker drove through and saw us in action, and the soldiers said we would be a great recruitment for the colonies. Apparently, they had yet to see civilians successfully defeat the creatures, and they applauded our resolve.

So, they are picking us up in about an hour. I am nervous and scared, and worried about what being around other humans will be like. We have come across people here and there, and slowly a sense of civility has started to propagate again. There is a new status quo, but I am just happy that everything worked out like it did. We survived.

I miss my mom, dad, and brother like crazy, but not a day goes by that I don't think of them. After all, it was my mom and dad who gave me the strength to defeat that creature that day. And I don't think I would have ever come up with my plan had it not been for the dream I had of my dad. My guardian angels watching over me.

We just finished packing the few things we felt we couldn't leave behind. We ended up making a good life here, and I am sad to leave it. Life has been great, actually. I know I wrote when Nick and I decided to marry last year. I don't know why we did, because it really isn't necessary now, but it just felt right. Just made things feel more normal (if normal is even a real thing anymore). It couldn't have been a more perfect fall day. The trees were vibrant with their shades of yellow, orange, and auburn. We were surrounded by the sounds of the forest. It was peaceful; just him and me with no pomp and circumstance. We exchanged rings that we had found hidden in a drawer in the cabin. I think they may have belonged to my grandparents, but there is no way of really knowing. We like to believe that is who they belonged to anyway. We just found that there was something nice about trying to keep an old-world tradition alive.

We knew each other before the world ended, beyond all odds we found each other in the middle of what was left, and we figured out how to start living once the world began again. I can't imagine doing anything in this life without him by my side. I look forward to what happens now, and what it'll be like moving forward. We live a simple life, in a world where monsters exist, and somehow, I feel like that is exactly where we were always meant to be.